The MERRY WIDOW MURDERS

The
MERRY
WIDOW
MURDERS

MELODIE
CAMPBELL

Cormorant Books

We acknowledge financial support for our publishing activities: the Government
of Canada, through the Canada Book Fund and The Canada Council for the Arts;
the Government of Ontario, through the Ontario Arts Council, Ontario Creates,
and the Ontario Book Publishing Tax Credit. We acknowledge additional funding
provided by the Government of Ontario and the Ontario Arts Council to address
the adverse effects of the novel coronavirus pandemic.

LIBRARY AND ARCHIVES CANADA CATALOGUING IN PUBLICATION

Title: The merry widow murders / Melodie Campbell.
Names: Campbell, Melodie, 1955- author.
Identifiers: Canadiana (print) 20220494479 | Canadiana (ebook) 20220494487 |
ISBN 9781770866928 (softcover) | ISBN 9781770866935 (HTML)
Subjects: LCGFT: Novels.
Classification: LCC PS8605.A54745 M47 2023 | DDC C813/.6—dc23

United States Library of Congress Control Number: 2023930805

Cover art and design: Nick Craine
Interior text design: Marijke Friesen
Manufactured by Friesens in Altona, Manitoba in March, 2023.

Printed using paper from a responsible and sustainable resource,
including a mix of virgin fibres and recycled materials.

Printed and bound in Canada.

CORMORANT BOOKS INC.
260 ISHPADINAA (SPADINA) AVENUE, SUITE 502,
TKARONTO (TORONTO), ON M5T 2E4
www.cormorantbooks.com

For Mike, my husband and best friend

CHAPTER ONE

DAY ONE AT SEA

I HAVE EXCEPTIONAL hearing. So when I heard my name being discussed in such a delicious way, it was impossible not to eavesdrop.

"Why, that's Lucy Revelstoke!" said Vera Horner, leaning as far to the left as she could without falling out of her deck chair.

"Who?" said her plump companion. Her head whipped toward me.

"You know, Amanda," said Mrs. Horner, waving a bird-like hand. "Married Lord Revelstoke's third son. Didn't expect to inherit a thing, and then the others got killed at the Somme. Even the father. My, doesn't she look smart."

Vera Horner wasn't wrong about fashion. The sleek amber shift with the handkerchief hem was Worth. Coupled with the matching scarf, it had cost me a bleeding fortune. Worth every penny, though.

I could feel their eyes on me. This type of scrutiny by women always made me feel uncomfortable. I resisted the urge to squirm. In my experience, gossip was rarely innocent. It usually came with a sting.

"Revelstoke. Wasn't that the fellow who raced automobiles?" said the woman called Amanda.

"That's the one," said Mrs. Horner. "Johnny Revelstoke. Rather a daredevil. Probably would have died in a crash if he hadn't been gassed in the war. Died a few years ago, of TB. Happy marriage, of all things."

"Really?" exclaimed Amanda. "Remarkable."

It could have been my imagination, but the ship seemed to give a slight lurch. I recovered my balance quickly. No one else appeared to notice.

"Look at that man with her now." Vera Horner peered through her pince-nez. "Reminds me of my nephew Edward. Tall and good-looking with the same dark hair, but a little too flashy. Where have I seen him before?"

The other woman shook her head sympathetically. "So frustrating, when you get older. So many memories, and you can't always come up with the right ones at the right time. Who was she before?"

"Well, that's a mystery. I didn't know her before," said Vera. "Johnny Revelstoke met her on a ship crossing. She had money, I know that."

"What was her maiden name?"

"Hamilton."

"That's a good English name," said Amanda. "Is she from the Devonshire branch of the family?"

Both matrons stared at their quarry, unaware that they were being equally measured.

It had taken some willpower, but I had kept my mouth shut. So funny, to hear them go on about my pedigree. Hamilton was a good name, a historically significant name. I had always liked it.

But I could hardly be from Devonshire. Surely they could detect that from my accent?

"Penny for your thoughts," said Tony Anderson, standing beside me at the rail.

I turned toward him. "Tuppence, and they're yours," I said.

Tony laughed. "Johnny told me you were a sharp business-woman." He produced two coins from his pocket and held them out. "Will American pennies do?"

I smiled. And took them. Even though I was wearing a Worth dress. Even though my young son had inherited a small castle and a title. Money was money, my uncles would say.

But I would give him value for his coin. "I was overhearing those two women talk. I know one of them. Vera Horner."

Tony glanced over. "The two fluffies over there?"

I choked back a laugh. "Those two fluffies could tear you apart with words alone, Tony."

I put a hand on the ship's railing and looked to my right. The dark blue Atlantic roiled in the distance. New York had receded behind us until the smoke from the city was no longer visible, the Statue of Liberty a fond memory. It was June, a hot and humid time in Manhattan, the thick air laden with toxic fumes that had become the curse of any large city in the modern age. In contrast, it was a beautiful time to be on the ocean. The warm air was fresh with salt, and I inhaled deeply in mild euphoria. I was going to enjoy the next five days. Strange, how I loved the power of the sea. It had been completely unexpected, this passion for ships. That had come after Johnny's death.

Beside me, Tony waited. I appreciated that about him. He didn't rush me, in any aspect of our relationship.

So I gave him more value. "They were talking about my past. Specifically, about whether I was from the Devonshire branch of the Hamiltons."

"And are you?" Tony raised an eyebrow.

"Nothing so dull, darling," I said. The breeze swept my hair off my face. It felt glorious.

Tony laughed. "Glad to hear it. God forbid there be anything dull about you, Lucy."

I lapsed back into my thoughts. Johnny had gone to war as he'd done all things: with great enthusiasm. Tony had been a fellow officer in the trenches, and they had become fast friends. It was easy to see why. They both had a similar zest for life and an irreverence for rules. That very irreverence had probably contributed to the circumstances that led to Johnny's illness and death, in the end.

It had been ten years since the war ended. Johnny had died four years ago. A long, lonely four years. Oh, how I had loved that man. Every bone in my body missed him. I had grieved hard for four years, and I was only just emerging from the dark. "Like a butterfly from the chrysalis," Tony had said.

Life had moved on, as it does. I had a son to think of, to love and nurture, to send on his way.

So for his sake, I had done my best to buck up and meet society's giddy expectations that I would become a Merry Widow. Why be boring? It was the 1920s, after all. Women had the vote in many places. Every day I thanked my lucky stars to have been born at a time that allowed women more freedom than ever before.

As for my slightly scandalous reputation? For a woman to be travelling alone with her maid was still slightly scandalous. Johnny would have approved.

Tony seemed to read my mind. "Do you miss him still?" he said.

"Of course," I said softly. "Why? Did you think I married him for his title?" I stole a sideways glance at him. The poor man looked shocked. I patted his arm. "Steady on, Tony. It's a valid question. Everyone else thinks I did."

"Lucy, you are the very devil," muttered Tony, looking off into the distance.

I smiled. "Funny you would say that. Reminds me of something. 'Dancing in the fire, laughing at the devil.'"

"Is that a quote? I don't recognize it," said Tony.

"Something Johnny said once." I leaned back against the ship rail and spread both arms to grip it behind me. "He was going to put it on my gravestone."

Tony started. "That's a bit rough."

I laughed and shook my head. "You should hear what I threatened to put on his!"

Tony didn't ask what that was, and I regretted my words the second they were out of my mouth. Oh, why had I mentioned gravestones? What a foolish thing to say. It put us both under a solemn cloud for a minute or two. In truth, Tony had more reason than I did to avoid such thoughts. He had witnessed so much death and destruction firsthand at the front.

"You met him on a ship crossing, didn't you?"

"Yes," I said. "Before the war." Little did Tony know how relevant his question was to the present. I was on this ship for a reason. I wanted to relive the crossing from New York to England that had brought me to this point. Even now, I can't be sure of my motivation. Was it to put the past to rest? Find some closure to my old life with Johnny?

And then there was Tony. He had been such fun in New York, showing me around town. I hadn't expected to have an admirer on this voyage to England. It was a complete surprise, this easy companionship.

I was raised to believe in fate. I had met my first husband on a transatlantic crossing. Could it be that I was fated to acquire a second husband in the same way? I liked Tony very much. My son needed a male role model.

But marriage? That thought should bring one joy. Not the sober, wary feeling that came over me now. I'd made a hasty marriage the first go-round and had been very, very lucky. Johnny was a whirlwind I couldn't resist. But I was older now and had seen enough marriages to know that they bound a woman to the whims of her husband. The law was not kind to married women. I'd have to consider very seriously before I made that leap again. Or be insanely in love.

"Tell me about when you met," Tony said. "Was it love at first sight?"

I chuckled. "I'm not sure I would call it that. I happened to see a young lad in an Irish scally cap relieve Johnny of his wallet, and called the alarm. Johnny sprang to the chase and tackled the fellow."

Tony sucked in a breath. "Now that is an unusual way to meet!"

I shrugged. "The unusual thing was that Johnny laughed it off. He let the poor wretch go and didn't report him. This was long before we had ship security on board." It was a new world after the war. Now, we employed security officers to ensure the patrons wouldn't be bothered by pickpockets, card sharks, or loose women, and to break up rowdy fights in third class, when need be. Prohibition wasn't a law on the high seas. Ships weren't dry, and if there was one thing you could always count on, it was the combination of men and liquor leading to fistfights.

"Sounds like Johnny," said Tony. "The chase would be sport to him. I wouldn't doubt he'd buy the wretched bloke a drink if he were skint."

"I think that's why I fell in love with him," I said, thinking back. "At least one of the reasons." Johnny seemed to understand that a man who would steal had been given a rocky start in life. That was an exceptional show of compassion for someone who had been born rich. He often said after the war, "We were all the same in the trenches."

"What happened next?" said Tony.

I watched an older couple walk past us, arm in arm. How wonderful that looked. It was hard not to envy couples who had been married for decades.

"Johnny insisted that I be moved to his table at dinner. I was travelling with only my maid, so one more at the table was easy to accommodate. From then on, we were inseparable. I taught him all the latest scandalous dances from America, and he taught me the constellations in the sky. By day four, he had proposed."

"That was quick work. But I don't blame him," Tony said.

"I didn't even know his father was a lord when I said yes." I had come from money in the new world, for sure. There was no other way I could be travelling first class. But little had I realized the usefulness of a title. It was an unspoken badge of respectability. Being on Johnny's arm meant instant acceptance everywhere.

"How did his family react?"

"With shock, I'm sure." My voice reflected my smile. "But you know how Johnny was. He could charm the stars out of the sky. He brought them around. And remember, he wasn't in line for the title."

"That makes all the difference," muttered Tony.

I looked at him swiftly. What story lay behind those words?

The chiffon scarf lifted off my shoulders and flew off into the sea.

"Bloody hell!" I yelled in a voice that was hardly ladylike.

CHAPTER TWO

I SPUN AROUND and watched helplessly as the scarf disappeared into the froth behind us.

"Making a sacrifice to Neptune, are you? Always figured you for a heathen," said Tony. "Don't worry. When we get to London, I'll buy you a new one."

"You can't," I said sadly. "It was one of a kind." Blast, but this was annoying.

"A portent of things to come?" said Tony. "Lucy Revelstoke swept off her feet?"

"As long as I don't end up in the drink," I said. I forced myself to unclench my hand from around the rail. It was irritating, but I could afford to replace it a hundred times over now. "Speaking of which. Cocktails beckon. Come on. We should get ready for dinner. Walk me back to my cabin, Tony." I pushed off from the rail and gave a cheery nod to Vera Horner. Her eyes went wide as I passed.

The *Victoriana* was the latest ship in the Empire line. Sleek and fast, she was a step up from the earlier models of the *Titanic* era. Huge improvements had been made in safety as well as speed.

My cabin was on the promenade deck where we walked, but on the other side of the ship. We had to pass through the grand foyer to reach it. Inside the ship, decor was firmly art deco, clean and modern, shunning the excesses of the *belle époque*. Instead of elaborate nature motifs, the lines were geometric, in some cases with a subtle ancient Egyptian graphic effect. Like so many, the investors in the Empire line were taken with the recent excavations in the Valley of the Kings. Egyptian motifs were all the rage.

Decoration might have been simpler now, but the first-class section was still a marvel in luxury. Lighting on board, particularly, had been greatly improved since the turn of the century.

We turned down one of those lighted corridors, nodding to other passengers as we went. My cabin was partway down to the left. I put my key in the lock. The door pushed open before I could turn the handle.

"That's strange," I said. "It didn't click."

"Maybe you forgot to lock it?" said Tony.

Not likely, I thought to myself. I was careful to lock up all possessions. For good reason, I was now cautious.

Tony seemed to sense my hesitation. "Let me go first," he said.

I was glad of his larger frame and chivalry. He pushed the wooden door all the way open and stepped in, stopping just inside. "Bugger," he said under his breath.

I moved quickly to his side.

The cabin was not as I had left it. Drawers had been dumped out. Their contents were strewn across the floor. The bed had been stripped and the mattress turned over. And something had been added.

"Jesus Murphy," I croaked.

On the cabin floor, next to the bed, lay a man. He looked

vaguely familiar, and not in a good way. His black hair was slicked back, and his suit was New York dandy. But it could have done without the dagger through the chest.

"Good gad, Lucy," said Tony. "Don't go any closer." He threw an arm up in front of me to block the way. "Who the devil did this?"

I stared down at the body. "Not me, darling. And if I had, it wouldn't be this way."

"SONOFABITCH," SAID MY maid, Elf. She leaned in from the doorway behind us. "Who is *that?*"

"Shut the door behind you," I ordered.

Elf — full name Elfreda — did as told, for possibly the very first time in her life. She came up beside me and peered down at the body.

"Know him?" I asked.

"Nope."

I glanced over to assess her visage. Everything Elf thought showed up on her face. It wasn't a particularly good quality for a servant to have. Mind you, calling her a servant was a trifle optimistic.

She barely came up to my shoulder, but that didn't seem to matter. A few of my would-be suitors had shrunk under her withering gaze, never to return to our townhouse in London. Which was probably to their advantage, as Elf had other, more painful ways of removing unwanted pests.

Which might explain why I was having uneasy thoughts about the man on the floor. Could this be someone from Elf's past?

"Why wouldn't you have done it this way?" asked a male voice.

Good lord! I'd forgotten Tony was there.

Elf answered for me. "Ruin a perfectly good gown, stabbing someone. Blood spray goes all over you."

Tony stared at her. "Yes, well ... there is that." He appeared to be choking back a laugh. Or maybe he was just choking.

Elf moved closer to the body. 'Hard-boiled, fer sure. Looks like a torpedo to me."

"A what?" asked Tony.

And here's where I had to make a decision. Could I trust Tony? I needed to take control of the situation. Bugger. That meant coming clean to a certain extent. I'd have to trust him.

"A hired gun," I explained.

"How do you ..." He stopped before finishing the sentence. "Should you be doing that?"

Elf had dropped to the floor. Both hands were checking the body for a wallet. "How else are we gonna find out who is this guy?"

I shrugged. "She has a point."

"No wallet." Elf sprang upright. "So whatcha wanna do?"

"Try for a tailor mark?" I suggested.

"Now wait a minute," said Tony. "Shouldn't we be leaving this for the authorities?" He drove a shaky hand through his hair.

Elf and I exchanged a look. She got my message and stood up.

I turned to Tony. "Darling, I know you didn't do this. But the authorities won't."

"Me?" Tony said, aghast. "Why should they think I did it?"

Elf shrugged. "On account of yer war record. Lot of kills. Sweet on her ladyship. Plus — you discovered the body. Probably go down for self-defence. Caught the burglar in the act. We could play it that way. Whatcha think, Luce?"

I glanced quickly at Tony to see if he'd noticed the slip. Maids did not usually call their employers by their first name, let alone a nickname.

"Or," said Elf, "we could make the problem go away." She glanced at me. "Pretend it never happened."

"Possible," I said coolly. "There are other options, being as we're here and not on land."

"What?" said Tony.

"But I really do want to find out who he is. Check for the tailor mark, Elf. We can make subtle inquiries after we reach port."

"Sure thing," said Elf. She dropped to the floor again.

And shoes, I thought to myself. We should check manufacturer, style number, and size. That might be the quickest way to identify him. I was thinking fast. What a mess. The last thing I needed was a dead man in my cabin. It brought to mind certain questions, like who on earth could be behind this? Was it a coincidence they'd picked my cabin to drop a body? And how concerned should I be about my own safety?

I'd feel a lot better if I could find out who the poor fellow was. That gave me an idea.

"Should I take a photograph?" I asked Elf. "I'd love to use my new camera." It was a beauty. Latest design, and one of my few indulgences beyond clothes.

"No photo." Elf shook her head. "Don't want no record. This guy is a ghost."

"I suppose you're right." I sighed. "That will make it harder. No matter. I've always wanted to do some sleuthing. Just like Tommy and Tuppence in *The Secret Adversary*." I almost clapped my hands.

A slight gurgling noise caught my attention. Oh, right. Tony. He was still here.

"Whatcha think," said Elf, getting up. "Wait until dark?"

I thought. "Yes, but let's clean this place up first." I glanced around the room. It was an unholy mess. "I wonder what he was looking for?"

"We'll never know," said Elf. She kicked my silk kimono with the toe of her shoe.

"If I could say a few words," said Tony. He seemed to be having trouble choking out those few words. "We should probably leave everything just as it is for now. In fact, we must, for the authorities."

Both Elf and I stared him. I decided, reluctantly, that it would be necessary to pull out the big guns.

"Tony, I don't think you quite realize the situation." I reached out to pat his arm. "If this gets out, the papers will have a field day. Can you imagine the headlines?"

"Viscount's Son Caught in Shipboard Murder Scandal," Elf offered gleefully.

Tony blanched.

"I expect this wouldn't be good for your financial situation," I said primly. It was wicked, but unfortunately necessary, to remind him. Tony depended on an allowance from home, I knew.

"The *pater* would have a coronary," he squeaked. I could almost hear the sweat beading on his forehead.

I nodded with satisfaction. "That would be tragic. We wouldn't want your father to have a coronary. So we will attempt to keep this among ourselves. Tony, dear, I think you should probably leave us. We both need to dress for dinner. Mustn't be late."

"Nope. Don't want to arouse suspicions," said Elf.

He was pacing now. "You can't ... Lucy, don't tell me you're thinking to hide a dead man in your cabin."

"Nonsense, darling," I said. "How long could that last? It wouldn't be sanitary." I took a deep breath. "Actually, I was thinking of the deep blue sea."

Elf nodded. "Seems the thing."

"At this point, we must think of Harry and what he would like," I said. "A romantic burial at sea? Or being torn apart while all exposed on a cold slate coroner's table?"

Elf shivered. "Bloody butchers."

"Harry?" said Tony. He was a sentence or two behind.

"Well, Tom, Dick, or Harry. He didn't look like a Tom to me," I said.

"Might be a dick," said Elf.

"We don't know that," I scolded.

Tony stared at me. Then he did something completely unexpected and burst out laughing. It was not the sort of laugh one expected to hear in circumstances like this. It seemed to go on longer than was normal in polite company.

Elf looked my way, hoping for an explanation. I shrugged my shoulders. "Strange things happened in the trenches," I said.

She nodded knowingly.

Tony finished off his laugh with a coughing fit. I raced forward, ready to help him.

"Damned mustard gas," he wheezed, shaking away my assistance. "I'm okay. Better now. Really. But honestly, Lucy. You and your sidekick here." He pointed to Elf. Then he was off on another round of laughing and coughing.

I hovered around him, cluck-clucking.

"Tony, go to your cabin. Leave this to us. We're more used to it," I said.

"More used to it?" He coughed again.

This had to end. Time was ticking away. "I'll explain when we're alone." I pulled at his arm with both my hands. "Right now, you need to change into formal attire and save a seat for me at the table. Don't forget we're dining with the captain tonight." I patted his back affectionately as I led him to the door.

Tony reached forward to twist the handle but turned around at the last moment. He gazed at me. He shook his head at Elf. Then he looked at the problem on the floor. "You're going to dress for dinner with a dead man in your cabin."

"Well, he's hardly going to notice, is he?" I said.

CHAPTER THREE

I WATCHED TONY'S back as he disappeared through the door. Frankly, I was surprised to see him go. It seemed out of character. Maybe it was the shock. In any case, I didn't want him turning around and coming back. At least not until I'd had a chance to think.

"Lock the door, Elf," I said. Then I sat down on the flipped mattress to work my brain cells. When I came to, Elf was watching me.

"You thinking what I'm thinking?" she said. She gestured with a short arm.

We both looked down at the body.

"Not enough blood," I said immediately. "He wasn't killed here."

She nodded. I knew that, like me, she had seen dead men before. Men who had been killed with similar weapons. It wasn't something I liked to think about now, but before I met my husband, both Elf and I had been on the run from dark pasts. Mine may have come with fur coats and massive protection, but the businesses that fed my lawless family were every bit as illicit as Elf's pickpocket career.

One thing we both knew was that if you are stabbed, your arteries keep pumping blood until your heart stops. There should have been masses of red stuff on the cabin floor. There weren't.

"Easier to clean up," said Elf. She touched the body with her toe.

"But why?" I said. "Why would someone kill a man and drag his body in here?"

She shrugged. "Puts us behind the eight ball. Maybe to plant the blame on you?"

"I haven't done anything that would warrant this behaviour, and no one but you knows about my past. So it's unlikely. More like, they wanted to put the blame on someone else. Anyone else. But how did he get in? And where was Harry actually killed?"

Elf got down on the floor and sniffed.

"What are you doing?" I asked.

"Checking how long he's been snuffed," she said. She put her nose down by the fatal wound.

"You can do that by smell?" I gave a little shiver. Elf was close to my age. She had an unusual and varied background, which included spending some time working for the mob. "Isn't it more usual to check for rigor?"

"Sure," she said. "But didn't know if I should touch the mug."

"Elf, I don't think you need to worry about leaving fingerprints."

"Fair dinkum," she said.

What? "Where did you pick up that expression?"

She lifted an arm to test for rigor. "Aussie sailor," she said.

I knew enough to leave it at that.

Jesus Murphy. We hadn't even spent one night on this ship, and we had a dead body on our hands. What were the chances of that?

Elf vaulted up from the floor. She wiped her hands on her apron. Usually, Elf wore what she wanted. But on this ship, I'd insisted she dress like an actual maid. "Pretend you're an actress playing a part," I had said, coaxing her. Which wasn't far from the truth. She was certainly a better actress than a maid.

"So how long?" I said.

"Not long," said Elf. "Hour ... no more."

"And the tailor marks?"

"Bugger. I forgot to do that." She dropped down to the floor again. Her hand lifted the cleaner side of his jacket. The side that didn't have a knife through it. I could see her check the inside pocket.

"Here," she said, pointing. "Can you read it?"

I moved over to take a look. "Manhouser, New York. Good thing they dropped him on his back."

"So we were right. He's American."

Manhouser was an upmarket men's tailor with a reputation for high style. Our Harry was quite a dandy. And American. That was a relief to me. At least he wasn't one of my relatives.

"Are we going to investigate?" said Elf, fingers lingering on the fellow's shoes.

"Don't you think we should?" I said. "The poor man was dumped right here in our cabin. Like he wanted us to find out about him." I sat back down on the bed. "Besides, we've already proved ourselves good sleuths."

She clapped her hands, all happy and chipper. "This'll be like when we got back those love letters for that lady friend of yours!"

"Bloody blackmailers," I muttered softly. "They deserve a thousand deaths by — oh, I don't know."

"Fish hooks?"

Why fish hooks? Honestly, the way Elf's mind worked.

"And the time we found out the maid didn't steal the brooch!" Elf was getting excited.

"I always knew Lord Duncival was a scoundrel. Stealing his own wife's jewellery to claim the insurance ..." I shook my head. "Too cliché. At least we got the maid off."

"That's the problem with unsolved crime," Elf said thoughtfully. "If you don't get the person who done it, everyone else stays a suspect."

And if you're a servant, how can you afford any stain against your name? We still lived in a world where young working-class women didn't have too many employment options. Rumours of theft could put a young female on the street. We'd prevented that, and we felt good about it.

So it stood to reason that we had a similar duty to try to find out about Harry. If not a professional duty, then at least a moral one. The first thing we needed to do was find out who he was. Then we could determine who would want to kill him.

"I'm thinking the shoes might help. Make a note of the make and size. Can you get them off? Or has rigor set in?"

She struggled a bit but managed to get them off. "Harry doesn't need them anymore. Gotta friend who might."

"Don't give them away yet," I warned. "If they're bespoke, we can use them to trace Harry."

Of course, we were going the wrong way. New York was rapidly receding behind us, and I doubted very much if Harry bought his footwear in London. After all, his tailor was in America.

"Wait a minute." An idea was coming to me. Something about the shoes. "I need a moment to think about this ..."

"No time, Luce," said Elf. "You need to change for dinner."

Rats. She was right. I scanned the floor for a suitable gown that hadn't been tromped on. "Maybe that one?" I pointed to a sapphire-blue velvet sheath. "It doesn't wrinkle like some of the others."

We spent the next ten minutes stepping around clothes and Harry while getting me ready for dinner.

I gave Elf instructions while I slipped on long gloves.

"Leave the body where it is. Maybe cover it with blankets. We'll deal with it when I'm back." *One thing at a time,* I told myself.

One of the things I'd always been able to do was compartmentalize. That is to say, put troubles aside to deal with later and not let them intrude upon the present. This characteristic has served me well. In the next few hours, I had to get through a very formal dinner with all the usual charm that was expected of me. The problem of Harry would simply have to wait.

She nodded. "I'll start cleaning up."

"See if you can find anything missing. I'm willing to bet not a thing. Doesn't look right." My eyes swept the room. It sure looked fishy. Professional burglars did their best to leave the premises looking untouched. Not only did it stall detection, it was also a point of pride. We both knew that.

"This so-called burglar did quite a number," I said.

She looked up at me. Way up, because I was wearing strappy heels. "You think he faked the burglary?"

I nodded. "Why flip the mattress?" That didn't make sense. No one puts their jewellery under a mattress. And other valuables, like clocks, cameras, and gold cigarette cases, tended to be bulky.

"Got it! Egg was making it look like he was after papers. Spy papers. Like in the pictures." Elf was an ardent moving picture fan.

"A bit of overkill, don't you think?" I searched around for my evening bag, careful not to step on garments. It was on top of a pile of underclothes by the dressing table.

Elf tossed her head. "Most cops aren't so smart. They go to the pictures too. Egg was covering all bases."

Egg. I knew it meant *man*, of course. But where Elf picked up these slang expressions ...

"I'm ready," I said. "Lock the door behind me and don't let anyone in."

"Not a cockroach," she said.

TONY WAS WAITING at the door to the salon. He gave me a stiff smile, came right up to me, and put his big hand on my upper arm. "You look stunning," he said.

"Thank you." I gave him a brilliant smile.

"I like that. Suits your hair." He pointed to my gold headdress. I wasn't surprised he liked it. It was the height of fashion and had cost me the earth in New York.

My hair is dark, but not black. Chestnut brown would be a good description, and the current style of bob seemed to suit me. I also wore a fringe that brought attention to my eyes, which are large and blue. They're my best feature.

He dropped his voice. "Are there still three in your cabin?" His smile was more of a crocodile smile, but I gave him credit for trying.

"Yes," I replied brightly.

"Will you require my help later this evening?"

We walked gracefully into the dining room, nodding to people as we passed. "I'm not sure. It would be nice to know you were on hand," I said in a quiet voice.

"Always," said Tony.

The first-class dining room was also known as the Grand Salon. The first time I had entered, several months ago now, it pretty well took my breath away. Enormous fluted pillars stood three decks high as the ceiling soared above us. The lacquered wooden floors and walls simply gleamed. All about us, paintings of historical ships — some mythical, others whimsical — graced the walls between the gorgeous art deco light standards. Tables were a mix of rounds for larger groups and squares for parties of four, all done up in immaculate white tablecloths with pristine bone china and shiny silver. The ship's monogram was on every piece of china.

This was our first dinner on board, and I knew the chef would make a special effort.

Tony escorted me through the salon to the captain's table at the far end, which was already fully occupied except for our two seats. Captain Elliot rose when he saw me approach, as did the other men at the table. The seat to his right had been reserved for me, I saw. He took my gloved hand at once when I offered it.

"You look stunning tonight, my Lady," he said. His warm brown eyes met mine with sincerity. I liked this tall, white-haired gentleman very much, and I knew the crew did too.

I thanked him and allowed him to help me to sit. How does one put that? A gentleman pulls out your chair. You make to sit in it, but somehow you have to balance your weight without really sitting down, to allow him to push the chair in. Quite a production, I always think, when it would be much easier for me to just sit, reach down for the legs at the front, and pull myself in closer. That's the way we did it at home. I had learned to adapt.

Tony had moved to the other side of the table to take the last remaining seat, which was situated between — good lord — Vera Horner and Amanda whatever-her-name-was.

I collected my poise and smiled brightly. "Good evening, Mrs. Horner. I saw you on deck earlier, taking the air."

She had the grace to recover quickly and leaned forward, eyes bright, ready for gossip. "Lady Revelstoke! Well, I do call that a bit of good fortune. So nice to actually *know* someone on this voyage. So many strangers." She looked at Tony hopefully.

Captain Elliot took his cue and did the introductions. Tony and I were introduced together, which caused the Amanda woman to expel an excited chirp. Her surname, it turned out, was Martin, and, not surprisingly, she was a recent widow. I tucked that knowledge away for later. It gave us something in common.

There was a pleasant-looking middle-aged couple at our table, the Johnsons — "Call us Drew and Florrie" — who hailed from somewhere in the U.S. of A. I smiled and declined to tell them that it would be like pulling teeth to get anyone in first class to use first names until they had been acquainted with each other for some time. That was another lesson I had been made to learn.

Our final dinner companion was a single man by the name of Sloan. He had the sort of polished good looks that never went down well with me. I know that sounds strange, but some men can be too good-looking. It makes them appear effeminate. I put his age at about forty. So, older than me but younger than the Johnsons. His accent was definitely British public school. I looked across the table to gauge if Tony knew him.

Tony was involved in the same process. His eyes were regarding the other man curiously. "You went to Eton," he said finally. I could see him eyeing Sloan's tie.

Sloan looked at Tony. "Many years ago. Did you?"

Tony shook his head. "Harrow. Then a quick tour of Oxford before I joined up."

Sloan nodded. He smiled then. My intuition told me he'd relaxed a bit. Something about the set of his shoulders. I've always been good at reading tension ever since I was a child. It had served me well then, living in a family where the men turned to violence so easily. And it served me well now, in these years past the war, when so many veterans like Tony suffered from shell shock. Damaged men can be dangerous even if they don't mean to be.

So. Why had Sloan tensed up when Tony asked him about Eton?

CHAPTER FOUR

VERA HORNER LIVED up to her London reputation. First she complained about the late departure from New York. Since we'd left late afternoon Monday, we'd be arriving in Southampton on Saturday morning. Couldn't be helped; it was just one of those things you had to accept if you were going to travel by sea. Ports got backed up. Cargo got delayed. In our case, another ship had caught fire leaving port. The resulting inferno had been visually spectacular, as men on the fireboats fought to control the flames and keep them from spreading to the dockland.

"Heroic effort," remarked Drew. "Not every day you see something like that. Pity the poor souls who didn't make it." He shook his head. "Such a tragedy."

"Disgraceful," said Vera Horner in her most upper-class voice. "Those foreign ships shouldn't be allowed into New York harbour if they are so poorly maintained."

My mouth flew open. I heard Tony snort across from me.

"You can't stifle progress, Mrs. Horner. We need trade," said Drew. "Those bananas you eat every day? They have to get here somehow."

"I don't eat bananas," said Vera Horner. "Apples and plums are good enough for me, and we grow them very nicely in England, thank you very much."

"Then tea. You'd miss tea, I assume." Drew looked across the table and caught my eye. I swear he winked at me. I gave him a small smile.

"Oh yes, Vera. We couldn't do without tea," said Amanda Martin, who almost gushed as she leaped in to the discussion. "And I'm almost certain they can't grow it in England. Not even in Cornwall!" I watched her animated face with interest. She clearly liked having everyone's attention. "I have a cousin in Cornwall. Or is it Devon? He grows all sorts of things you can't grow in London. I hope to be able to go down there —"

Vera whipped her head to the side. "This is a ridiculous conversation, Amanda. I don't know why you are continuing it."

A blush spread across Amanda's face, and she looked down at her lap.

I was searching for something to say when the captain stepped in, apologizing sincerely for the delayed departure. The shipping line realized what an inconvenience it was for everyone. Vera wore a smug smile.

But soon it became apparent that rather than food, she fed on gossip. This was a woman who liked to hold court. Before long, she had captured everyone's attention and demanded patronage.

"So what brings you on this voyage, Mr. and Mrs. Johnson?"

I noticed with a smile that she'd started with the Americans. Vera Horner was cunning. They would be the least likely to consider it an affront to be questioned.

"It's our thirtieth anniversary!" said Florrie. "Thirty years with this man here, can you believe it?" She punched his arm, and they both grinned.

"Promised the old girl I'd show her the old country," he said with a chuckle. "Meant to do it for our twenty-fifth, but we had a wedding that year."

"Our eldest daughter, Marian," said Florrie, leaning forward, eyes bright. "She had eight bridesmaids!"

"And you know how expensive weddings can be." Drew gave us a cheerful smile. "Took me damn near five years to get back on my feet."

"Drew! Language," said Florrie.

"Sorry, pupcake," said Drew.

Pupcake? I had to smile. Drew and Florrie seemed to be oblivious to how vulgar they appeared to others at the table. And yet, I couldn't help liking them, myself.

Drew took over the conversation then. "What about you, Mr. Anderson? What brings you on board?"

Tony gave a lazy smile and held up his gin cocktail in a toast. "Going home," he said. "Had a bad time of it in France. Got out of hospital and didn't fancy a trip back to the continent. Been touring America as a way to forget." He swung the glass up to his mouth and took a large swallow.

That should have put a damper on the table, and indeed there was silence for a moment. I was shocked that Tony had been so forthcoming. There was something of the "don't-give-a-damn" about Tony, and I was still learning all his moods.

The captain cleared his throat. "We owe a lot to you men who fought. Glad you made it through." More silence. I'm sure most of us were thinking of the thousands of young men who hadn't come home.

When the silence got awkward, Vera stepped in again. "And you, my dear?" Her piercing eyes looked directly at me.

I already had my story. "I needed to go to New York to sign business papers. When Johnny died ..." I let the sentence trail off.

"Of course, dear," said Vera. I think she would have patted my hand if it could have been reached.

"I was left with his business interests to make sense of. But also ..." Again, I trailed off. I could see her eagerly waiting for more. "I'm revisiting the time I first met Johnny. We were engaged to be married on just such a crossing from New York."

"Oh, how romantic!" chirped Amanda.

I heard Tony grunt across from me.

I didn't wait for more questions and instead turned the tables and addressed the woman opposite me. "And you, Mrs. Martin? What brings you on this ship?"

Her sallow face lit up. "I'm going home too!" she said. "My dear husband passed away, so I'm returning home to England where I grew up. So fortunate to meet up with Vera almost as soon as I boarded the ship. I didn't know a single other soul on it! We recognized each other immediately, even after so long. Vera and I went to school together, oh, it must be nearly fifty years ago! Wasn't it, Vera?"

"Fifty years?" croaked Vera.

For a brief moment, I thought she was going to dive for Amanda's throat. It took everything in me not to giggle. The one thing you did not ask a society matron was her age, and Amanda had all but spilled it.

"Not that long ago, dear. Don't age us so." It was clear to me Vera Horner was exerting every bit of control she possessed.

Had to admire her for that, at least. I decided to help them out.

"And you, Mr. Sloan? Why were you in New York?" I gave him a cheery look.

"Business," he said. We waited for more. Odd, that. He didn't seem to want to elaborate. Most men were eager to talk about their work. Luckily, our American tourists weren't about to leave it at that.

"What business are you in?" asked Drew.

"Import-export," said Sloan. This time he looked up and smiled smoothly.

Drew launched into the subject of automobiles, and the prospect of more American cars being shipped to England.

I watched them discuss this and rolled it over in my mind. Import-export. What a clever catchall; that could mean anything. It also — as I knew — served as a cover for many smuggling operations. Liquor mismarked in barrels. Cocaine masquerading as baking soda. I'd even heard of counterfeit money being hidden in coffins. And then there was the spectre of tax evasion. Slippery, how our Mr. Sloan had evaded the question. If he was into something illicit, could he have had something to do with the body in my cabin? It was worth considering. I wondered if Drew would get much more out of him.

Dinner passed by quickly. I prefer eating to talking when good food is put before me, and the cuisine on this liner was superb. First course was a lovely consommé, followed by sole almondine and filet of beef with a lovely buttery sauce. Dessert was rum baba. It had been liberally infused with rum, so much so that the aroma reached my nose. I wasn't keen on rum, so it was easy to resist dessert this time. I pushed it away from me. My figure would thank me for it.

A sudden movement to the left caught my attention. Tony had jerked back from the table. His face was alarmingly white. He vaulted to his feet unsteadily, mumbling, "Excuse me."

With that, he rushed from the room.

I stared after him, in shock. I wasn't alone. The whole table went quiet.

"What on earth?" said Vera Horner.

"Is the poor man sick?" said the captain.

"Sozzled, more like," offered our Mr. Sloan.

I threw my napkin down on the table and rose. "I'll just go check. Excuse me." I picked up my evening bag and wrap and followed in his wake.

I checked the salon bar as I went through it. No sign of him. I stood outside the water closet for some time, an adequate amount of time to complete any usual functions. When he didn't emerge from there, I wondered if he had bolted for his cabin. That presented a problem. We hadn't progressed to that sort of relationship. Hence, I didn't know where it was located.

Then I had an idea. If I had been taken ill, cabin air would not be what I was craving. I retraced our steps from earlier that day. Through the main lobby, up the grand staircase to the promenade deck. I turned left at the wide landing and stepped through the double doors to fresh air.

Tony was there, where we had been before, leaning over the railing, looking out to sea. His head was down. I joined him at the rail.

He looked over. "So sorry," he said quietly. "That was rude of me."

I searched his face. It was still too pale, and the long lines that creased alongside his nose and mouth were more pronounced than usual.

"Are you ill?" I said, putting a hand on his upper arm. "Can I help you back to your cabin?" His arm was stiff, the muscles hard. I dropped my hand.

He shook his head. "Better now." He looked off into the distance. "Sorry to interrupt your dining."

"I was done anyway. Dessert was not to my liking," I said.

He laughed coarsely then. That's when an idea popped into my mind and constricted my throat. "Was it the rum?"

He nodded. "Can't stand the stuff. Even the smell sends me back to the trenches."

I waited for him to explain. Even though I already knew what he was going to say.

"We gave it to the boys before we went over the top."

Johnny had told me that on one of his leaves. Tin mugs full of rum. They called it liquid courage. The sort of courage that was needed to charge into an onslaught of enemy machine-gun fire.

"Funny how it is. I can't bear it. Yet some blokes can't stop drinking the stuff, now that they're back in Blighty."

"It helps them to forget," I said.

"Wish something would help me," said Tony. He stood up straight, his whole height of six feet. "Strange how it comes on. The quacks call it shell shock My heart starts beating like crazy, and I've got to get out of wherever I am."

"I'm sorry, Tony," I said. "It's so unfair."

He shrugged. "A lot of blokes have it worse. At least I pull out of it."

That was true. A lot of fellows had it worse. Blinded, disfigured, missing limbs. Missing minds. Some were still in hospital these many years later, and probably always would be.

"Nighttime is the hardest. To be honest, I'm not much fun to sleep with." He gave that low, coarse laugh again.

I had heard about that too. A lot of men returning from the trenches couldn't sleep with their wives. Too much thrashing. Of course, a lot of couples in our set had separate bedrooms anyway. I'd never understood that tradition of the English. But then, my background was completely different.

I looked out to the place where the sea met the air, and couldn't find it. It was a cloudy night, already shrouding us in darkness. Waves were tame right now, coming in steady rolls. The wind had shifted direction, sending plumes of smoke our way.

"Ah, the wonderful odour of bunker fuel," I said, pretending to take a deep breath.

That coaxed a smile out of him. "Better than the old days of coal soot."

"I remember that," I said. "First boat I came over on was coal-fired. In some ways, I feel bad about the switch to oil. No need for all those stokers now. And men need jobs."

It was true. I did feel bad about that. If only there was something I could do about it.

"You can't stop progress," said Tony.

He echoed my thoughts. Progress was a good thing mostly, but not always, for all people. The war had taught us that. Progress led to the development of better and faster killing machines.

"Up for a walk?" I said, determined to change this sad conversation. I pushed off from the rail.

Tony faced me. "Don't we have something to do back at your cabin?"

I stopped moving. "Good lord! I completely forgot about Harry. Let me think."

I tried to do so, as Tony carefully watched my face.

"I haven't entirely decided what to do about Harry," I said finally.

"You mean, whether to involve the authorities." Tony's voice was soft and low.

"That would be a last resort. In any case, there's no reason to involve you. Best for your sake that I don't." I patted his arm. He tensed at my touch.

"Nice of you to think of that," he said. He gave a small, crooked smile.

"Well, it's not a problem for me, to the same extent," I said. This was a small fib. It could indeed be a problem if investigators looked into my past. Tony didn't need to know that, however. "I'd rather not be involved in a formal investigation. So can I count on your discretion?"

"Of course," said Tony. "I'll stay on standby, shall I? You can call on me if you require my assistance." He gave me his cabin number then. Not too far from mine, after all. That could be a good thing. Or it could make things even more awkward, depending on what I decided to do about Harry.

We parted at that. I hurried back to my cabin, ready to confront the problem. Elf met me at the door. She had done a good job of clearing up my clothes from the floor.

"Left the mattress overturned," she said. "Until we decide for sure what to do."

"Smart thinking," I said, looking down. The body had been covered by a rather magnificent gold and black bedspread. "We'll have to do something soon. Before there's an odour."

Elf scrunched up her face. "Hate dead bodies. Never got used to the smell."

"So let's discuss our choices," I said. "I could call for the purser. Do we know who he is?"

Elf shook her head. "Some new guy."

"Unfortunate. Then we don't know if he'll be loyal. And I'd really prefer not to involve the authorities. It's too risky for us." I didn't need to look at Elf to gauge her agreement. She was allergic to the law.

"Storage is a problem. I really don't see how we could get Harry down to the cold cellars without being seen."

Elf shook her head.

"So." I started to pace, but there wasn't much room with Harry in the centre of the floor. I trod around him a few times like a dog circling the floor to lie down. "Either we move him somewhere else close by where he will be discovered soon, or ..." I looked at her.

"... we shove him out the porthole," said Elf.

I left my circular march and moved to where she pointed.

"It's dark enough," I said. "As long as someone isn't looking out their porthole at exactly the same time ..." *Then they wouldn't see a body dropping over the side*, I finished in my thoughts.

"Do we know what's directly below us?" said Elf.

"More cabins, I think. But perhaps we should do a small check?" It wouldn't be too hard to go down the stairs and try to find the corridor directly below us. Just one problem. The level below was likely second class. What reason could I give for my little walk on the wrong level?

"I could pretend to be inebriated, I suppose. Or attempting to reach a lover." Neither appealed to me.

"Leave it to me," said Elf. "I got friends I can ask."

Friends? What friends?

"Need something to grease the wheels," she said.

"Money?" I said.

"Nah. Let me think." She sat on the edge of the mattress with her legs tucked up under her arms. I could see her forehead crease with thought. "Got it. You got any perfume you don't need?"

I tilted my head. "Not the L'Heure Bleue, Elf. You're not taking my favourite perfume." Johnny had bought me that when it first came out, in 1912. I didn't always wear it. The memories were too bittersweet. But I carried the beautiful bottle with me wherever I went. Sometimes I'd sniff the scent right before bed.

Basta! Enough. Back to business.

"Any smelly stuff. Don't matter which," said Elf.

I headed to the water closet and switched on the light there. The shelf above the sink held all my toiletries. I reached for the bottle of My Sin, a new scent by Lanvin that was too husky for me. It was hardly touched. I could donate that to the cause.

I came back into the room and handed it to her.

"Perfec'. You want I should go now?"

I nodded.

"Back in a jiff," she said. She disappeared out the door.

I stared after her. Then I looked down at the floor. At Harry, under the bedspread that served as a shroud. Poor fellow. Here he was, dead on my floor, and I had been treating him as a nuisance to be dealt with. That horrified me. Someone should be mourning him. Did he have a mother still alive? A sweetheart?

I wondered who he had been and what had brought him onto the *Victoriana*. Had he survived the war only to die at sea on a luxury liner? And then I remembered that he was American. He probably wouldn't have been in the trenches with my Johnny.

Still, I felt it was my duty to find out who he had been. If there was a woman waiting for him, it would be a kindness to let her know that he wouldn't be coming back. If there was one thing I could relate to, it was that. Grief did not care about class barriers, and it could be far, far worse not to know what had happened to your loved one.

Besides, I needed to know what was going on in order to feel safe.

Bile rose in my throat. I quickly discovered that I didn't like being alone in cabins with dead bodies. I wrenched the door open and lurched into the hall. Tony had given me his cabin number on our walk back from dinner. I headed there without thinking.

It was further down, on the far side of the ship. A small centre hallway connected the two corridors.

"Come in," said Tony when I knocked on the door.

I twisted the handle, pushed the door in just a bit, then stopped. "Are you decent?" I asked. Then waited. He would be expecting the porter, not me.

"Just barely," said Tony. He continued to pull the door open. A crooked smile replaced the surprise on his face. He was down to shirt and evening trousers.

I looked away, feeling the flush creep up my face. My eyes surveyed his cabin. "It's the same layout as mine," I said, stalling for time.

"So it is," he said. "Aren't they all?"

I shook my head. "This is the first time I've seen the standard staterooms. I had intended to take the Victoria stateroom at the stern, but I waited too late to book, and it was already taken. My current one became available, luckily."

He nodded. And waited.

"Elf had to run an errand. I didn't like being alone with Harry."

I saw comprehension and then concern cross his face. He nodded. "Completely understandable. Can I offer you a seat?" He gestured to the two tub chairs between the portholes.

I walked all the way into the cabin and sat down primly. He took the chair opposite. I glanced around. Tony's bed was neatly made up with the same black-and-gold patterned bedspread that currently served as Harry's shroud. That brought me back to the problem.

"You'll have noticed that Harry wasn't killed in my cabin," I said.

Tony sat back. Again, that amused smile. "Yes, I noticed that. Though I'm a tad surprised you did. Were you a nurse in the war?"

I shook my head. "Not exactly. I drove an ambulance. Elf worked in a funeral home."

Tony barked a laugh. "Of course she did."

"I heard a lot of stories," I added.

The laughing was followed by a coughing fit, as before. Tony didn't like comments on his coughing, which he saw as a weakness, so I waited quietly, looking around the room. It was in the same art deco style, with geometric shapes repeated in the art and furniture, but a slightly different, darker colour scheme of slate and grey.

"So that's what you meant earlier by 'We're more used to it,'" he said finally.

I smiled innocently. If Tony thought that, it was just as well. I'd have to watch my tongue better in future.

I fiddled with the hem of my gown. "I thought it might be good to address the big questions," I said. I leaned forward to meet his gaze.

"Such as ...?"

"Where was Harry killed? Why was he moved, and particularly, why did he show up in my cabin?" I paused. "Was it deliberate? Meaning, was I a target? Or was it simply a crime of opportunity?"

"Any reason you can think of for you to be a target?" asked Tony.

"No, of course not," I said quickly. I could feel Tony's eyes on me.

"I know at first you said you didn't recognize the fellow," he said. He reached for the silver cigarette case on the table. "But could you be mistaken, on second thought? Someone from years ago? Now that you've had a chance to think about it."

I had to admire Tony's technique. He was giving me an opportunity to change my story without making it seem like I had lied. But that wasn't necessary.

"I truly don't know who the fellow is," I said. "And I would swear, just by the way he's dressed, that he's American."

Tony raised an eyebrow. "So?"

"Johnny didn't tell you?" I said with a small smile. "I'm from the colonies, darling. I'm Canadian."

"Really?" He seemed pleased by that, for some reason. His hands continued to play with the cigarette case. "I assumed you were American, even though your accent is pretty well gone."

"Most people do." I sighed. For the most part, it really annoyed me. Canada was so overlooked. People just lumped us in with the Americans. And yet we were quite different, probably because of our harsh northern climate and the way we were settled. For instance, our national slogan was not "Life, liberty, and the pursuit of happiness." We were "Peace, order, and good government." And while we might be known for being extremely polite, we are *not* pushovers. Canadians have won every war they've been in, I like to remind people. We even burned down the White House in 1814 …

"So. Canadian. But really, that explains so much," said Tony. I waited. His eyes went cloudy with memories.

"Your wicked sense of humour, for one. I knew some Canadian officers. They were with us from the start, unlike the Yanks. Good men. The best. Uncommonly good-natured. And good lord, were they tough. Nothing fazed them. The weather. The conditions."

"It's the winters," I said quietly. "Once you've lived through a prairie winter …" I paused. I'd heard it before. Our big prairie farm boys, accustomed to baling hay all day, were a welcome sight on the battlefields of France.

"Are you from the prairies?" Tony asked.

I guessed I had invited that question. "No. I'm a city girl, from close to Toronto," I said. Again, I followed the family mantra. Be truthful whenever you can be. There is less to remember.

He seemed satisfied with that. "I'd like to hear about it sometime."

Not likely, I said to myself. I sat back in the chair and let my eyes wander. Tony's jacket and tie lay on the bed, but everything else was orderly and neatly put away. A single cufflink box sat on the solitary set of mahogany drawers. The top was clear of any bottles or jars. No whisky bottle in sight. No seltzer bottle. Tony appeared to be man who appreciated order and simplicity. I couldn't see into the water closet from here.

He watched me until the silence became awkward.

"Elf should be back by now," I said.

"I'll walk you back," said Tony. He stood up and retrieved his jacket and tie from the bed. "Give me a moment and I'll put these back on, for propriety's sake." He disappeared into the water closet.

I couldn't sit still, so I stood up and continued my assessment of Tony's character via his cabin. A book lay on the bedside table. This was something that drew me like a fly to honey. Always, when visiting the homes of my social peers, I hoped for a view of their library. Books were like sweets to me, almost impossible to resist. Not to mention, you could tell a lot about people from the books they read. Or didn't read, and just had on display. That was almost more interesting.

My curiosity got the better of me. A book on a bedside table would be read. Was it lurid fiction, like I enjoyed? Agatha Christie or something high-minded? Or boring non-fiction? I stepped over to read the cover, hoping to find something with which to tease him.

That's when I noticed the handle. Only the butt was visible, peeking out from behind the lampstand on the desk. You had to get up close to the bedside table to see even that. I got closer.

When the past creeps up on me, it comes with a cold feeling. I felt the chill now, looking down at the handgun.

I backed away swiftly. Thoughts went tumbling through my mind. Obviously, I didn't know Tony as well as I thought. I reminded myself that Harry had been killed with a knife. Tony could have had nothing to do with the body in my cabin. He had been with me at the time of the murder, thereby giving us both perfect alibis. But all those thoughts didn't explain what I had just seen.

Why would Tony have a handgun?

CHAPTER FIVE

I REACHED MY chair just as Tony opened the door of the water closet. He smiled.

"Ready to go?" he said.

I nodded and managed a small smile. What sixth sense possessed me to keep my knowledge of his gun a secret? Why didn't I mention it then and ask for an explanation? Even now, I can't explain it. If only I had.

He poked his head out the door. "The coast is clear," he said.

I appreciated his concern for my respectability. A single lady leaving a man's cabin? At any time of the evening, that was certain to set tongues wagging.

We walked along side by side, meeting no one until we passed through the centre hall into the far corridor. There, a steward was just leaving a cabin. He nodded to us and then knocked on the next door. I waited until I saw him enter before turning toward my cabin. Once there, I bent over to peer at the door lock. I let my finger trace the keyhole, then straightened.

"Doesn't appear to be scratched or forced," I said. "Perhaps the killer is good with picking locks?"

"Possibly." Tony shrugged. "Let me go first." He stepped in from of me and put his hand on the doorknob. "Any chance your cabin might have been left unlocked? Like apparently it is now?"

He twisted the handle and swept the door open.

I groaned. "Well, that's me, feeling an idiot. I rushed out to your cabin without my bag or key." We both walked in. And there was my bag, on the set of drawers where I'd left it.

"Honoured to be held in such esteem," said Tony. "But promise me you won't do it again."

We both stared down at Harry. Or rather, at the black-and-gold bedspread that covered the recently deceased. Elf had not returned. I contemplated what to do. The mattress was still flipped over. There wasn't a lot of walking room with the middle of the floor occupied. I considered circling the body like I had earlier, so we could at least sit on the chairs between the portholes to wait for Elf.

Tony's voice cut through my thoughts. "Could that have happened earlier today? Forgetting to lock the door?"

I nodded miserably. "Yes, only then the culprit would have been Elf. She left the cabin after me this afternoon." Elf had her own key. But she was notorious for turning keys the wrong way and not checking. That had happened more than once before when we were in new environs. I told Tony so.

"So. Probably the killer tried a few doors and found yours unlocked." Tony latched the door behind him.

"That seems likely," I said. I leaned back against the wall, cursing Elf in my thoughts. "What miserable luck."

"But you must admit it's probably better than someone targeting you personally, Lucy."

Tony had a point. It *was* better. If I had been targeted, it was likely by someone from my past. Not a pleasant thought. I'd worked hard to cover my tracks. And I didn't need that sort of ghost following me around after all these years.

So yes, it was better if I hadn't been specifically targeted, but it made other things more difficult. "So if leaving the body in the cabin had nothing to do with it being *my* cabin, we don't have as many clues," I said.

"That's true. Still," he said, gesturing with his arm, "you can't drag a body far in broad daylight. Probably the killing took place on this deck, in a cabin not far from yours. In fact …" He opened the cabin door and stepped out. "You have a recessed entry. It's perfect, see?"

I could see. My cabin was down a short hallway leading off the main corridor. Mine was at the end. Two other cabin doors faced each other, perpendicular to mine.

Tony walked to the main corridor. "The killer had only to come as far as here and look both ways to see that no one was coming. Your hall is halfway down the corridor. If all was clear, he would have had ample time to drag the body from his room to yours without the risk of someone walking by and peering down this recess."

"You mean if the killer was in one of those cabins next to mine. Oh goody," I said with a deep sigh. "When we finish dumping the body overboard, we can break into these cabins to find the scene of the crime. Elf will be delighted."

ELF WAS BACK in a jiff. She nodded at Tony and then came to stand beside me.

The three of us looked down at Harry.

"He's a slim man, thank goodness," I said. "Are you thinking what I'm thinking?"

"Burial by porthole?" Tony's voice was grim.

"It's foggy out. No one would see," said Elf.

"I know it sounds heartless," I said quickly. "But it really would be most expedient and do the least social damage. I'm not just talking about me here."

Elf harrumphed. "None of us killed him. Why should we get fed through the wringer?"

Sometimes silence can be stressful. Even worse than unrelenting noise. I found my hands twisting the fringe on my wrap again. Tony stood with his own hands in his pants pockets, clearly assessing the situation. He turned and walked to the closest porthole. "This one, I think. Easier access. We won't have to move furniture."

I saw what he meant. The other porthole was over the small table, framed with easy chairs. We'd have to rearrange things and then put them back. Always risky, if people hear you doing it or if we didn't get it exactly right. First rule of burglary: always leave things exactly as you found them. I learned that at my grandfather's knee.

Tony opened the porthole and looked out into the distance.

"Can't see a bloody thing," he said. "The fog is too thick."

"Surely that's a good thing," I said, rushing to his side. "A dark, foggy night. You can hear the waves." I loved the sound. We both stood there for a few moments.

"Can't see what's directly below," said Tony.

"Elf took care of that," I said. Then I let her explain.

"Second-class cabins below us. Then steerage. No public rooms."

"Are you sure?" said Tony. "How could you see?" He frowned in her general direction.

Elf shrugged. "Maggy said so. Told me herself. No public rooms. The main promenade is on the other side."

Therefore, no one likely to be looking out at the romantic sea as Harry went by.

"And who is this sage Maggy?" said Tony.

Elf sniffed her disapproval. "Maggy's not a cook. Doesn't use sage. She does for the cabins in second class."

Now I knew where my perfume had gone. And why Elf had come back smelling like a brothel. Obviously, My Sin had made the rounds of the female servant class on this ship. I shuddered to think how much they had put on. Not to mention how the ship corridors would smell tomorrow.

"Shall we get right to it, then?" said Tony. "I'll take his head and shoulders, if you two want to help with the legs."

Tony removed his jacket and placed it neatly on the bed.

I felt bad about it. I really did. But it truly didn't seem like we had much choice. At sea, when someone dies, they are always buried en route. Whether Harry left the ship here or by the stern would hardly seem different to him, at this stage.

Despite his slim physique and lamentable shell shock, Tony was a strong man. He had no trouble hoisting the body up to porthole height. I tried to busy myself organizing Elf with the leg-carrying so that I didn't have to look when Tony placed the head out the porthole.

"Ready, everyone?" said Tony. He managed to hoist Harry's shoulders through the frame of the porthole. Elf and I held the legs as high as we could.

"Tallyho," said Tony. With a herculean effort, he grabbed Harry's hips and followed through. Elf and I let go. For a moment, Harry seemed to hang there, legs suspended on our end. There would be a splash. Would we hear it? The waves were quite loud.

I watched in morbid fascination as Tony completed the task and heaved Harry over the side.

We waited for the splash.

THUD.

Elf raced to the other porthole. She twisted the handle until it was fully open, standing on the small table for support. Her shoulders disappeared through the opening as she leaned out as far as she could.

"Bloody hell," said Tony, also leaning out and looking down.

I stood frozen to the floor.

"Bull's-eye," said Elf. "Right in the lifeboat."

CHAPTER SIX

I SLUMPED TO the floor. "We dropped a dead body into a life-boat." I groaned.

"There's a certain classical irony to that," said Tony. He seemed to be enjoying this a tad more than the rest of us.

"Maggy didn't tell me 'bout no lifeboats," Elf grumbled.

"Did you ask her?" My voice might have been a tad strident.

She shrugged again. "Asked about the rooms below. Didn't think of anything else."

"Well, neither did I, for that matter," I said. "Can't be helped."

Tony started to laugh then. It wasn't a nice laugh, and as usual he struggled for breath after it. I was a tad alarmed he was going to go blue.

"Sit down, Tony," I said, getting to my feet. Elf rushed forward to help. We tried to guide him to the bed — or rather the sloping mattress — but he shook my hand from his arm.

"I've been meaning to ask. What on earth is that cloying odour? It smells like someone broke a bottle of perfume in here."

Elf backed away.

A small giggle escaped me. "Ah, yes. We bribed them with My Sin."

Tony looked blank.

"Elf's friends in service. Maggy et al. She bribed them with perfume, and they kind of went overboard."

Elf whooped. "Just like Harry!"

Too late to regret my unfortunate choice of words.

"One good thing," I said brightly. "At least the liberal use of perfume will cover up the stench of poor Harry in here."

WE SEPARATED SOON after that. As Tony declared, there wasn't much we could do until morning.

I stood at the porthole thinking about fog. It struck me how convenient a murky mist could be. And that if only we had the ability to harness it, we could accomplish a lot that we didn't want known or, for that matter, cover our sins.

"*I couldn't tell who he was. There was a fog ...*"

"*Sorry I'm so late. There was a fog ...*"

"*Sorry, darling, I couldn't find my way home. There was a fog ...*"

"*I didn't see the lifeboat ...*"

"Damned shame about the fog," said Elf, at the other porthole.

A strangled noise escaped me. Elf set about straightening up the room, and I turned to join her.

"Maybe they won't discover the body until we get to port," I said hopefully as we moved the mattress into place.

"Maybe they'll think he did himself in," said Elf.

"Without his shoes?" I gave her a glare. "Who takes their shoes off before they jump?"

"Forgot about that," Elf mumbled. "Maybe should I throw them out after 'im?"

I straightened up. "No, that won't work. Too risky. Shoes

wouldn't come off in the tumble. They'll know someone tossed them over after. Besides, I have an idea about those shoes. Did you put them in a safe place?"

She nodded.

I started to pace. My mind was working on a really cunning idea. So cunning, it reminded me of stories I used to hear at the knee of my bootlegger grandfather. "You checked his pockets, right? Nothing there."

"Not a bean," she said. "Did a full check when you were at dinner. Searched hems and linings too."

I knew Elf used to sew coins into her hems, back in the day. For all I knew, she still did so. It was standard practice for street urchins. They didn't have the use of banks or even regular mattresses for hiding cash.

But our Harry had had nothing on him but his clothes. No identification. No currency.

Unless ...

"Elf, where did you put those shoes?" I said.

"Eh?"

"Harry's shoes. Bring them here."

One of the luxuries of being in first class is they provide you with fresh fruit in your room. A small basket containing apples, bananas, and one orange sat on my bedside table. Things that might require peeling. I moved over to look at it better and found what I was after. A paring knife.

Elf came back into the room with the shoes. "Wanna know where I hid them?"

"Later," I said. "Put the shoes on the coffee table."

She did so, and I sat back down in one of the easy chairs. It took some effort, but I was able to use the knife to pry the heel off one shoe. Instead of a solid heel, this one was hollow in the middle. The cavity was packed with stuffing to keep the contents from rattling. I carefully removed every bit of it. Rough greyish rocks spilled out onto the table.

"Just as I suspected. Diamonds!" I cried.

Elf peered over my shoulder. "Don't look like very good ones."

"They're uncut, Elf. The real thing. And look at the size of them." I poked with my finger. "Must be worth a fortune."

I knew a thing or two about diamonds. Something the size of these rough rocks would cut down to at least one carat each. Maybe more.

"See?" I said to Elf. "A master splitter will cut each of these in half to make two diamonds. Then he'll start carving facets. It's precise work and takes years of practice and skill."

"Looks like grey gravel to me. That why they call these things rocks?"

I smiled. "Probably. I hadn't thought of that before." I counted them. Seven. I set to work on the other heel.

"So. Was Harry doin' a deal?"

"Most likely a deal that went wrong," I said, putting extra pressure on the knife. "It may not have been about the diamonds specifically. By that I mean, diamonds are used as a type of currency internationally. In some circles," I added. Elf would know what circles I meant. "And this lot, looking like common gravel, would attract much less attention than the cut gems."

"You mean if they fell out of the heel of his shoe by mistake," she said.

"Yes," I said, as more fell from the second heel onto the table. "It would certainly be a great deal safer to transport the uncut version."

We both sat in silence for a moment, staring down at them. My eyes were swimming.

I yawned. "It's late. We need to find a safe place to put these. Somewhere no one would think to look."

"Leave it to me," said Elf. I watched her sweep the gems with both hands into a little pile.

"And let's keep this to ourselves for now, Elf." I got up and made my way to the water closet. "Lord, I'm tired. This day is done for me."

CHAPTER SEVEN

DAY TWO AT SEA

THE NEXT MORNING dawned bright and fog-free.

"Blimey," said Elf, peering out the porthole.

"What?" I said sleepily.

"Birds."

I groaned and rolled over.

THE CIRCUS STARTED soon after that. Elf had opened the porthole so we could hear what was going on rather than stick our heads out.

The commotion reached us several stories up. Clearly, Harry had been discovered.

"Let's stay here for breakfast and monitor the situation," I suggested. "We have fruit here. How about you run down to the dining room and pick up a few buns."

"Sure," she said. "And coffee." As she pulled on some clothes that might pass for a maid's, I was getting an idea.

"Elf, I've been thinking. We need to find out who is on the other side of us. The two cabins," I said. "It would be easier if we didn't involve the purser quite yet. Can you do that?"

"Sure thing," she said. "I'll drop by the servants' dining room. Pick us up some grub there."

"You're a treasure," I said.

She just grunted.

While Elf went on her covert mission, I busied myself with dressing. It would have to be things I could wiggle into myself, without help. So I did without a full corset and chose a drop-waist day dress with side zipper, long sleeves, and a matching scarf. Both were in magenta, a colour that suited me. I was long past the mourning requirements of black and then dull mauve. These last two years, colour had become a treasure for me to embrace. To this day, I can't bear to wear black for evening wear.

I had the perfect pair of shoes for this ensemble — grey suede with crossover straps — and a matching clutch bag.

Elf returned as I was finishing my makeup. I practically leaped on her for the tray of warm biscuits, butter, and jam. We sat on the chairs by the portholes, sharing the pot of coffee between two cups and happily munching away at the food. I took a banana from the fruit basket and split it in two, giving her half. That made me think about Vera Horner, and the banana that would go to waste in her basket. I would have to mention that conversation to Elf.

I always enjoyed meals, savouring each new taste and sometimes lingering over favourite things to make them last longer. My companion was very different. Elf finished her share before me. Like many children who grew up with never enough to eat, she had a habit of wolfing down her food. It always broke my heart a little, watching her. I was reminded of a dog that lived in fear of starvation.

She stayed quiet until I had finished licking jam off my fingers and raised my head. I waited for her to spill the names.

"Dame by the name of Martin is in cabin twenty-six. The girls call her fussy-muss."

I groaned. "Oh no. Not our Amanda, right next door! She's Vera Horner's friend. I sat with them at dinner. They both specialize in gossip. I'm going to be ducking around pillars to avoid her." What rotten luck! It also meant we would need to behave and keep our voices down. The walls between these cabins were not as soundproof as I would like.

"The other side is booked in the name of some gent called DeBeers," she said. "From Antwerp. But it's a queer thing. Steward hasn't seen the man at all. There's no luggage in the cabin. Looks like he didn't make it."

I thought for a moment, then laughed out loud. "Oh, Elf. How amazingly clever. I think we have our culprit. The name gives it away."

"What's so special about DeBeers?" she asked.

I grinned. "Listen and learn. DeBeers is the name of a huge diamond enterprise based in South Africa. Probably, the man who booked the cabin isn't named DeBeers at all. It was simply a code name to help Harry find the right cabin for a rendezvous. Too obvious to, say, look for Mr. Diamond. But Harry would recognize the name DeBeers."

"That means they wouldn't even have to know each other. Just each be given the code name." Sometimes Elf surprised me. For a person who never made it beyond third grade, she had a good working brain. That's likely what kept her alive all those years before she met me.

There was a knock at the door.

"Take these dirty plates into the water closet, Elf. I'll see who it is." I watched her disappear from the room before I opened the cabin door.

Tony stood there, with a steward beside him. Neither of them looked happy, but the steward took the prize for misery.

"Darling, it appears you have been summoned," said Tony.

"Bugger," I said.

The steward nearly fainted. Whoops! My lady mask had slipped.

"I'll go with you," said Tony.

"No need," I said. There really wasn't. I had my story straight, and Tony had no idea how resourceful I could be.

"Nevertheless," said Tony. His face was firm. I could see he was itching to play the hero.

I smiled and relented. Tony had influence all his own, when he chose to use it. It wouldn't hurt to go in with extra firepower.

I grabbed my flimsy wrap and led the way to the corridor. From there, the unfortunate steward escorted us to a small lounge by the bridge, used by the officers. I'd been there before. It was a room most men would feel comfortable in. Club chairs and two games tables fit the old naval atmosphere. A portrait of the king graced the short wall between the portholes. Numerous nautical drawings from the last century lined the other walls, all framed with wood. Similar wood covered the walls, with wainscoting that was not as elaborately carved as that in the first-class card rooms and bars where men gathered. And of course, one couldn't miss the inevitable ashtray on every flat surface.

There were two men in the room. I recognized the captain, of course.

"Ah, Lucy! Er, Lady Revelstoke. Mr. Anderson. This is unfortunate business. Very unfortunate." The captain came across the room and reached down for my hand. I wasn't sure if he was going to hold it or kiss it. He decided to hold it in both his hands, as if I were a sweet young thing needing comforting. The concern in his eyes was genuine. I was beginning to feel a teeny bit guilty.

"I expect you have already met the purser. He is detained at the moment. Mr. Mason is in his employ as our security officer."

He gestured to the other man, who stepped forward. I gave him a thorough look. This was not the sort of man I mixed with these days. However, his type wasn't entirely unknown to me.

Brown hair turning to grey. Worn face that had seen a lot of the seedy side of life, I'd wager. Solid body that in the past might have been muscular but had softened with time. I put his age at about fifty.

"Mr. Mason was previously a police detective in America," said the captain. "He has joined our crew after sadly losing his wife this year. We're very lucky to have him."

I nodded to the American, glad to see I didn't know him. "I'm sorry about your wife," I said.

He smiled warmly and gestured with a rough hand to the leather easy chair. "Thank you, miss, please have a seat."

I waited for Tony to explode. It was fun to see his face go red and his throat produce sizzles.

"'Miss'?" he croaked. "Have you lost your mind? If this were a century ago, I would demand satisfaction."

The poor American looked utterly mystified.

"By 'demand satisfaction,' he means meet you at dawn with pistols loaded." I gazed fondly at Tony. "We don't do that anymore. I think you will find he's referring to how you addressed me. 'Miss' isn't one of the acceptable ways."

"She's a countess!" Tony was practically spitting.

"Dowager countess," I corrected. "I may still reside in the old pile, but I am a widow now." This was starting to be fun.

The captain stepped in. "Lady Revelstoke, my apologies. Our guest is American and wouldn't know. Mr. Mason, forgive me, I should have told you. Please address her as Lady Revelstoke."

"Of course. My apologies," said Mr. Mason, who appeared sincere, if rattled. "But if I could ask —"

"Don't be ridiculous, my man," said the captain, clearly irritated. "She's the picture of delicate womanhood. Look at her. She couldn't lift a twenty-pound dog out a porthole, let alone a two-hundred-pound man."

Elf isn't the only actress on this ship. I can play a part when I need to. I gasped. "Then there really is a body in the lifeboat? My maid told me about it this morning, and I could hardly believe her. You aren't honestly suggesting I had anything to do with it?"

"Of course not, my Lady," said the captain, sweeping an arm. "Ridiculous."

"Of course I meant no such thing," said the American policeman earnestly. "Please understand that we are just trying to make sense of it all. You see our dilemma. It isn't logical that someone hoisted the body up *into* the lifeboat."

"Really, Mason. Is it necessary to go into detail with a lady present?" The captain was outraged. Good for him. I like a man who will underestimate me.

I waved his concern away. "Please don't worry. I have war experience."

The captain raised an eyebrow at that. I hadn't told him.

"But you see my point," said the American, looking directly at me. He had kind brown eyes. "Much more likely that the body was dropped from above. And from what I can see, there are three suites that could have been used for this purpose. Yours is one."

"You're suggesting that the body was thrown from my suite?" I gasped convincingly. "Surely we would have noticed. Wouldn't there be blood?" I looked to Captain Elliot for answers.

"Yes, Mason. Think of that. The steward would have noticed this morning." The captain nodded in satisfaction.

Tony caught my eye. We were both thinking the same thing. *Unless the body was butchered elsewhere.*

"Most definitely, it is unlikely. And I apologize for any distress we are causing you, my Lady." Mason looked more distressed than I felt. I was having the time of my life.

"You will understand I have to ask these questions, merely as a process of elimination. Lady Revelstoke, is there any possibility that someone could have gotten into your cabin when you weren't there?"

I let that one sit for a short while. Better for emphasis.

"Oh dear," I said finally.

"Yes?" said Mason, keyed up.

I turned to Tony. "Tony, you remember Elf yesterday."

Tony groaned. I was pleased. He caught on quickly.

I turned back to the captain. "You see, we have servants at home."

"I'm sorry?" Mason would need more explanation than that, it appeared.

"They follow one around and lock up after one," I said. "It's simple, really. You need a key, correct? The cabin doors on this ship don't automatically lock when you close them, do they?"

The captain shook his head.

I leaned back into the chair. "Elf left the door unlocked yesterday. We discovered that when Tony walked me back to my cabin."

"Who is this person 'Elf'?" said Mason.

"Lady Revelstoke's maid," said Tony. "She isn't used to locking doors in the castle. The butler does that."

"So your door might have been left unlocked?" said the captain.

I shrugged. "Quite likely."

"Damned careless of you, Lucy. You need to train that girl better." Tony folded his arms as he scolded me.

I felt Mason tense.

"Oh, he's allowed to call me Lucy," I said sweetly. "You see, his father's a viscount."

I'm going to hell, no question.

CHAPTER EIGHT

THE CAPTAIN SEEMED to think I had been badgered enough by the American. He suggested I could use a medicinal brandy. I acquiesced graciously and promised to sit beside him at dinner. I followed Tony out into the corridor.

"That went well," I said.

Tony started. "This must be some new definition of the word 'well' that I am not acquainted with."

My face wore a smile, and I had a spring in my step. "It did go well. We learned heaps. For instance, we know that they are focusing on three cabins, not just mine. And that their American detective is out of his depth. Plus we managed to insinuate that my cabin door is frequently left unlocked. I'd call that a good hour's work."

"Subterfuge, you mean," muttered Tony.

"Don't quibble," I said as we descended the grand staircase. I nodded to an older couple going past us in the opposite direction. "I think I earned my brandy. But first, a short trip back to my room to visit the plumbing."

Tony snorted. "Think I'll do the same. Shall we meet at half past the hour?"

Before I could answer, Elf came barrelling out of my room. "Lor, there you are. Tell me, and be quick about it."

We stood in the empty corridor as I gave her the abridged version. She got a big kick out of the security officer who had been a detective.

"Known a few of them types," she said. "I'm no Dumb Dora. He won't get nuttin' out of me." I shivered to think what would happen when they met in person.

But Elf had other things on her mind. Seems she had been doing a bit of investigating on her own. You might say it fuelled her somewhat exaggerated delight in the macabre. She pulled us into the cabin and shut the door behind us.

"Checked out egg, best as could, with all them sailor knobs standin' guard. Wouldn't let me close, but I snuck up to the lifeboat and had a peep while they were swatting away at the birds. Then they threw a tarp over the poor sod, so couldn't see no more. Birds had done a number."

"That's awful," I said. I truly felt bad about it. If only we had managed to dump him in the ocean, where he would have been eaten by fish instead.

"Can't wait to tell the others back home. This beats Mamie Murgatroyd's death by a long shot." Elf was practically wringing her hands.

"Who the devil was Mamie Murgatroyd?" said Tony.

"Devil is right," I muttered. "Deserved everything she got."

"Hoity-toity cousin of our Lucy here's husband. She died in a bizarre undergarment accident," said Elf.

"You mean she worked in a garment factory?" said Tony, clearly puzzled. Cousins of the aristocracy did not work.

"Nah," said Elf. "She fell while playing tennis and broke a bone in her corset."

"Stabbed through her black heart," I added.

Tony made a sound like a donkey.

"Blimey. Plum forgot to tell you," said Elf. "Purser wants to see you, Luce. You can beard him in his lair, says he."

I raised an eyebrow. "That's odd. Did he actually use that expression?" I hadn't heard it in years.

Elf shrugged. "Sure did."

"Do you know him?" said Tony.

"No idea. Do we know him, Elf?" I supposed not. Otherwise she would have said his name, surely.

"Not from Adam. Handsome bloke, though. Wouldn't kick him outta bed for naught."

"Elf!"

Tony made that donkey noise again.

I sighed. "I'd better go see what this is about. Tony, I'll meet you in the salon bar at noon." I shooed him on his way, then headed to the loo.

Elf was peering out the porthole when I returned.

"Elf, in the meantime, why don't you ..." I stopped there. Better not. I didn't want to think what Elf could get up to if I set her loose to investigate on her own.

"On second thought, take a break. Do whatever you like, visit your friends. I'll be back after luncheon." I turned around and gave a little wave. "Toodle-oo."

I made my way down the first-class corridor, across to the grand stairwell, and down a level. All manner of well-dressed people walked by me, the fashionable women nodding and the men tipping their hats. I smiled at everyone and stopped to talk to one or two who were known to me.

By the time I found myself down another flight and across another corridor, it appeared I was completely lost. I'd had a vague idea of where the purser's office should be. Everyone knew that. And I'd been on this ship before. But the blasted office wasn't where it was supposed to be.

A young steward found me looking around, all alone and absolutely bewildered.

I accepted his help with grace. He was delighted to squire me down another flight of stairs, past several other official-looking cabins, to the man himself. On the way, he gave me a running commentary about how the purser was "the goods" and how I wasn't to be flustered or anything. He was "quite a gent."

All the stewards reported to the purser, of course. On a ship, the purser was a very important person. He was the money man. You have no idea how many financial transactions and thousands of pounds it takes for a ship to sail. All the food supplies, fuel, linen, salaries … pursers handle all negotiations and payments and manage all of the staff except for the naval officers, who report directly to the captain. A big job, and a necessary one.

The steward knocked three times on the door.

"Enter," said a deep voice from the North American side of the pond.

The young man opened the door and held it for me. "Excuse me, Mr. West. This is Lady Revelstoke."

I swept by him into the cabin.

This office was similar to the captain's, but less decorative and much busier. There was a central desk bolted to the floor, with two chairs on my side. A ship's clock and barometer hung on the wall to my right. That and the opposite wall were lined with tall file cabinets. Piles of paper claimed every flat surface. I smiled at that.

"Lady Revelstoke. Thank you for coming," said that deep voice.

I looked up and started. I'd been accustomed to middle-aged officers. The man opposite me was like nothing in my experience, and it shook me for some reason. I had to steady myself with a hand on the chair back.

He had been seated behind the desk. Now, he vaulted up, in a move that was both powerful and controlled.

He had what I like to call Saxon good looks. Above-average height, broad in the shoulders, light eyes, honey-blond hair. It was the kind of body you could imagine wielding a broadsword or mace on a medieval battlefield. I had to shake that vision out of my mind.

He was dressed in the incredibly sexy and immaculate uniform of a naval officer. Sexy to me, anyway.

We stared at each other for a moment longer than polite. My sixth sense was tingling. I could swear ... no, how could I have met him before? Yet he seemed familiar. Like I had met him in a dream somewhere, which wouldn't have been a hardship. Maybe it was the way he held himself that reminded me of someone else?

He seemed to be struggling to keep emotions in check. His mouth opened to talk, then closed again. The room seemed uncommonly still and stifling.

Finally, he broke the silence. A thin smile spread across his face.

"Bessie says hello," he said.

I froze.

Funny how the world can give way in one single moment. Terra firma becomes a slithering mound of quicksand. There was only one Bessie. Bessie Starkman, the most powerful mob woman in the world. Who just happened to call Hamilton, Ontario, her home.

"Rocco sent you," I said flatly. I dropped into the chair I had been holding.

He had a nice smile. "You don't recognize me. Think back."

I stared at him. Oh lord. So I *had* met him before. But when? And how could I forget such a dominant male presence? It was more than just good looks. Lots of men had that.

I thought back. *Mr. West*, the steward had called him. Could be a false name. Did I know any Wests?

"Way back," he said.

I slipped back in time to before my first ship crossing. To before Elf. To before I met Johnny and started a new life. Back to my school days, running in the streets of Hamilton with the other kids. Catholic school, the nuns, the other girls ... but mainly the boys. Me and the boys, me and that blond kid a few years older, watching my uncles sling cases of bootleg gin into the boats that would speed them across the lake to towns that had embraced the Temperance movement ...

"Graham West," I said finally.

"Just Gray now," he said, obviously pleased that I remembered him.

The world shifted back into place, and I felt a chill slide down my back. "You work for Rocco?" Rocco Perri was Bessie's husband. Another close relative I'd left behind.

"Not anymore. Not for a decade. I work for this shipping line. Rocco just asked me to do Bessie a favour."

I didn't like the sound of that. "What kind of favour?"

Gray shrugged. "Watch your back."

I hadn't thought I could be any more flustered, after the events of last night. But I was wrong. This was news I didn't need.

"Why do they think it needs watching?" I said cautiously.

"Perhaps you need reminding. A man has been murdered," he said.

Crap, I thought. What did he know? I stared at him with my mouth open, not even attempting to play innocent.

"You've heard about it, I'm sure," he said.

I breathed a sigh of relief. "Of course I know. My maid got a look at him in the lifeboat. Said he looked like a torpedo. Is that what got you concerned?"

All this time, he stood tall with his hands behind his back, watching me. Distinct military bearing.

I went on, looking down at my hands in my lap. "Elf said he was stabbed. Knife went deep into the chest. Would have taken strength I don't have."

"I know that," said Gray, finally lowering himself into his chair. "I never thought it was you. That's why I arranged for this meeting. You needed to know I'm here if you need protection."

At that, I looked up and nodded. "Thank you. And believe me, I appreciate it. In a way."

He grinned with straight white teeth. "Understood."

There was a long silence between us. So Graham West had been watching out for me. Just like he had when we were young. I'd had no reason to doubt his motives then, but were they still as pure?

"Anyone we know?" I asked, referring to the body.

He shook his head.

Good. I drew a breath of relief. Gray would know better than I who worked for the family. I'd been gone longer.

I thought back to those lively days, when I was just a kid and didn't seem to have a care in the world. Life had been grand then, just one big adventure. How long ago that seemed.

"How's your sister?" I asked. I remembered a sprightly girl a few years younger than me, with similar honey-blond hair.

"Dead of the flu," he said.

My heart squeezed. "I'm so sorry."

"My fault," he said quietly. He was talking about the Spanish flu that came home from the war in Europe. Millions had died of it. Survived the war, only to die of the flu. Defined the word *irony* in a way never before seen.

"The flu was over home already," I said. "You didn't bring it."

The silence between us was heavy. Everyone had lost loved ones to the flu. Hardly a family had been spared, on either side of the Atlantic. Two of my brothers had died of it, but the people dearest to me had been spared: Johnny, Elf, and my son, Charlie. Johnny was already ill with tuberculosis by then, so we had retreated to the country estate, which was secluded.

"She was sweet," I said. "A good kid. I liked her."

"Thanks."

So he had served in the war. I should have expected that, but most of the non-British men I met these days were American, not Canadian. Did America have conscription like we did in the colonies? I wasn't sure. But one thing had been certain: you simply couldn't replace the thousands of dead bodies in the trenches with volunteers anymore.

"Allied Merchant Navy?" I asked.

"At first," he said. "Then the Royal Canadian Navy. We had only two boats to start. Three hundred and fifty men."

I nodded. The navy had just been getting started, which was surprising considering Canada is a nation bordered by ocean on three sides.

"I signed up immediately. It seemed a way to get out, if you catch my meaning."

I got it. "Ah," I said. He wasn't the only one who'd wanted out and managed to find a way.

"Exactly." A moment passed as we grappled with our respective pasts.

"How did you manage it?" I asked finally.

He shrugged. "The timing was good. War came along just at the moment I was barely into my twenties. I was basically a runner, but that was about to change. Rocco had his eye on me. Mom hated the work I did for your uncles, so she encouraged me to sign up. They accepted it, grudgingly. They're a patriotic lot, which might surprise some. Quite proud of me, as it turned out. *One of us should go and beat the Hun,* that sort of thing."

I nodded. That made sense. And better Graham West risk his life in the trenches than one of their own sons.

He leaned back in the chair and wrapped his big hands behind his head. "When the war was over, I didn't go home — for good. Stayed in shipping. Liked the supply side of the business, and I'm good with numbers. A crusty old gent took a liking to me and made me his assistant. He retired last month. So here I am."

"Here you are," I repeated. *And how am I supposed to feel about that?*

"Rather young to be in this job, aren't you?" I said.

"Rather young to be a dowager countess, aren't you?" he countered.

I laughed. "Touché. It was meant to be a compliment, by the way."

He grinned at me. I started to relax, finally.

"So," I said. "About this murder. Do you think there's a connection? Am I in danger?"

His arms came down on the desk, and his fingers linked together. "Not sure yet. Can't see it being likely. But it is one hell of a surprise. Excuse the language." His one eyebrow raised in a way I remembered from way back. "I don't like surprises."

The clock on the wall ticked its way toward noon. I felt every awkward tick. "I should go," I said. "People are expecting me."

"Of course." He rose from the chair. I waited for him to cross the floor to open the door.

When a man holds a door for you, you are forced to pass quite close to him. It can be too close for comfort. I often wondered if that's why men invented the courtesy in the first place.

As I approached Gray, the scent of him reached me. A sweet smell of hay and tobacco, plus something much more dangerous.

He blocked my way at the last minute. "Lucy," he said in a very low voice. "Send for me day or night, if you need me. Promise me."

I froze for a second. Nobody had called me Lucy in that tone for years. But I nodded my promise and skittered by him as soon as he stepped aside.

CHAPTER NINE

I WAS RUSHING. For some reason, I felt the need to put distance between me and the man who held the purser's job on this ship.

Too close. There had been a time when I would have welcomed a little closeness on the part of Graham West. That had been years ago, when I was barely into my teens. He had stood tall and blond then, a stark contrast to my Italian brothers. Even at sixteen, he'd had the shoulders and muscular physique of an older man. Easy to let my girlish imagination run wild. Better yet, my family had trusted him, my brother Paolo had trusted him, and so had I. Nothing would happen to me with Graham West around. And Gray had been smart enough not to put any moves on me, much as I might have liked it at the time. Girls can be dreamy.

Gray had been my friend in the past, or more accurately, my brother's friend. But was he a friend now? Yes, he'd said he had left the mob, but could I believe him? How could I know for sure he wasn't still working for Rocco?

A purser is in a unique position to know everything that happens on a ship. Every cabin number, every passenger. All supplies are ordered through his office. All the invoices run through his hands. He would have numerous contacts at either end of a voyage. Who would be better placed than a purser to run a little smuggling on the side?

I didn't want to think of it. But truth be told, I wasn't quite sure I could trust our Mr. West.

This new complication shook me. So I probably wasn't as alert as usual, which is why I didn't see Mr. Sloan from our dinner table last night until he was almost on top of me. By the look on his face, I got the distinct impression that was a place he would like to be.

"Lady Revelstoke!" he exclaimed in a very plummy voice. "How fortunate for me. I was hoping to ask you for a drink before lunch."

I looked up in mild shock. How could I get out of this? There didn't seem to be a polite way. And then my good sense kicked in. Could Mr. Sloan be a suspect? He had mentioned being in the import-export business but wouldn't elaborate. In fact, this opportunity was too good to resist. I could find out more about our Mr. Sloan without his being suspicious. I smiled.

"Of course," I said. "That would be delightful."

He gave me a brilliant smile and put out his arm. I wrapped my own around his elbow, as was the custom. He was average height, at least three inches shorter than Graham West. No denying he was an extremely attractive man. His dark good looks suggested a bit of Black Irish in his background.

"The Britannia Bar, I think. It's on this level. Do you play bridge, by the way?" He walked with an easy gait, so I had no trouble keeping up in my heels. Some men aren't as considerate.

"I do, but I much prefer conversation. Or poker," I said wickedly.

He chuckled. "I was right in thinking you would be entertaining company."

I let him guide me into the nautical bar at the bow of the ship. I'd always loved this retreat. You had a gorgeous view of the ocean from almost every chair, as the second row of tables were on a raised platform.

It was moderately busy, but with several seats available. By late afternoon, it would be packed with couples. The Britannia Bar reminded me of the new speakeasies in New York. Very flash and upbeat, with jazz music playing on a gramophone. The fresco above the long, sleek bar consisted of mermaids frolicking with Neptune in a lively pastel sea. In contrast, the other bar near the Grand Salon was more like a traditional British men's club, with dark wood panelling and aged military drawings on the walls. Indeed, that's where the men gathered for their cigars and port. Women ventured in with escorts only, whereas here in the Britannia Bar I could see a few tables where ladies sat alone together. I felt comfortable here.

We sat, and Mr. Sloan asked me what I'd like to drink. I gave him points for that too. So many men just took it upon themselves to order you a dry sherry. I hate sherry.

"A whisky sour, please," I said.

"Make it two," Sloan told the young waiter. He turned to me. "Isn't it refreshing to be free from Prohibition on this ship? Registered in England, no doubt."

"I believe, since we are on the high seas, we would be free to indulge regardless," I said. "But yes. You can be sure the liquor here is of much better quality than the bathtub gin we've been drinking in New York." In fact, I knew it was.

I sat back, and listened to "Bye Bye, Blackbird." My companion made no secret he was looking at me. He appeared to be searching for something to say, or the best way to say it. I decided to help him out.

"Is this your first transatlantic voyage?" I asked.

"No," he said, appearing to relax. "But my first time on the Empire line. I'm quite impressed. First-class outfit."

"Yes, isn't it," I said with a secret smile. "Wonderful chef on this ship. The food can't be beat. I believe the owner is most particular about that." That, I also knew to be true.

He nodded agreement. "My steward is quite a decent chap. Devil of a thing, travelling without a valet. Mine announced he was getting married right before we were to set sail."

"How romantic. But inconvenient," I replied. And I waited.

"Do you travel with a maid?" he asked, all innocence.

I had been waiting for that. "Yes. She shares with me. Since my husband died, she accompanies me on all my travels. With fashions as they are these days, one can't get dressed without help."

"I can imagine," he said. And I got the distinct and chilly feeling that he was imagining exactly that: me getting dressed. Or rather, undressed.

I was revising my opinion of Mr. Sloan. No doubt, he took me for a high-born English lady and a relative innocent. I was hardly that. Asking after my maid was a deliberate attempt to determine if I was alone in my cabin at night. How I replied would determine his chances at seduction. I would have to watch this man.

"Well, your maid does you credit," he said finally. "You are by far the most beautiful woman on this ship. Not to mention intriguing."

Yes, he was a playboy, this man. I smiled gratefully and said thank you.

Our drinks arrived. I lifted mine to clink with his and was rewarded with a brilliant smile. I wondered how many young women and rich widows had fallen for it?

He reached in his pocket and pulled out a silver cigarette case. It was engraved with scrolled initials and looked old. I watched him open it and offer me one. His hands were smooth and the nails manicured. Interesting ...

"No, thank you," I said. "I quit smoking when my husband got back from the war. He had TB. The smoke bothered him. But you go ahead."

He shook his head and placed the case back in his pocket. No mention of his being in the war, which was unusual. Almost every British man his age would have been over in France, and they made a point of telling you if you raised the subject. So it made me wonder: how had he dodged that bullet?

I sipped more from my glass, nearly finishing it. Sours were powerful, but there wasn't much liquid in those squat glasses.

"Are you from the north?" I asked.

His blue eyes darted over to me. "Now, how did you guess that? Did my accent give it away?"

"Not really." I smiled to show innocence and interest. "I assumed as much, as we hadn't crossed paths before. A man like you would be much appreciated in the London set I run with. I'm sure I would have heard of you." Because that was the real thing, of course. I hadn't heard of him before.

"I've done a lot of business overseas since the war," he answered smoothly. "Not a lot of time for socializing. That's why I enjoy these voyages so much." He waved a hand through the air. "It's an opportunity to mix with charming people like you."

I made myself look flattered. "What sort of products do you import, Mr. Sloan?"

Before he could answer, another voice cut in. "Lady Revelstoke! And Mr. Sloan. How agreeable running into you here." Vera

Horner appeared at Sloan's shoulder, eyes beaming. "Amanda darling, look!"

Sloan rose to his feet. "Mrs. Horner. Mrs. Martin. We were just about to leave for lunch. Join us please." He stuck out his arm, and Amanda grabbed it.

I had to hide my smirk. How smoothly he had done that. Obviously, he didn't want to get saddled with tiresome, gossipy matrons over pre-lunch drinks. At least at lunch, we had food to keep our mouths busy.

I rose, collected my bag and wrap, and joined the others as we exited.

Amanda Martin was clearly struck with the man. Obsessed might be a better term. She clung to him on the way back from the bar, chatting away like a teenager making her debut. I wasn't about to take a chance at being trampled out of the way, so I held back to walk with Vera.

We made a leisurely pace down the corridor, nodding to people as we went. I felt a hand on my arm, and I slowed.

Vera pulled me aside to talk low. "You watch that one, Lady Revelstoke. I'm sure you know this, but I'm going to say it anyway. You are an uncommonly good-looking woman, and I'm sure I don't have to tell you that men will be after your money. That one strikes me oddly. I don't like his looks. He reminds me of that fish — what's the name of it? Not shark. The other one."

I nearly giggled. Like there were only two types of fish in the sea. But I understood her. "Barracuda," I said.

"That's it!" she exclaimed, almost hissing. "Watch yourself with him. I don't know him or his people, and neither does Amanda. That may be an Eton tie, but I have a good intuition, and my instinct is telling me he may not be the original owner of it."

Interesting. This was a side to Vera Horner I'd not seen before. Vera may have been a wicked gossip, but she had a head on her shoulders. "Just what I had been thinking, Mrs. Horner. The very same."

Something else bothered me about him. It wasn't only the lack of background. That might be possible for someone who lived in Northumbria or thereabouts and didn't mix with London society. The war and its aftermath had upset many social patterns. No, it was something else that didn't sit right, but I couldn't put my finger on exactly what. Perhaps it would come back to me later.

We walked together through the doors of the Grand Salon.

LUNCH WAS A delightful affair. Because there was assigned seating, we were sitting with everyone who had been at dinner last night. It was fun to say hello to everyone and receive their return smiles.

The main course was chicken à la king in those delicate pastry shells, one of my favourites. The others had pie for dessert, but I finished with a fresh fruit cup, another favourite. One of my uncles owned a produce store back in Hamilton, so I come by my love of fruit honestly. Or perhaps "honestly" is the wrong word for anyone in my family to use.

I gazed around the table, watching the others eat, enjoying my coffee and the company. The discussion had moved to music, and the new jazz tunes coming out of the American south that had been playing in the Britannia Bar. Amanda Martin quite liked the sound. "It's all the rage in Chicago," she said, nodding enthusiastically.

Vera Horner sniffed, nose in the air. "I find it quite uncivilized," she said.

Drew and Florrie, being American, were, not surprisingly, huge fans. Drew took up the challenge. "You probably haven't heard the best. It's incredibly complex to play — quite sophisticated in structure, really. Requires a true master. Louis Armstrong, for instance. And Gershwin, of course. 'Rhapsody in Blue' will become a classic, you mark my words."

"How about you, Lady Revelstoke? Do you enjoy a hot jazz tune? How about 'Let's Misbehave'?" Tony winked at me across the table. Really naughty of him to refer to our last night out in New York. I heard someone — probably Amanda Martin — gasp out loud.

"Wonderful to dance to," I said, lifting my wineglass. "I like some of the sweeter songs too. 'Blue Skies,' even 'It All Depends on You.' You've spent a lot of time in the U.S., Mr. Sloan. Don't you find the new music diverting?"

He paused with his fork in his right hand. I watched him put it down on the plate, considering. "I prefer a good brass band, actually. Something military. Or maybe Perry or Elgar."

"Exactly," said Vera, poking a finger at us. "Something where you can hear the tune and they don't try to hide it under a cacophony of notes that have no relation to real music! Honestly. Sometimes I think the composers have run out of ideas for melodies, so they simply string notes together in order to get paid more."

Tony laughed out loud. "Nice one, Mrs. Horner."

Vera preened under his praise.

Meanwhile, I had been watching the man beside her. The one from the north of England. And I knew now what had bothered me so.

CHAPTER TEN

AFTER LUNCH, TONY excused himself to play cards. It seemed like that was becoming his main occupation on this ship. I was surprised, as he'd never played when we were in New York.

There wasn't a lot to do on a ship, but even still, it bothered me. Coming from the family I did, I was no stranger to gambling. If you let it consume you, it can overwhelm all aspects of your life. Nothing is more important. I've seen men willing to sell their souls to the devil for yet another hand of cards. It was close to home, and it messed with my ethics, I'll admit. My uncles had made a small fortune off the misery of others who couldn't resist games of chance.

But Tony was a grown man and entitled to live his life the way he wished. Certainly, he had already met the devil on the battlefield and seen the worst that men could do to each other. I was not in a position to interfere with how he spent his time. But this new side of him was a revelation that made me sad. Besides the card playing, I rarely saw him without a drink in his hand now. True, he didn't drink rum, but I had never seen him turn down a gin.

I'd also seen men with addictions promise the world to the women they loved. One last drink … one last roll of the dice. They meant it too. But the demon was too strong.

I would need to be cautious about getting further attached to him.

I MADE MY way back to my cabin slowly, taking in the grandeur of the Grand Salon and its attached rooms. I poked my head into the card room, which was already foggy with cigar smoke. That couldn't be doing Tony's lungs any good.

I continued on my way into the main hall, admiring the mural on the long wall. More sea motifs, but these ones were lighter in colour and theme. Large clamshells and waves suited the curving lines of modern style, and the surface of the mural almost had a shimmer to it. I can be happy looking at beautiful art. It brings me out of melancholy.

I turned to my right and carried on down the corridor, following the lovely carpet, which reflected the undulating blue theme of the sea. I marvelled, as I'd never seen this carpet before.

Oh no! That brought me up with a start. I'd made a wrong turn somewhere. I groaned in frustration and embarrassment. Had I taken the staircase up to my deck level? I couldn't remember. Why couldn't I pay more attention to my location? I stopped where I was and gazed around in a daze.

Where was a steward when you needed one? I scolded myself for being so inept and remembered that I had only to turn around and attempt to retrace my steps. If that didn't work, I'd simply have to shelve my pride and beg directions from a fellow passenger.

No need to worry. Further down the corridor, I saw a familiar shape. It was a woman, and not a young one. That ensemble in dull purple looked familiar. I sucked in air. Surely not. That couldn't be Amanda Martin knocking quietly on that door, could it? Before I could be sure, the door opened, and the woman disappeared inside.

I must have been mistaken. Amanda Martin had the cabin next to me, and this was not our corridor, nor even our deck, as far as I could tell. What could she be doing on this floor? She had made a point of saying she didn't know anyone other than Vera Horner on this voyage.

I shook my head and scolded myself. Probably, I was mistaken. There had to be other middle-aged matrons dressed in purple on the ship.

"Are you ill, ma'am?" The shaky male voice came from behind me.

I turned and smiled. "No, just lost. Most definitely lost. I took a wrong turn somewhere."

He was an older steward, probably close to or past retirement age. His smile was kind. "I thought as much. Please, come with me."

I did so, and had to stop myself from giggling while we travelled, because how could I ever explain to this white-haired gent beside me what was going through my mind. Could our Mrs. Martin be having a love affair with the only other single man at our table? It was too outlandish!

But curiosity is a wicked thing. I am an absolute slave to it. No doubt about it, I would simply have to find out the number of Mr. Sloan's cabin.

THE KINDLY STEWARD left me in the main hall, where I had started. He'd offered to walk me back to my room, but I'd assured him I could find the way from here. Much better to say that. I was embarrassed enough to have been found lost and wandering the corridors. If the dear man were to realize — as I had just — that I had left my wrap in the dining room … Well, I didn't want him thinking what a Dumb Dora I could be, as Elf would put it.

I didn't have to go far into the salon. My fringed shawl was draped around one of the full-size nymph statues just inside the door. I groaned to myself while flicking it off. One of the stewards had definitely had some fun at my expense.

I looked around, hoping no one had seen me. The dining hall was mainly vacated, except for a few of the staff setting tables for dinner service.

I turned around and left the salon with the shawl in my hand. Oh no! Mr. Sloan was coming right toward me, and the look on his face showed feral determination.

"Lady Revelstoke?" said a female voice.

I turned in relief. A lady was coming out of the lounge to the left of me. She smiled and then stopped.

I gave her my full attention, eager to have a reason to avoid Mr. Sloan.

I tried to place her, as she seemed vaguely familiar. Well-dressed in a soft green two-piece ensemble, maybe Chanel. Bobbed honey-blond hair, pretty face, lightly made up. Perhaps a few years older than me.

"We met briefly at Eton's open house. I'm Patricia Everley. My son Richard knows your son there?" She ended her sentence as a question.

I came alive. "Oh, Richard's mother! Charlie talks about him all the time."

She beamed with pretty blue eyes. "Your Charlie is a delightful lad. I believe they are the best of friends. Would you like to sit and talk for a while? I have some time to kill. My husband has abandoned me for the men." She nodded to the room across the hall.

I acquiesced gratefully, relieved to see Sloan disappear behind us. It was disturbing, this reaction I had to him. Usually a good-looking, attentive man did my ego good, but that man just made me uncomfortable. And he seemed to be turning up everywhere I was, which made me further suspicious of his motives.

We sat in the pretty Veranda Lounge. I'd first thought, when seen from a distance, that it appeared to be decorated as an underwater garden. On closer view, it better resembled a deserted South Sea island lagoon. Painted vines and tropical flowers graced the walls, framing a cerulean blue waterfall. We settled into plush green chairs with a glass table between. I put my small bag on the table and made sure to keep the wrap around me, knotted loosely in front.

"I know school is good for them, but I miss my boy dreadfully, don't you?" said Mrs. Everley.

She couldn't have opened with a better line. "Every minute," I said, meeting her eyes. "But I was glad to know he has made friends and is having a wonderful time."

"That helps," she agreed. "I wanted to talk to you about Charlie coming for a visit to Sundrings, our country place, in school term break. I know you'll want to see him, so perhaps just for part of the time? Perhaps for a month?"

I knew Charlie would love that. His first venture away from home and school! At the same time, I was greedy for his company. "I'm not sure I could manage a month apart from him, but perhaps we could do a trade? You take the boys for one week, and I'll take them for another?"

She agreed to that, and we spent a few minutes talking about how we could manage the travel between our homes. The Everleys lived in York, some counties away.

"Are you enjoying the voyage?" I asked.

"Very much. It's a lovely ship, isn't it? Delightful to have a band playing every night after dinner."

I agreed, and we went on to discuss the people we had met thus far on the ship.

"Your tablemates seem interesting," she said. "I've never met Mrs. Horner, but she was pointed out to me. Of course, I know her by reputation." She leaned back and waited for my reaction.

I smiled at that. "I like to think of her as one of the Furies. I'll introduce you when I get a chance."

"Thanks," she said. "I think." We both laughed at that. This was a woman I could like.

A steward came at that moment to take drink orders. Mrs. Everley opted for tea; I asked for a Coca-Cola. It was all the rage back in New York, and I was assured it was now easily available in the UK. With luck, we could stock it at home, and Charlie would be in for a treat.

"I've met Mr. Anderson. He knows my husband. But who is that single man at your table, the dark, good-looking one?" She leaned forward. "I thought I saw him in the hall just now, watching you."

I gulped. "Yes. Thank you for that interruption. I was trying to avoid him."

She smiled. "Men can be insistent. I noticed he was wearing an Eton tie, but that is no guarantee of much, these days."

"His name is Mr. Sloan," I said. "Do you know him? He mentioned he was from the north."

"Not from my part of it," she said, shaking her head. "And believe me, I would remember. A handsome man like that." Her laugh was impish, and her eyes held a twinkle, as if we were sharing a special joke. "But he may be from the Lake District, or further north in Northumberland or Cumbria. Our social circle is rather limited in York. That's why we wanted Richard to attend Eton, even though it is a distance. He'll meet so many new boys that he wouldn't otherwise. People it will be good to know when he makes his way in the world."

I nodded. So Sloan wasn't from York. That didn't mean he wasn't from somewhere else close to Scotland. But none of that explained what I had observed earlier at dinner.

We spent a convivial hour discussing her husband's passion (racehorses, which is how they knew Tony), the management of his large estate, and our mutual love of fashion and books. When I mentioned that I was friends with Agatha Christie, she seemed delighted.

"You must know all about her mysterious disappearance then," she said, leaning forward, keen with interest.

I didn't blame her. Not just mystery book lovers but all society had been captivated by the story. Back in 1926, Agatha had gone missing for eleven days. Truly missing, in that absolutely no one, including her wayward husband, knew where she had spent those days. The papers were full of it. So romantic, a mystery writer going missing!

"I don't, actually. She doesn't speak about that time at all. Which one has to think is a clever book marketing strategy."

This wasn't true, actually. She had told me, but I had pledged my secrecy, and I don't break promises.

Patricia nodded her head. "A mysterious story surrounding a mystery author. All very delightful!"

Which was one way of putting it. The true story was a little grimmer than that.

We discussed our favourite books, and it wasn't long before she suggested I stay for the weekend when I delivered Charlie to Sundrings. Johnny's title made me particularly desirable to hostesses outside our immediate circle, and I could see there were no flies on Patricia Everley.

Still, I enjoyed our conversation and looked forward to more.

It wasn't until much later that I realized with a start that it was she who had introduced the topic of our Mr. Sloan almost immediately.

ON THE WAY back to my cabin, I thought about the Mrs. Everleys of the world, and the gilded life she must lead. We had discussed her husband's passion of horse racing. Not for the first time, I felt my ire rise. I liked Patricia very much from our conversation today. But like so many women I knew, she seemed to define herself through the interests and endeavours of her husband. It made me wonder what Patricia's passion would be, besides fashion, if she had had an opportunity to have one. Because that was the problem, of course. Men with money had the freedom to indulge in any interest they wished. Women in British high society — even if they had money — were confined by prescribed roles. Yes, they could be passionate about gardens, artistic pursuits like music and painting, or other "feminine" pleasures. But if Patricia's passion had been horse racing, would she have been allowed to indulge in it if her husband did not share that interest?

Of course she wouldn't. Women like her lived a restricted life.

I mulled this over in my mind as I walked the last corridor back to my cabin. Johnny had been a wonderful husband who had allowed me unusual freedom to express myself. He had happily tolerated my insistence that Elf was always to be a part of my life. He'd raised a toast to us when we'd solved the little minor mysteries of the blackmail letters and the lost brooch.

Being a widow now gave me certain freedoms, perhaps even more than I had enjoyed as his wife. But even now, if I failed to behave to the minimum required of a dutiful dowager countess, English society would shun me. I had no doubt of that.

I had left the confines of my family in Hamilton because of the control those people had exerted over my life. They loved me, but they sought to control me. Now, as we cruised across the Atlantic to another world, it disturbed me to think that perhaps I had traded one restrictive social confine for another.

"SO, ELF, FOLLOW along with me on this reasoning. A man claims to come from the north of England. He has a plummy accent. But neither Vera Horner nor I have heard of him before. Also, he claims to be in the import-export business but won't elaborate. Reasonable?"

It was sometime later, and I had just awakened from a nap, remembering several things about our enigmatic Mr. Sloan.

Elf shrugged. "Might be. Could be he ain't as posh as he sounds. The accent could be put on a bit. Maybe he's gentry but not enough to roll with your highfalutin set. Or maybe he's a cake-eater, hoping to sweet-talk lonely widows with money." She looked at me pointedly.

"Fair enough. But this man doesn't appear to have been in the war. At least, not in a battle role, which is unusual to say the least for an Englishman, given his age. And there's more."

I had her attention now. "Go on."

"He uses his right hand to hold his fork."

"Huh?" she said.

I looked hard at her. "He cuts with the knife on the right and then transfers the fork from left hand to right."

"Blimey," she said. A light appeared in her eyes. "He's a Yank."

I nodded, smiling in satisfaction. "That's what I thought. Only an American would do that. It's innate, the way we learn manners. We can't unlearn them. If you're taught to transfer your fork to your right hand, you can't switch it up. It becomes habit." I frowned. "Well, you can try. But you'll slip up every now and then."

"So Sloan is a Yank?" she said.

"I'm pretty sure of it. I saw him with that fork eating dessert and then remembered that last night while we were at dinner, I noticed he put down his knife in order to eat. At the time it niggled at me, but it took a while for me to figure out why."

"A Brit would never do that."

"Exactly. And so we have an American most likely masquerading as an Englishman. Highfalutin, as you would say."

"You think he's our man? Harry's killer?" she asked.

"He's certainly a prime suspect," I replied.

CHAPTER ELEVEN

DINNER THAT NIGHT was a cheerful affair. I wore a sparkly green beaded gown with matching beaded headband and bag.

"Knock 'em dead, you will," remarked Elf when I waved goodbye.

Tony was — once again — in the card room. I made my way through the smoke to his side.

"That time already?" he said. He looked at me, frowning, and then he *really* looked at me. His eyes went wide. "Wow. You look stunning."

"Introduce us to the lady, Anderson," said the man to his left. He was a big man, not bad looking, with a prominent nose and even more prominent wedding ring. I nodded to him as the introductions went around, without bothering to register the names to the faces. Card sharks were not the sort of people I planned to spend time with after the voyage.

In addition, I hadn't liked the way he'd looked at my gown and what was obviously underneath it. There are some men who can send you a compliment by the way they look at you. Others … well, their gaze will give you the creeps.

I managed to get Tony away and moving toward the dinner table. When we entered the dining room, it was filling up. I could see Patricia Everley at a faraway table and gave her a little wave. She smiled and waved back. I saw her poke the balding man beside her and prompt him to follow her gaze. The husband, no doubt.

I approached our table and stopped in surprise. Mr. Mason, the security officer, rose from one of the chairs.

"We have a new man," chirped Amanda Martin to me. "His name is Mr. Mason, and he's from New York."

"Amanda! Let the poor gentleman introduce himself," said Vera, with obvious disapproval.

Mason's deportment was impeccable. He bowed to me with a secret smile and then shook hands with Tony, who caught on quickly and pretended to meet him for the first time.

I sat in the chair Tony pulled out, and he slipped in beside me. When we were all seated, Tony turned to me. "The captain has planted a spy at our table," he said quietly.

"I prefer to think of it as providing us with additional protection," I said. Although I thought to myself it was quite a clever move by the captain. Or was Gray behind it?

Tony harrumphed. "As long as he doesn't police our drinking."

I smiled. Prohibition had made the best of us suspicious of the long arm of the law.

It was clever, bringing Mr. Mason to the table. I wondered if this was the future: having security officers blend in with guests. It would allow them to ask innocent questions and not raise suspicions that they were being watched.

The others were clinking glasses, and only Sloan was missing. I smiled across to Amanda Martin, but her eyes were elsewhere.

I followed them to see Mr. Sloan approaching. She popped up from her chair excitedly.

"Mr. Sloan!" she said. "Over here. I saved you a chair."

Sloan was already pulling out the empty chair next to Drew. He gave that slow smile. "Not tonight, Mrs. Martin. I need to talk business with Mr. Johnson here." The two men immediately engaged in conversation, and Amanda was left standing.

She sat down slowly, her face red. I was full of sympathy for her. What a rotten thing for him to do, embarrassing her like that in front of everyone! Sure, she might be a little pushy. Obviously, she had a crush on him. But a gentleman would have taken the cue and done his duty.

Sloan was not a nice man, I concluded.

I looked over at her to see how she was managing the slight and was about to say something soothing when I noticed her eyes. They stopped me dead. It seems remarkable now as I recall it. Her face had cleared, but there was something hard and unsettling in her eyes that gave me the strangest impression that I had it all wrong. But for the life of me, I couldn't put my finger on how that could be.

Talk filled in quickly to cover the awkward moment. The captain wasn't joining us tonight, apparently. Drew introduced Mason to Sloan. I listened with interest, waiting for the inevitable question.

"And why are you suddenly at our table, Mr. Mason?" said Vera Horner.

I smiled that she had the nerve to ask and waited with interest for the reason Mason would give. No doubt, he had rehearsed this beforehand.

He cleared his throat. "I was asked if I would give up my seat at another table in order that two elderly ladies who were travelling alone could sit together. Of course, I was more than happy to do so."

Vera nodded in approval.

I thought about being naughty and asking Mason what he did for a living, but Drew beat me to it.

"I'm retired now," said Mason. "But I was a civil servant until my wife died this past fall. This voyage is a trip of a lifetime for me."

That got the other ladies clucking! Another unmarried man at the table was something to celebrate. Meanwhile, I was smiling at the cleverness of choosing civil servant. It sounded boring as the devil, so not likely to elicit further questions, and yet there was some truth to it.

Florrie was keen to tell us about the dolphins she and her husband had seen following our ship. Vera Horner watched her with disdain. "Porpoises," she corrected. I wasn't sure if she was right.

Meanwhile, my mind was drifting back to Harry. We were almost two days out from New York. It would take another three days to get to Southampton, if the weather was favourable. Three days before the murder of Harry got turned over to the police there and, likely, buried. By that I meant the case would be shelved. I had no doubt that Harry himself would meet a burial at sea long before we reached port. It just wasn't sanitary, keeping a dead body on ship for long. And without the body, would authorities bother to investigate a killing that had taken place outside of their jurisdiction? Everyone was short-staffed these days. The chance of solving a case like this was slight. The suspects would have dispersed. No police body would want another unsolved crime on their books. It looked bad.

So my guess was the murder of Harry would stay in jurisdictional limbo, body gone to the sea. Probably, for the sake of the shipping line, I should be glad of that. No bad publicity. I'm sure that's what Mr. Mason was trying to prevent. But it made me sad to think that Harry wouldn't get justice. I simply had to try my best to find Harry's killer.

Conversation had taken a different turn. So I was dismayed when Vera Horner asked the following question.

"Was it your cabin that was broken into last night, Lady Revelstoke?"

CRASH!

The steward behind her dropped a tray.

We all jumped in our chairs. Buns scattered everywhere across the floor, the round ones rolling away like they were critters escaping with their lives. In a way it was comical, and I was sorely tempted to pick up a few and lob them across the room, as we had done in the Catholic school lunchroom years ago. I felt sorry for the poor distraught fellow. He looked a bit like my older brothers, with wavy, dark brown hair and average features.

"Good thing it wasn't the soup course," said Drew with a hearty laugh.

After the fuss died down, Vera turned back to me.

"The stewards were gossiping," she said by way of explanation. "Mrs. Martin overheard them, didn't you, Amanda?"

Amanda had turned to help the hapless steward behind her, pointing out runaway buns under chairs.

I glanced at Tony, who was no help at all, gulping another cocktail. So I decided to be somewhat open.

"Yes, the cabin was broken into while I was at dinner. My fault. I forgot to lock it. Nothing was taken as far as I could tell, except possibly some perfume." It was wicked saying that last bit, but it did make for an explanation of the cloying odour that had been stinking up the corridors.

"You're suggesting a woman?" said Drew, clearly shocked.

"More likely a man stealing something nice for his lady-friend," said Florrie with a wink.

Vera simply sniffed.

I found it interesting to observe the action — or rather lack of it — behind her. The steward was still crouched down, almost out of sight. He seemed to pause in his cleanup to listen to our conversation.

"Very odd," she said, harrumphing. "What is this world coming to? No one is safe in their beds. I blame it on the war."

We all knew she was referring to the body in the lifeboat. But what that had to do with the war …

"Certainly, a lot of things have changed since the war," Mason said.

"Too right," said Tony, his voice morose. He followed the statement with another slug of his drink.

No question, it was the thing upon which we laid all blame. Government run to ruin? Blame the war. Couldn't get good servants anymore? Blame the war. Short skirts? Lack of morals?

My eyes continued to watch the steward behind Vera Horner. He appeared to be lingering. I saw an older staff member come over to help speed things along. His violent arm gestures were silent but easy to interpret. I looked around to see if anyone else at our table was observing the steward. Only one. Mr. Mason. I smiled to myself.

The rest of the dinner went ahead with no mishaps. I was delighted to see roast duckling on the menu. I skipped a few of the courses (really, why do they think we need eight courses?) but left room for peaches in Chartreuse jelly and a small chocolate eclair. I hoped Elf was enjoying her meals as much as I was. Her menu would be different, of course.

I was tired, so I excused myself right after dinner. Tony didn't appear to be in good shape, leaning heavily on one arm of his chair. I'd observed that his glass had been replaced several times this evening. I said good night to the others and promised Tony I'd see him tomorrow, and no, he didn't have to walk me back. I could find my way. He smiled sheepishly. No doubt he would wander to the card table before long.

Sleep hadn't come easily to me last night, so I made my way directly back to the cabin to make up for it. Of course, dinners on board ship didn't start until eight and went on for two hours, so it was nearly eleven before I had removed my garments, done my ablutions, and laid my head down on the pillow.

I thought of Charlie and how I would tell him about meeting Richard's mother. He'd enjoy that. I missed his easy affection and exuberance. We'd done something right in raising that lad, Johnny and me. I loved him to pieces, and I couldn't wait to get back to England to see him. Plus all the dogs he had collected in the last few years. Never a dull moment if you love dogs, and we both did. I smiled and turned over on my side.

As I was falling asleep, my mind lingered on the scene at dinner, and I found myself wondering: Why had the young steward in the dining room been listening in so intently?

"WAKE UP," SAID Elf. "I hear something." She squeezed my upper arm over and over in the dark.

"What?" I grumbled, swatting at her. It couldn't be morning. Surely, we'd just gotten to sleep. I forced my eyes open to see her face looming over mine. It wasn't a pleasant experience at the best of times, but in this darkness …

"Shhhhh." She held her index finger to her lip. "Some guy's moving in the cabin next door."

"Which one?" I said. Thoughts of Amanda Martin making whoopee with a man like Sloan tumbled through my mind, giving me the shivers.

"Not the Martin dame. The other cabin." She was on her feet, pulling on slippers.

"Elf, wait." I pulled myself up to sitting. "Maybe it's just a steward or the cleaning staff."

"And maybe it ain't." Elf looked at me. "Aren't you coming?" She looked as determined as a hungry ferret.

"Oh, all right. Just let me grab my dressing gown." This didn't make me happy. I hate getting up in the night. It's always cold in a castle before dawn, no matter how much money you have. Impossible to install central heating. It's hard for me to sleep in a strange bed, away from home and Charlie. Even more so with an eccentric Elf right beside you. I continued to grumble.

Elf was already peering out the door when I crept up behind her. Sure enough, it sounded like things moving in the cabin next to us.

"What should we do?" she said.

I was a lot taller than Elf and could easily see over her shoulder into the empty vestibule.

"No idea," I said with little enthusiasm.

"Maybe it's the murderer," whispered Elf. "Maybe he's coming here next, to finish us off."

"Oh, for crying out loud. Come away from that door." I took her shoulder with one hand and tried to pull her back.

Just then, the cabin door next to us started to open.

Elf whipped back with a hiss. I caught the door with my left hand so it wouldn't click shut and give us away. We both stood perfectly still. I swore I could hear Elf's heart beating. After a few moments, Elf put her face up to peer through the crack, and I followed suit.

The corridors were dimly lit at night, and the vestibule not at all, but we couldn't miss the slight male body that slipped out of the cabin next door. He turned, twisting a key in the lock. Then he moved swiftly down the vestibule to the corridor and turned right.

I pulled Elf back and shut our door.

"Not someone breaking in. Just a steward after all," she said, clearly disappointed. "He even had a key. What a bust."

"A steward? At this time of night?" I shook my head. "Got an idea," I said to Elf. "How are your lock-picking skills? Good as ever?"

"As ever," she said. I could see she was intrigued. "What's on yer mind?"

"I've wanted to find out where Harry was murdered, and we finally have a chance to do a little exploration without interruption. That steward was up to something just now. We know the body couldn't have been dragged far."

"And since fussy-muss is on the other side of us —"

"Hmm ..." I was lost in my own thoughts of how to proceed.

"The Martin dame," Elf reminded.

"Right. Exactly," I said. "Get your tools and gloves, and let's go."

I had tools myself. But it pleased me to see her so excited to take charge.

We snuck out of the cabin together. I closed the door quietly behind me while Elf got to work on the lock to the door a yard down and to the right of us. Handy, that we shared a little side corridor. It allowed us to stay out of sightlines. But then, sharing that side corridor is probably what led to Harry being dumped in our cabin in the first place.

I stood sentry in front of her, pretending to search for something in my handbag, which I had grabbed on our way out. But it wasn't necessary, as it turned out. No one ventured down the hall on our side, and Elf had the door open within a minute.

She pocketed her tool and led the way into the neighbouring cabin.

"This is a different layout than ours," I said. Smaller than my cabin, and not quite so posh, although the paintings were very nice. School of Turner, I noted. There was a double bed with a single nightstand. A fine set of drawers took up space on the other side of the bed. Across from it, one easy chair faced a small, highly polished wooden table.

There was a throw rug in an odd place. Not on either side of the bed, where one might put one's feet when getting out of it, but instead at the foot of it. Elf crouched down, grabbed a corner, and pulled it back.

"Here's your blood, Luce."

I dashed over to look. The floor was stained a dark colour, and it still looked sticky. "Definitely looks like it. Good work, Elf."

Elf dropped to her knees. She leaned forward to sniff the stain. "Blood, for sure," she said, wrinkling her nose. "Smells like ironworks."

"Probably the rug prevented all the liquid from evaporating," I mused. What a macabre thing to think of! I gave a hoarse little giggle. How strange our conversation would sound to normal people.

"So the question is, why did they move Harry to our cabin? Why didn't they just do what we did, and use the porthole?" I said, still staring at the bloodstain.

"Easy," said Elf, waving an arm around. "It was daylight."

My eyes swept the room. "Jeepers!" I said. "You're right. They would have crossed to the porthole, opened it ..." I did so now. "And what did they see?" I looked down into the darkness.

"Lifeboats," said Elf from behind me. "We couldn't see them, 'cause it was night. And foggy."

I groaned out loud. "So simple. If only we'd looked out our porthole before I went to dinner."

I turned around to survey the room, and while doing that, something else came to me. There was another possibility to explain why they hadn't used the porthole to get rid of Harry. I played with that idea for a few moments, trying to visualize it. In the end, I didn't voice it out loud to Elf. That couldn't be it. I couldn't make it jive with the way Harry had been murdered.

We both stared at the floor. I wondered exactly how it had happened. There didn't appear to be blood spatter anywhere else. Likely, our poor Harry had dropped to the floor and bled out there.

I pointed to the rug. "Put it back," I said. "Just the way it was."

She did so, then stood upright. She asked the question I was thinking.

"But why not just leave the bloke here?" said Elf. "Why move the body?"

"Well ..." I gave it some thought. "A dead body raises questions even if the cabin is unoccupied. Whoever was running the show didn't want any connection made between the person who booked and paid for the cabin and our Harry."

"So they make it someone else's problem."

I looked straight at her. "And picked my cabin because it was left unlocked."

Elf groaned at that.

I giggled then. "Just think, Elf. What a shock they must have had when we didn't report the body!"

"Cor," she said. "Too right."

I laughed out loud. "Waiting and waiting for there to be a fuss, and instead, dead quiet. We did the dirty deed for them! How they must have fretted, wondering what had happened."

Elf snorted. "Till the body was found in the lifeboat."

"And even then, they must have wondered how the heck it had gotten there." I shook my head. "That gives me some satisfaction, knowing we caused Harry's killer some grief."

"Wonder what they think now?" said Elf.

"What do you mean?"

She sat down on the edge of the bed. "We're respectable peoples. Killer must be wondering why we dumped the body and kept it secret."

I gaped. "You make a good point. Don't know why I didn't think about that before. The killer knows we know about the body."

"Sure he does, 'cause he's the one who put it there, in our space."

I sat down on the bed beside her. "What's going through your mind, Elf? Spit it out."

She gave me a shrewd glance. "Sure know what I'd be thinking." She swung her short legs back and forth.

I waited with mine firmly on the ground.

"Keeping in mind our killer's a crook, see? So he'd think like a crook. Not like us."

That made me smile. Elf had turned herself respectable. "Go on," I said.

"Probably figures we're out to blackmail him. If only we knew who he was," she said.

I whistled low. "Good thinking, Elf. So he'll want to remain hidden from us. But chances are, he's watching us."

"Count on it," she said.

I pushed off from the bed. "Let's get out of here, then. But do a quick search of this cabin first. I don't expect to find anything, but you never know." We spent the next few minutes looking under, behind, and in things. Nothing.

"She's emptier than a tart's heart," said Elf.

I led the way out the door, looking out to make sure the coast was clear.

"Shall I trap it?" she said.

"Couldn't hurt," I replied. "Make it quick." I opened the door to our own cabin and slipped through it.

Elf followed behind me a few seconds later and shut the door behind her.

"You think it's that steward what killed Harry?"

"No," I said with conviction.

She frowned at me. "Then what do you suppose the steward was doing there?"

I shrugged. "Perhaps the same thing we were. Looking to do a bit of sleuthing."

"Or maybe he was the murderer, cleaning up after his deed," said Elf in a bloodthirsty tone. Really, I think she was enjoying this more than I was.

"Perhaps," I said, pausing to think. "But more likely, he was looking for something. You heard him moving things around. If that boy was the killer, why didn't he look for whatever it was right after he stabbed our Harry? He had the opportunity."

Elf wasn't convinced. "Still. He's up to no good." She sniffed.

I sank down to the bed. "Could be. Might have surmised the murder was about something valuable and set about to see if he could find it. A bright lad would know which cabins were unoccupied and figure that could be the murder scene. Just like we did."

I stared into space, trying to find the words to voice my misgivings.

"He could be someone's lackey, I suppose. But I really don't think a steward is behind all this, Elf. The fellow we saw was pretty young, hardly needing to shave. You know the way this works. Those rocks are worth thousands. The mob wouldn't give that responsibility to a youngster. No, this enterprise smacks of brains, experience, and a cool head. Not to mention ruthlessness."

We both took a moment to let that sink in. "Go to bed, Elf," I said finally, throwing my dressing gown on the chair. "Go to bed, and don't wake me until noon."

She did as told, and within minutes, she was snoring softly. I lay awake, uneasy in my thoughts. The light had been low, so I couldn't be sure, but it had seemed to me that the steward coming out of the cabin next door was the very one who had dropped the buns at dinner.

CHAPTER TWELVE

DAY THREE AT SEA

ELF LET ME sleep until half past eleven, not twelve. It's not that she deliberately poked me awake. Her particular way of banging about the place did the trick. A few times, I had stirred in the morning to find her mysteriously gone from the room, and I had lapsed back into a restless dreamland. It wasn't a nice place to be. At one point, my Johnny was fighting a fire-breathing dragon that had the face and bosom of a disapproving Vera Horner. No question, I really needed to lay off those dinner cocktails.

Elf did her best with my clothes and hair, but I had to scramble to make it in time for lunch. Even then, I arrived late and missed the general gossip and the first course.

Tony had saved me a place beside him, as far away from Mr. Sloan as possible. I had to smile at that. It was clear he didn't care for the man. Even more, he didn't like the attentions Sloan had been giving me. The seat put me beside Florrie and Drew and away from Vera Horner, which suited me fine.

Our American friends seemed to enjoy their meals as much as I did, which made me feel a certain kinship with them. Certainly,

Tony was no fun at all when it came to gastronomic talk. He seemed to live on gin and cigarettes.

I glanced across the table to see Mr. Mason engaged in conversation with Sloan. I suspected Mason would find opportunities to speak with everyone, perhaps by changing his seat with every meal.

Today, I had slept through breakfast and was ravenous. Never do I skip meals, and dinner had been over fifteen hours ago. One of these days, I was going to have to start watching my weight.

"You seem deep in thought," said Florrie from beside me. "Penny for them?"

I turned and smiled. "I was just thinking that I've always been astonished by those women who say, 'Oh, I was so busy, I forgot to eat.' Who *are* you people, I want to say!"

Her laugh was a wonderful thing to hear, completely delightful in its spontaneity. Her husband turned at it and gave her a nice smile. I liked the way he looked at her; it always seemed to be with pleasure. How nice to see a good marriage.

"What are your plans for today?" I asked Florrie. Jeepers, I needed to remember her last name, for I had clearly forgotten it. This was going to get embarrassing if I ever had to make introductions.

"I thought I might trip down to the hair salon and make an appointment," she said. "Such a nice thing to have on board."

"Yes, it's a very new thing for ships," I said. "The French lines started it, I believe, when the new shorter hairstyles became popular. Very convenient with so many women travelling without their maids now. I hear the *Olympic* and a few of the older ships have been retrofitted for them. Ours has a small gift shop right in the salon you might want to check out."

She clapped her hands. "I'm sold! Drew can do without me for a while. Will you join me?"

I shook my head. "My maid is my hairdresser, and believe me, she would kill me if I strayed." *Ain't that the truth.*

Florrie laughed again. This time, Vera Horner caught it. "What's so funny?" she said, frowning with disapproval.

I shook my head. "The men," I said vaguely.

Our steward came then, to remove the main course dishes. I smiled up at his lined face, which relaxed briefly at my friendly visage. He was a fellow I hadn't seen before, much older than the one from last night.

I waited until he had moved away before saying, "I notice we don't have that young steward serving us today."

Vera jumped on it. "The fool who dropped the buns? He's been moved to second class." She gave a satisfied nod.

Amanda Martin gave a small gasp. "Oh, Vera. You didn't have anything to do with that, did you? The poor man."

Vera turned on her, waving a finger in the air. "I will not tolerate carelessness, Amanda, and neither should you. In first class, we expect an exemplary level of service. Furthermore, we should all —"

I was distracted by Mr. Sloan, who had come up behind me and put a hand on my shoulder. "Perhaps you would save a dance for me at the fancy dress ball tonight, Lady Revelstoke." He had leaned over and spoken very softly. I didn't think Tony heard.

"Perhaps," I said between clenched teeth. I did not like men who put their hands on me without an invitation. I could see a problem brewing. My desire to find out more about Sloan for our investigation was warring with my primal instinct to avoid him.

He smiled with very white teeth and moved off, leaving the salon before dessert was served. Definitely not my type.

Across the table, Amanda Martin gave me a startled look that changed to a frown. Oh dear. The last thing I wanted was to make another woman jealous for no cause.

She wasn't the only one who noticed.

"What did he want?" Tony asked in a grumpy voice.

"Just a comment on our tablemate," I said quietly. A little white lie is sometimes the only peaceful option.

AFTER LUNCH, I found myself in the library lounge for an hour, lazily scanning the shelves. Really, it was an excuse to escape the others and just think.

It was inconvenient, the steward having been moved to a different dining room. I had planned to observe him more closely, and perhaps even question him after the other diners had left. It would have been easy, since he served our table. We could have talked naturally. Now, that would be impossible. I could think of no excuse that would allow me to go down to second class to inadvertently strike up a conversation with a young steward.

Oh well, it had been a long shot, as my brothers were apt to say. I truly couldn't believe that young fellow was Harry's killer. It didn't make sense that he would come back to the scene of the crime. No, much more likely he was just an opportunist. Probably a petty thief, lifting what he could easily pocket from the first-class cabins.

I took the outside route back to my cabin, intent on getting fresh air. No sooner had I turned the corner than my stomach took a different turn.

Trapped! Vera Horner saw me immediately. She was seated in a deck chair, holding a teacup, unfortunately alone. Unfortunate, because I knew there was no way she would let an audience pass her by.

"Lady Revelstoke!" She leaped up, fully prepared to trip me, if necessary. "Do join me. I've been dying to ask about your gown."

Horsefeathers, I thought to myself. *You could have asked me at lunch.* But I did sit down on the chair beside her and forced myself to smile.

"Another Worth?" she asked slyly, referring to the first time she had seen me on deck.

"Clever you," I replied. "I've noticed you appreciate fashion. That's a lovely suit you're wearing right now. Gorgeous colour." I wasn't lying. It was cranberry. Vera was quite fashionable, in a respectable way that befitted an older matron. Her hair was bobbed and styled, unlike her more matronly friend Amanda, who wore her hair pinned up in the old-fashioned way.

Vera Horner preened. "I feel it's important to set a certain style for one's circle. Did I guess right?"

"No, actually. This is a new designer. *Schiaparelli.* American."

"Ah, yes, New York," she said, leaning back. Her beady eyes took in every fold and layer, as if summing the parts to reach the cost. "Is that your home?"

So that was the purpose of this discussion! But she laboured in vain. I refused to give this woman any information on my background. "I like to think of it as a second home. The castle in the West Country is where I am most at home."

"Of course," she said in a satisfied tone. "Although I much prefer our London townhouse over the Devon property. So isolating in the country, don't you think?"

"There are advantages," I said. "I like the quiet."

"But it's lonely, surely. You must miss the season."

I shrugged. "I get tired of people. They tend to gossip so." I waited for the response. Whoosh! Completely over her head and gone.

"Of course, when one travels, one misses the *right* sort of people." Vera Horner sniffed. "So many Americans on this voyage."

"And at our table," I added wickedly. It was just the juice to get her going.

"Yes!" she exclaimed, and leaned forward. "That's why I was so fortunate to meet up with Amanda. And Mr. Anderson, of course."

Poor Tony, I thought. No wonder he was ducking her at every corner. But this gave me the chance I'd been waiting for. "Have you known Mrs. Martin long?" I obeyed the convention. Vera might call her Amanda, but she was still Mrs. Martin to me in formal company.

"Oh, forever!" she twittered. "It's true, we were girls at school together." She gave a long, sentimental sigh. "So many years ago. We were both painfully young then. Seems an age."

I sat quietly, leaving her to her silent recollections. This was a first-class guarantee of respectability. The word of Vera Horner was one I could depend on, at least to this end. Meaning, Amanda was who she appeared to be, a not-so-handsome matron of the old school. That made my sleuthing a little easier. One person eliminated.

Maybe Vera did have a purpose in life after all.

"Of course, I hadn't seen her in an age. Not since she married that American and moved to the Midwest of the United States."

I perked up. "So you haven't seen her for a while?"

She snorted. "Must be thirty years! Not the fifty she referred to, upon my soul. We came out together. I was married after my first season, of course," she said proudly. "Amanda was not so desir— fortunate."

I could hardly contain my amusement. No doubt the word Vera had intended was *desirable*. *Fortunate* was a last-minute switch. Whether intentional or not, I could not tell. These high-born British women seemed to think it a contest to get to the altar the quickest.

She went on. "Howard stood for the Conservative party in the early years of our marriage. I was a busy wife with full enter-taining responsibilities when Amanda met her American husband a few years later. She was an Honourable, you know. They like titles in the colonies. I never met her husband, but from what I heard, he was well *off*, but not well *bred*. If there is such a thing in America."

"Boston," I said, holding back a smirk. "You're forgetting about the Boston Brahmins."

"Cows? What on earth are you talking about?"

Cows, indeed. I smiled. "Surely you've heard of the Boston Brahmins. The wealthy elite who claim to be descendants of the earliest English colonists. Very upper-class and traditional. Scads of money."

"Oh, them," she admitted, sniffing. "He wasn't from there. Some windy, dusty place in the interior. They left England almost immediately." She paused, and her eyes went dreamy. "Those were busy years. I didn't have time to keep track of classmates, even if I'd had an inclination to. You know how it is. I had my children in quick succession, and they took all my attention."

No mention of her husband claiming her attention. The gossip I had heard put their marriage clearly in the lukewarm category.

I thought back to Amanda Martin. Could she be having an affair with Sloan? She certainly seemed to follow him around like a lost dog. It was pathetic to watch. She was way older than him, but I wouldn't put it past him, if she had money. He seemed the type to take advantage of women. And it may sound cruel, but I couldn't imagine their friendship being for any other reason, if indeed they were seeing each other. Amanda was at least a decade older than him. She sure didn't seem like a femme fatale, but you never can tell.

"Has Mrs. Martin changed much?" I asked, just to make sure.

"Hardly at all!" said Vera Horner. "I recognized her immediately. Always was a plump, mousy little thing. No sense of style. But then, if she's been locked away in the middle of who knows where, for years and years, what can one expect?" Her face took on a smug expression. "One must make allowances."

"Must one?" I said. The devil was in me today.

She looked right at me. "My dear. It's important for our class of people to have compassion for those less fortunate. When you are older, you will realize this."

I nearly laughed out loud.

CHAPTER THIRTEEN

I STOPPED ON my way back to the cabin to look out at the sea. It was a dark blue colour, rolling now, with a life of its own. Many days I would look out and it would be beautiful, almost feminine, reflecting the sparkles of the sun. Not today. The waves had a masculine heft to them, as if nothing could stop them.

It made me think of my late husband. Johnny had been a rough-and-tumble sort of man, easily confident. Rugby had been his sport, not cricket. And, of course, cars. Always cars. I smiled, remembering how excited he would get talking horsepower and displacement, along with other words I barely knew the meaning of.

With Johnny, I never feared anything. He just radiated confidence. I remembered him saying that some older fellow had tried to bully him at school. Johnny had decked him with one punch, broken his nose, and that had been that. No one challenged him again.

The way he died had sucker-punched me. TB is a cruel disease. It strips you of your strength, and for Johnny, that was central to his being. But no, I wouldn't think any more about that. I'd cried enough.

I'd been a widow for nearly four years. The first six months, I can't describe the grief except to say I wanted to kill myself. No question about it. I wanted to be dead. Elf kept me alive then. She forced me through all the steps required to live, every hour of every day. She made sure my son, Charlie, knew I loved him, even when I didn't have the strength to do so myself. The next six months, I overcame the urge to kill myself, but I didn't care if I lived or died. Then, at about the year mark, something changed. I was still shrouded with sadness, no mistake. So sad that Elf was prompted to say something that saved me.

"It's okay not to have hope about the future, Luce. Blimey, with my start, I know all about that. So here's what I say: It's enough just to be curious about what will come."

That changed me. Hope was beyond me at that point. But I could be curious, I decided. And I was curious to see the sort of man my son would become. I should stay around for him. No, I *must* stay around for him. When a year passed, I could see that clearly. I would stay alive for my son, and if I happened to have a little fun along the way, then that would be a bonus.

Charlie was thirteen now and had been dying to go away to school, so I'd let him for the first time. Johnny's old school. He would have approved. And how nice that Charlie had made a good friend there. But I missed them both. Oh, how I missed them.

I shook myself from the sadness. There were things to do now, and I couldn't allow myself to get distracted.

We weren't any further ahead. From what I could infer, the investigation had stalled. For my own part, I had learned very little useful in a full day. It looked very much as if the murderer would get away with it.

I couldn't bear that. First, it was wrong — very wrong. True, I came from a dubious background where the law was something that could be ignored or at least avoided. But even in a family like mine, murder had its price. We had our own code of right and wrong. And it was wrong that this murderer should go scot-free.

Second, this was a personal affront. The murderer had had the gall to leave the body in my stateroom, thereby implicating me. It was either amazing bad luck or — as I was coming to think — a personal challenge. I had yet to determine which.

Something had to be done. If this was a challenge, if someone knew who I was and had chosen my cabin deliberately, I couldn't rest. That person was a danger to me. I would have to step up. A plan was forming in my mind.

Tony joined me at the rail. "There you are. Elf was getting concerned."

"She sent you?" I was amused.

"Always at your service. At anyone's service, apparently, including recalcitrant maids." Tony shook his head. "'She don't come soon, I'm goin' down to have my tea, and that's all there is to it,' I believe was the exact phraseology. Honestly, Lucy. Are you sure she's the best maid for you?"

I smiled. "Yes, darling. For anyone else? Maybe not. But for me, she is priceless. I can count on her to do the one thing I've always prized most of all."

"And that is?"

"Watch my back," I said into the wind.

"Humph." He didn't sound convinced. "She's waiting back at the cabin. Something about a 'bloody fitting' you missed. Would this be for the fancy dress tonight?"

"Great Scott, I forgot!" I pushed back from the rail. "That damned costume."

Tony snorted. Whoops. The lady wasn't supposed to swear. Even though it was a new world order after the war, polite society (and I could say a few words about that term) was still back in the 1800s.

"Are you dressing up?" I asked quickly.

"Of course," said Tony. "Can you guess?"

"Something military," I said. "Probably historical. Maybe Roman?"

Tony looked shocked. Then disappointed. He grumbled something that sounded like, "You should go as a witch."

I smiled and turned back to the sea. It was a safe bet. Almost all the men dressed up in the costumes of political or military leaders at these things. There must be a psychological desire for males to play at taking on the roles of great men from history. Never a slave or subaltern. No sir. Always a leader. Always the general.

Women didn't have many such role models, of course. Our choices were limited.

"What are you going as?" he asked.

"Not a witch," I said. "But still, you won't be surprised." Although he might be shocked.

I remembered the question I had been going to ask him. "Do you happen to know where Mr. Sloan's cabin is?" I said it as casually as I could.

"Not a clue. Why do you want to know?" There was a dark tone to his voice.

I smiled. "So that I can avoid him."

He grunted. Apparently that was the right answer.

Tony walked me back to my stateroom. He didn't need to. I was pretty sure I could find my way. Eventually.

I was explaining this to Tony, in hopes of lightening his mood. "There are advantages to having a horrid sense of direction, you know."

It worked. He brightened. "Name one."

I walked with a spring in my step. "It's enlightening. You get to experience many parts of the ship that other people never see."

He laughed right out loud.

"Truly, it's educational." I counted on my fingers. "I've seen the second-class reception rooms, the kitchens, the laundry, various passenger corridors ... oh! Even the captain's cabin."

"As long as you haven't been visiting other cabins," he said.

I raised an eyebrow. What was this? So Tony saw Mr. Sloan as a possible rival. He couldn't mean anyone else. As far as I knew, Tony hadn't even met Gray.

Elf was seated in the light by the porthole, doing some rare darning, when I got back to the cabin.

"Where you been, Luce?"

"Don't call me Luce," I reminded her half-heartedly.

Tony excused himself with a "Pick you up at seven."

CHAPTER FOURTEEN

THE BED WAS tempting, and I found myself lying back on it. I must have drifted off for a while, as I woke to find Elf rustling around.

"We should be getting you ready for dinner," she said, a mite loudly.

"Really? I slept that long?" I smacked a hand to my forehead. "Oh lordy! It's fancy dress night. I am *not* in the mood," I grumbled.

"Got that lovely dress for it. Come, I'll do you up nice." One thing about Elf. She may not have been a good maid from the point of view of behaving like one, but she really liked the dress-up part of our relationship. With a better accent and some poise, she could have worked in a good salon.

An hour later, I looked quite different. In fact, I hardly recognized myself. Makeup can transform a face. No longer were my arched brows the centre of attention. Eyeshadow in shades of green and blue reached all the way up to my brows. Eyeliner took the place of primitive kohl. My eyes popped. I had taken a little liberty from history myself and dressed as the one queen I would have given a lot to know.

"Theda Bara, from *Cleopatra*! My God, Elf, how did you do that?"

Elf grinned. "Saw that movie in 1917. Got a thing for Theda Bara. You gots the hair, so I just gotta make up the eyes to match. Easy peasy." But she was obviously proud of herself.

"You did a splendid job. First rate."

Elf came over with the costume piece I had planned to wear on my head. I waved one arm at her. Because I had a plan ... a cunning plan.

"Get the diadem with the side drops, Elf. The new one, from New York."

Elf sucked in air. "That? But it's real. You said we weren't showing off our best stuff on this voyage. Twasn't safe."

"I'm tired of being safe," I said. "Pile it on, Elf! I can be safe when I'm dead."

Elf snorted.

We did indeed pile it on. An Egyptian-style lapis and diamond necklace circled my neck. Big gold hoops fell from my ears. Wide bracelets covered both my wrists. I wore every ring we had brought with us. It was an arsenal. Never before had these items walked out together.

The only thing not real was the gemstone leopard brooch that adorned the shoulder of my white gown. It had come with the costume.

"You wearing all the goods tonight? That smart, Luce?" Her voice held doubt.

I gave her a mischievous grin. "The better to tempt you with, my dear."

Her dark eyes lit up. "Bloomin' hell. You're setting a trap for the thief!"

CHAPTER FIFTEEN

TONY ARRIVED A short while later. I met him at the door. As expected, he was wearing the purple-edged toga of a Roman senator.

"Caesar, I presume?" I said.

"Don't," he said. "I'm speechless." His eyes were full of admiration and something perhaps a little more carnal.

"You know I'm not the Marie Antoinette type," I explained. "Why play a dimwitted pawn when you can be the greatest queen who ever lived?" I reached back for my wrap on the chair. Tony took it from me.

"Our Virgin Queen might take offence at that."

"Bosh," I said. "Elizabeth the First probably took lessons from her. Cleopatra came centuries before Liz and did it with panache and a much better wardrobe."

"You're right about the wardrobe," said Tony, gazing at my garb. "What do you call that, exactly?"

"Chilly. Hand me that wrap." A problem with ancient Egyptian sheaths is they were sleeveless. In fact, this version had only one shoulder, as was often the style for high-ranking women. Another common style was to let the fabric fall below the breasts.

I had cautiously avoided being too accurate. The effect on Tony was strong enough.

"What do you wear under those things?" Tony sounded breathless.

"What do you wear under a kilt?" I replied.

I entered the ballroom on his arm. Sure enough, there were a dozen Marie Antoinettes accompanied by their powdered-wigged escorts. I counted several Napoleons plus a few Nelsons.

"No slaves or subalterns," I murmured.

"What did you say?" asked Tony.

The only people not in costume were the servers and naval officers. I spotted Graham West at our table. He stood as we approached.

"Did you get a promotion?" I asked him.

He smiled. "The captain sends his regrets. The ship requires him elsewhere."

"She is a demanding mistress," I said, easing into the vacant chair to his right. I introduced him to Tony.

"Good evening, sir," Gray said, addressing Tony.

"Mr. West," Tony said in response. I was pleased that he'd addressed Gray in the naval way, with respect. Maybe there wouldn't be bun fights after all.

"Would you sit between the ladies, sir." Gray pointed to a vacant chair on the other side of the table.

"With pleasure." Tony strode to the chair. "Ladies. You look very fetching."

Amanda actually giggled. I had a long look at her outfit, which was quite accurate, if somewhat larger than the original would have been. Amanda was one of the Maries. Vera Horner had settled for Queen Victoria. Mr. Mason had made a small effort.

He had a patch over one eye and a white dinner shirt undone at the neck. I glimpsed some red scarf-like fabric tied around his waist, which lent some doubt to the intent of the costume. He could have been a pirate or a highwayman.

Some of the men, I noticed, had not dressed up. Graham West, as the duty officer, was in his naval dress. My eyes swept around the table. Mr. Sloan wore an elegant evening jacket, as did Florrie's husband, Drew.

The room seemed to sparkle more brightly tonight. Light from the great chandeliers made dazzling designs upon the walls and tables. Or maybe it was just the diamond jewellery I was wearing, which caught the light with every move of my head and wrists.

Dinner conversation was polite and cheerful. After the first compliments on one another's costumes, we settled into the comfortable atmosphere of diners who have been previously introduced and could relax to some extent.

Or perhaps it was the silliness of dressing up that made our evening companionable. While I actually love costume balls, one has to wonder at the childish nature of it all. I have found the British upper classes take themselves alarmingly seriously. Perhaps this is one of the few ways they can allow themselves to play?

All that musing aside, I marvelled that Amanda Martin's corset didn't seem to stop her from eating with gusto.

As I watched them, it appeared my dinner companions were also watching me.

Vera Horner finally couldn't contain herself and gave me the opening I was waiting for. "That is a stunning headdress," she said. You could hear the naked hunger in her voice. "I don't think I've seen anything like that before."

"*Vogue* magazine," said Florrie, who appeared to be decked out as a rather plump Statue of Liberty. She pointed her teaspoon at me. "Last month, they featured one just like that. Didn't they, Drew. You remember. Copy of an Egyptian diadem found in the tomb of that young pharaoh. I pointed it out to you."

Drew grunted. "Pretty thing." He stared for a good few moments. I could see him assess the gemstones with a banker's eye.

"Thank you," I said. "This is the first time I've worn it in public. I don't seem to have many occasions for wearing such a piece." I played with my empty cocktail glass to show off my wedding ring. The large pear-shaped sapphire was set with a halo of diamonds that blazed under the new electric lights.

"Is your husband's family in the diamond trade?" asked that enigma, Mr. Sloan, who hadn't missed the ring either.

"No. That would be my own family," I said. This was true. My relatives had many businesses. Stealing diamonds was one of them.

I heard Gray struggle to conceal a snort. In contrast, Vera gave me a satisfied smile.

I smiled back. This exchange had done double duty. First, it had established the fact that my own family had substantial money, which is something I rarely had the chance to demonstrate. I wasn't the gold digger some believed, and everyone would soon know it. How? Vera Horner. This amounted to valuable gossip in high society, which was something she could dine out on for weeks.

More importantly, the seeds of temptation had been sown.

Amanda whispered something to Vera, and the attention of the table turned elsewhere. I sat back, wondering who would take the next step. I didn't think Harry's killer would rest until he had the gems from the shoes in his hand, and if I knew anything, it was how underworld characters reasoned. Why not pick up a few choice additions from my cabin?

"What do you think, Lady Revelstoke?" Drew's voice brought me back to the table.

"I beg your pardon? I was woolgathering," I said by way of apology.

Drew smiled. "We were discussing how the latest developments in shipping are making transatlantic trade more viable. Less than a week to cross the pond now. Soon it won't matter where something is produced. They could just as easily peddle it to foreign markets abroad as at home."

"Does that affect the business you're in, Mr. Sloan?" I tried once again to wheedle the nature of his trade from him.

Sloan watched me with steady eyes. "Any way of moving goods faster can only be good for all of us. We can manufacture things where they are cheapest to produce. Grow things where they are easiest to grow."

"That's it exactly," said Drew with excitement. "Easier and cheaper transportation will allow countries to specialize in what they do best."

"Or cheapest," I said uneasily. "What you suggest means that countries with cheap labour will dominate manufacturing."

"Goes to reason," said Tony, waving his brandy snifter in a careless manner. "They called it 'economies of scale' at Oxford. Good ole Adam Smith, I believe. Fancy my remembering that." He took another swig from his glass.

"But we already have massive job shortages in the British Isles. Surely, this won't help," I said.

"Well said, my Lady," said Mason. "It is just as troubling in America."

"You can't stand in the way of progress. Business is going global. The world will be one big market soon, Lady Revelstoke," said Drew, pointing his finger at me. "You mark my words."

I didn't like it. How would the average person have the money to buy these goods from foreign countries if they had no jobs at home?

But I had to face the truth of it. Why, it stood to reason in these modern times that even crime would be going global. In fact, it suddenly dawned on me that it already had. The gems in Harry's shoes. They were being transported from one continent to another, as easily and as swiftly as a crate of oranges.

It made me consider: would local crime families become a thing of the past? I shivered thinking what could happen when syndicates stretched the globe. Territory wars would be commonplace and even more widespread and destructive.

Someone called Tony's name from two tables away. He smiled, excused himself, and rose from his chair. I watched as he shook hands and laughed with the other men seated there. These were his card-playing opponents, I recognized. After dinner, he would end the evening with cigars and cards, and more brandy, no doubt. I wasn't keen on those friends of his, nor this pursuit of gambling that seemed to have snared Tony. Amazing how that hadn't been obvious in New York. Maybe he had been on his best behaviour there. Or maybe I had just been too enamoured with the attention he gave me to notice it. I grimaced at the thought.

When it became obvious Tony was going to sit down with them, Gray signalled me to turn in the chair so it appeared we were looking at something behind us. He spoke softly, so others wouldn't overhear. "We used to play poker, remember?"

I nearly choked. The mention of poker after I had been

thinking of gambling caught me off guard. "Of course," I said, wondering if Gray could read minds.

Growing up, we were often in the pool hall with the card room at the back. No one seemed to mind. It was a safe place, with so many of the men of the family around. At least they knew where we were.

"You were good," said Gray. "Real poker face and nerves of steel. No one could tell what cards you held. You aren't the type to wear your heart on your sleeve."

I held my cocktail glass stiffly.

"So I'm a little surprised to see you decked out in all this armour." His voice had dropped low. "Showing all your cards at once."

I didn't know what to say. He was right. It was out of character.

"Smashing effect, I'll grant you. I particularly like the thing on your head."

"It's called a diadem," I said, relieved at the change of topic. "As Florrie pointed out, it's a copy of one found in the recent excavations in the Valley of the Kings."

All things Egyptian were popular these days.

"I know what you're doing." Gray spoke low.

I shot him a glance, then looked off to the right, all the time playing with my empty cocktail glass. "And what might that be?" I said finally.

He kept his voice quiet. "You're setting a trap."

"DAMNED DANGEROUS THING to do," said Gray.

I could have denied it. Played dumb. But what was the sense? Gray wouldn't have believed me. So I shrugged and spoke quietly. "The investigation has stalled. I needed to do something."

"By setting yourself up as bait? This isn't Hamilton. We aren't kids playing a game. Lucy, the man has already killed once." He stole a quick look at the table. No one was listening in that we could see.

"You have a better idea?" I said, struggling to maintain a nonchalance I didn't quite feel. "I'm all ears."

Silence.

"No? Well, at least this plan might work. It's only a little bit of temptation." I leaned forward. "Gray, look at it from my point of view. The body was thrown into my room. I was meant to be the prime suspect. Can't you see why I want the damned case solved quickly? Before we get to port?"

He seemed to mull it over. "So you think you were targeted on purpose?"

"Not sure," I said. "It could be coincidence. Maybe the killer just picked me because my room was close. Or …"

"Or maybe he knew your background," said Gray. He sat back suddenly. The wooden chair rocked under his weight. "Some sort of retribution? But for the family. You haven't been associated with them for years, and you haven't committed any crimes."

Best he think that, I thought. After all, it had been a long time.

"I don't like it," he said finally.

"I don't either," I said, pointing to the headdress. "I don't want to lose this." Nor my life.

"You think he won't be able to resist trying for it," said Gray.

"He's a thief, Gray. As well as a murderer. Once a thief …" I gave a cautious tilt of my head and waved a hand. If there was something I knew about, it was theft and the people who committed it.

"Really," Gray said. He was smirking now. "A thief. I thought so."

"Thought what?" I asked. It was something in his face. I was starting to get a bad feeling. What had I said to bring that on? *What?*

"That it wasn't just a murder. Murder was simply the outcome. What did you find on him, Luce?"

Crap. Gray hadn't known about the stones in the heels of Harry's shoes. No one but Elf and I knew about that.

My face must have given it away.

"Come on, Lucy. You think I didn't get the training you did? Awfully convenient, heels. You don't forget things like that." His fingers drummed on the table. "The shoes weren't found with the body. Ergo, someone kept them. I put my money on you."

Silence. A whole lot of silence.

"You don't have to answer. But hear me out. This tells us something," said Gray.

"What?" I played with my linen napkin.

"Our killer didn't have our training. He didn't know to pull apart the shoes. That implies he wasn't one of us. Did you think about that?"

"Not until now, actually." I raised my eyes to meet his. "By one of us, you mean he couldn't be from our hometown family. Seems you're not just a pretty face after all."

I've never actually seen a crocodile. But the smile across Gray's face made me think of one.

I tore my gaze from his face and stole a look around the room.

Gray had been wrong. This didn't just tell us "something." It told me a whole lot more, and I was relieved. Just the way Gray had broached the subject made me think he wasn't involved. For if he had been behind the attempted theft, why would he have brought it up and chided me? Far smarter to keep mum about it all.

I couldn't be sure, of course. This wasn't proof. But my gut told me Gray had gone straight, as he had insisted.

Patricia Everley saw me across the room and gave me a small wave from her chair. I smiled and lifted my hand in response.

Gray had turned back to face our table. I followed his example.

"How are you doing?" said Gray in a normal voice. "Can I get you another drink?"

I turned to him. "No, thank you. I am one cocktail away from proving my mother-in-law right about me."

Gray chuckled. "That's the ship rocking, surely. Which reminds me, the captain asked me to invite you up to the bridge after dinner," he said. "You might want to slip away now, before your pet dog comes back to the table," he added softly, so others couldn't hear

I snorted in spite of myself. Tony as a pet dog! Well, I could see how that might appear to be the case to some men. Gray was an altogether different type, much more of a loner.

"Tony does have a habit of always being there," I replied equally softly.

"The man is a bloody leech," Gray practically growled. "I don't know how you stand it."

"Maybe I like a little mindless male devotion," I said.

"You didn't used to," he shot back.

My back stiffened. He was referring to the reason I had left Hamilton so quickly and completely. Not many people knew that tale, and I wasn't keen to revisit it.

"Kindly tell Mr. Anderson where I've gone, when he gets back," I said in a normal voice. I rose from my chair, nodded to the others, then began to weave my way through the tables. Timing, I've always believed, is everything.

CHAPTER SIXTEEN

THERE ARE TIMES when everyone is gathered together having fun, and I just want to be alone. That last exchange with Gray had put me in a downhearted mood. To put it bluntly, I was sad. I missed my son. I missed Johnny.

Grief is a funny thing. You'd think after four years, I would be inured to it. It's true, the tears come less often now, but melancholy can steal over me within seconds, and there doesn't seem to be anything I can do about it.

Dancing is a trigger. We'd loved to dance, Johnny and me. He was surprisingly light on his feet for such a big man, and I'd had fun teaching him the latest dances. We took advantage of every society occasion to dance with sheer abandon and shock the elders, until it got to the point he didn't have breath for it anymore. Tuberculosis strips a man of his dignity before it ruthlessly takes his life. Even after all these years, it hurt deep down that we would never dance together again.

The band would be starting up after dinner, and I didn't mind missing it at all. Perhaps this trip to the bridge was just what I needed. And indeed, the cheery welcome that greeted me there was just the tonic I needed.

"Ah, Lady Revelstoke! You are a lovely sight for these sore eyes," said the captain. "Cleopatra herself could not compare." His ruddy face beamed with pleasure.

I smiled in return. "Thank you for inviting me here tonight. I never tire of visiting the bridge."

It was true. I'd camp up there, if it were possible.

The captain smiled. "Were you a man, I'd be in fear of my job. You surely would have taken to the seafaring life."

I cocked my head. "Perhaps my soul is still partly in Sicily, the land of my forebears? Sicily is an island nation too, just like England."

The man nodded. "It's in our blood." He gestured to a quiet corner. "We won't be disturbed here."

I followed his hand. Instinct had me lean back against the wall such that I could look out upon the sea still. How can I describe the way it makes me feel? The night was pitch-black, but the waves roared with an energy I found intoxicating. That great poem by John Masefield says it so well: "I must go down to the seas again, to the lonely sea and the sky; and all I ask is a tall ship and a star to steer her by ..."

"I wished to talk to you about Mr. Mason. Do you think perhaps it's time we shared with him who you really are?"

I thought about that. He wasn't talking about my background. Not even the captain knew about my family in the colonies. But still, he had a point.

"Not yet," I said. "I've learned that privacy is a dear thing, and I've come to value it. If we let on ..."

The captain smiled. "I can imagine the requests."

"And complaints." I shivered, recollecting the last time I had travelled with Elf on one of the Empire line. A secret, once let loose, can constrict one like a snake.

"Obviously, if the man insists on pointing the finger at you, I'll have to step in," said the captain. "Please permit me to do so."

"Of course," I said. So that was the reason for his asking me to the bridge! How thoughtful. And at the same time, worrisome. I wondered who else thought I might be a suspect?

"My purser is an interesting man," the captain said.

The training kicked in. I stood very still and kept my mouth shut. And waited.

"Mr. West has offered to be at your disposal at any time, and I have agreed to this. I understand you are comfortable in his company, having known him as a child."

"True," I said carefully. "It was rather a surprise to find him on board."

"But not an unpleasant one," said the captain. He said it as an inquiry.

"Not at all," I replied.

"Good," he said. "You should know that I trust him. And my trust doesn't come easily."

Neither does mine, I thought to myself.

I GOT BACK to my cabin nearly without incident. It was only one wrong turn, and the flustered steward was really very kind when he found me in the linen room.

It's funny how my brain does not retain directions yet serves me well in so many other ways. For instance, when I was a young girl, the family used to call me *la strega*, which is Italian for witch. At times I seemed to have an uncanny ability to detect lies, find things that were hidden, or sense that something bad was happening somewhere else. Roma blood, my cousins claimed. It could have been true. One of my grandmothers had been left on the church steps as a babe.

I paused at my cabin door, feeling funny. I couldn't explain it exactly. "Silly broad," I said out loud and gave myself an imaginary shake. I turned the handle and felt the door give.

Damn that Elf! The door had been left unlocked. Again.

I took one step inside and looked around suspiciously. Nothing appeared out of place. And yet that cold feeling down my spine didn't dissipate. *You're imagining things,* I told myself. I stepped in further.

All appeared tidy. I am a pretty neat person, more so than Elf. And yet, I could swear things were a little different.

It's hard to describe how I felt, looking around. Like I was looking at an exact copy of my room, but it wasn't my room. I know it sounds insane, this feeling, but the best way I can describe it is like this: it was as if someone had taken out all my things and replaced them with exact replicas.

"Hello," I said, a tremor in my voice. "Anyone there?"

Not a sound, of course. *Too many cocktails at dinner,* I finally concluded. Not only that, my feet were hurting. I sat down on the edge of the bed, thinking to take off my shoes. And stared.

I was up in a flash, across the room to the small dresser. It was subtle, but I was certain. The jewellery case had been shifted. Not much, just by an inch or so. But enough that I knew. I like things to line up. This didn't line up. I held my breath and lifted the lid.

Then let the air out. Not empty! I did a quick inventory in my head. Everything that should be there appeared to be. Maybe I was going crazy.

I closed the lid, sat back down on the bed, and cursed. Stupid, that I hadn't followed the family training. I knew ways to tell if a room had been entered. Little traps you could set that no one else would even notice. Next time, I would be smarter.

But that didn't help now. My inner voice wouldn't keep quiet. Something had disturbed this room; the very air was telling me that. I frowned and bent down to undo the straps of my shoes.

Shoes! Jesus, Mary, and Joseph! Then I was up again, racing across the floor. Elf had told me the location. I knew how to access it and how to cover my tracks after. In less than a minute, with the strategic use of a hat pin, the hiding place was revealed.

It was empty. "Sonofabitch!" I yelled. Harry's shoes were gone.

CHAPTER SEVENTEEN

ELF APPEARED AT my shoulder. As usual, her timing was exemplary.

"Stole the bloody shoes, 'e did. Wanker."

I swung around and plunked my butt on the floor.

"Just the shoes, Luce? You checked the rocks?" she added.

"Not yet," I said. "You do it, will you? I need to catch my breath."

She did some digging in the trunk off to my left. "Rocks are safe," she said. "Nobody tried to get inside. I set a hair. Still there, see?"

I groaned. Elf had done what I had neglected to do. "I'm losing my touch," I said.

She shrugged and dropped the lid of the trunk. "Lots goin' on," she said kindly. "Did you just get back?"

I nodded. "The captain wanted to see me."

"Convenient for the thief," said Elf.

What she said was true. Who could have done this? I needed to think. A stranger of course, who got lucky. Or unlucky, if you wanted to look at it that way. He got the shoes but not what had been in them. Still, it was very convenient that the shoes were stolen at a time when neither of us was in the room. Since I'd stopped off to meet with the captain, I was later getting back.

"Elf, this could have been someone at my table. It could have been done right after dinner. Mr. West didn't make a secret of the invitation to visit the captain. Amanda heard us, for sure. Anyone at the table could have overheard him."

Elf faced me. Her odd little face twisted. "People at the table could scamper here while they knew you were away. It wouldn't have to be planned. They took a chance, maybe."

"That's what I'm thinking." I grabbed at my diadem, yanked it from my head, and placed it on the bed beside me.

"So they have a fair shot at it. Timewise. But Luce, you're forgetting something."

That cold feeling again. I wasn't forgetting it. It was foremost in my mind.

"Not forgetting." I smoothed down my hair with a hand. That was the real question, of course. And I loathed it. I hated what I was thinking.

"They didn't take my jewellery," I said reluctantly. "The case is intact. So it wasn't my showing off the family jewels tonight that prompted the break-in."

"Nope. The only thing snatched was the shoes." There. She'd said it. We weren't dealing with a normal burglar.

"You got a list of suspects in mind?" said Elf. "I gotta ask, though. Who would even know about the shoes?"

"Harry's killer?" I posed it as a question.

"Maybe. But see here," said Elf, plopping down on the corner of the bed. "Killer would have taken the shoes when he offed the guy. And he didn't. So goes to reason he didn't know about them shoes hiding the rocks."

That was exactly why I was panicking. The killer had left the shoes behind. He hadn't known they were valuable at the time of the killing.

"So who *would* know to go for the shoes?" she asked.

I was quiet. Elf, damn her, said out loud what I was dreading.

"Sorry, Luce. But it's kinda obvious. You gotta face it. Your friend Tony. He was at the table. He knew the shoes were missing. He helped us toss Harry into the drink."

I'd thought of that first, of course. It was highly unlikely, though. I'd seen Tony laughing with his card-playing friends at the other table, and no doubt they had made a plan to play after dinner. He would have an alibi for the time, I was sure. Tony never missed a game now, to my sorrow.

But that wasn't why my heart was thumping so wildly. It came down to this: there was something I knew that Elf didn't. Tony was a possibility we couldn't overlook, but he wasn't the only one.

I felt panic spread deep into my heart. One other person knew about the shoes, and also knew when I was going to be missing from my cabin.

The very person who had sent me off to meet the captain.

Graham West.

"Wait here," I mumbled.

I sprang from the bed and grabbed my wrap. Then out the door and down the corridor. I had to know. And if it meant bearding the lion in his den … well, I have claws too.

It was late. Would he be in the purser's office or his cabin? I'd try the office first.

No wrong turns. How could it be that I found an office I had only been to once? Could it be that I was concentrating on just that and nothing else ... or that my own subconscious drove me to the place I needed so desperately to be?

He was in the office, but he wasn't alone. Gray sat behind the wooden desk with his eyes down, immersed in paperwork. To his right, the assistant purser pointed to documents on the desk.

Both looked up, startled, when I blundered into the room.

"Gray?" I said, not thinking. "Are you ...?"

I was breathless, with one hand on the door frame for balance.

Gray stood immediately. He signalled his man to go. For a few moments, I couldn't move. The poor bewildered fellow had to squeeze past me through the doorway.

"What is it? Has something happened?" He leaned forward, both hands on the desk.

I moved to the chair opposite and sat with a graceless plunk.

"That was silly of me," I said. "Unpardonable."

"Using my Christian name?" he said, smiling. He seemed pleased. "It will get a few tongues wagging in the mess. Nothing more. I'll see to it."

I blurted it out. "My cabin has been broken into."

You couldn't fake the shock on his face. Then the swift change to anger.

"Are you hurt? Were you there?" For a moment I thought he was going to leap right over the desk.

"I'm fine." I waved a hand to reassure him. "Just shaken. I wasn't there at the time. Don't know what came over me. I just panicked and ran here." I gulped. "I feel better now."

A lot better. Incredible relief, for that was real shock I had seen on his face. I'd been trained to read expressions. The sensitive side of me gave me an edge in that as well. And I'd stake my life that Gray wasn't involved in this burglary.

"When did it happen? While we were at dinner?"

"I think right after, when I was with the captain." I looked down at my hands. "Elf was in the cabin for the early part of dinner." Not all, I realized. Curses. I hadn't waited around to establish when she had left.

"And your guard dog? Where was he when this outrage occurred?"

My throat closed for an instant. Good lord. Was he thinking what I'd been thinking? "Don't be ridiculous. Tony's father is a viscount."

Gray grunted. "Surprised you haven't snapped him up then."

My eyes narrowed. "I'm not in the business of selling myself. And I don't need the money."

"Steady on." He raised a hand. "I apologize. It was a foolish thing to say, especially considering our backgrounds."

I relaxed a bit. At least that had sent him off track, and I planned to keep him there.

"I don't, you know."

"Don't what?" His gaze was quite earnest now.

"Need the money," I said, looking him innocently in the eye. "I live in a castle."

Shock again. I almost smiled. Yes, it was a teeny bit wicked. But I was tired of feeling out of control.

Gray started to speak but garbled it. Then he did the most extraordinary thing. He threw back his head and laughed.

"She has a castle." He coughed as he said it.

"Well, technically it's only mine until my son comes of age," I said primly. "In typical British fashion, the property is entailed. Luckily, I have other investments in my own name."

"A castle." He was off on another round of mirth. But with an edge to it.

I tilted my head, curious.

When he finally finished laughing, he wiped his eye with the back of his hand. "Oh lordy. You know, I almost feel sorry for the poor bugger."

"Who — the thief?" This made no sense at all.

"No. Your Tony. What chance has any poor mutt got to woo you when you already have a castle?"

I waved a hand at him. "You're being absurd."

"I'm not," he said, looking away. "Fellow can work hard from nothing and amass a small fortune, but what can it matter? It's nothing to her. She has a castle."

Very suddenly, I realized we weren't talking about Tony anymore.

The silence between us was suddenly charged, dangerous. I worked fast to change the subject. "Aren't you interested to know what was taken from my room?"

Gray cursed. "Dammit, yes. Tell me."

I leaned forward. "Harry's shoes."

He looked blank. "Who's Harry?"

I watched him with astonishment. He stared back at me, looking completely out to sea.

I was beyond frustrated. "The dead man in my cabin that you helped me send overboard!"

The silence was heavy. Oh no! That's when I remembered it was Tony who had helped me with the body, not Gray. Crap crap crap! Why was I getting the two men mixed up?

Gray rose swiftly and moved to close the door. All the time

he kept his eyes on me. When he went back behind his desk, he said, "Start from the beginning. Tell me all."

So I did. Or at least most of it.

IT TOOK A while. Gray listened silently, with no expression on his face. When I finished, there was a long pause. I waited nervously, having now bared my soul and the numerous laws I had broken. How would Gray react to all this? Yes, we had been childhood friends, but he was a different man now. Was a shared past enough to ensure he wouldn't slip an anonymous word to the authorities?

I fiddled with the fringe on my wrap and waited.

The first words out of his mouth were, "You called him *Harry?*"

I expelled my breath and relaxed. "We had to call him something. I just picked Harry after Tom, Dick, or Harry."

He shook his head. A slow smile spread across his face. "Were you sozzled at the time? Or should I be doubting your sanity?"

"Definitely the latter." I smiled back. "Perhaps your own too, since you're taking this quite well."

He laughed then. "Good hiding spot for the rocks." He nodded his approval.

"It was Elf's idea. She used to work in a funeral home," I said.

"Of course she did." He snorted. "And your family supplied the customers."

"Actually, my family had nothing to do with it. She worked there during the war. After we arrived in England together."

Gray looked back at me, quizzical. "Tell me about that. I only know the bones."

I thought about how Elf and I had met. It was a closely guarded secret, in that I would never disclose it to my society crowd. That meant Tony as well. It wasn't that Elf and I had discussed it and agreed on silence. But her background might prompt someone to look into *my* background, and all in all, it was better laid to rest.

But Gray was different. He would understand and appreciate it, and it wouldn't hurt to have Gray on her side. Knowing her story would put him there. Elf might need a champion other than me after this trip.

Not to mention Graham West knew how to keep a secret. He had plenty of his own.

"I'll tell you about that," I said. "But you might want to finish that drink first."

He did that thing with his eyebrow.

"Okay, make it the whole bottle," I said. "This could take a while."

He raised both palms up in the air and leaned back. "I've got all night."

CHAPTER EIGHTEEN

MAY 1912, NEW YORK CITY

THE TRAIN TRIP to New York City was uneventful. As we stopped at small towns on either side of the tracks, I felt a sense of euphoria seize me. Lucy Perri, free at last! Free from the stares of regular people passing me on the street. Folks who knew my background and stepped aside or around me.

Oh yes, I saw what they did. Crossing the street. Looking the other way. You didn't want to get involved with the Perri girl. Too dangerous, what with *her* family.

For almost eight hours, I'd been free from the constant surveillance by brothers, cousins, uncles, and associates. Well-meaning, of course. Because kidnapping a Perri girl would be the perfect kind of hold to have on the family. Except that you'd have to be crazy to snatch a female relative of Rocco Perri. Talk about asking for death, and not a nice one.

But it was more than that. The family chose what you did with your life. They chose your husband and your destiny. Yes, they would love you to pieces, keep you safe and financially well-off. You wouldn't have to worry for anything. The women of the family wore the latest couture designs and sported serious jewellery.

But it wasn't the life I wanted, and I'd known that for years.

In fact, it was that jewellery that had allowed me to plan this bold escape. I'd inherited my mother's collection when she died. Strands of pearls, heavy gold bracelets, and a choker of diamonds, not to mention the rings. She used to call it her "get out of town" jewellery. You could always peddle gold and jewels when currency wasn't worth much. She also left me a bit of money, which no one knew about.

I'm a fast learner. Since I'd turned twelve, I'd asked for gold and gemstone jewellery for every birthday, Christmas, and special occasion. The old men in the family liked to indulge that feminine side of me. Little did they know why I was collecting it all.

By eighteen, I was ready. When the family decided I should marry Marco Battalia, I knew it was time to leave.

I figured it had to be someplace far away. Not Italy, even though I spoke the language. We had relatives there. Ditto with America. No, it had to be somewhere far away and completely different, where we had no connections.

I settled on England.

Once in New York, I found my way to the docks and booked a last-minute cabin on the very next voyage to Plymouth. I had dressed to the nines and made sure I looked the part, so when they offered me first class, I didn't hesitate. They were happy, and I was happy. I had a few hours to kill before the ship set sail, so I left my luggage with them and decided to take a little walk around. I'd never been out of Hamilton before. Didn't want to miss the opportunity to see New York.

It was foolish, of course. I was carried away by the excitement of escape, and I should have known better. The dockland was hardly safe for a single young female wearing expensive clothing. It wasn't long before the sixth sense feeling came upon me. I was in the wrong place. Didn't need to read any road signs — the other, more subtle clues were all there. This was my side of town, my sort of people. I glanced down the alley to my right and flashed to alert. On instinct, I took off my gloves.

I felt it then, the feather-light touch of a hand. Immediately, I turned into the alley, dropped the gloves, and moved like lightning. My hand closed over a small wrist and held it in an iron grip.

"Gotcha," I said.

It was a girl, maybe twelve or thirteen, waiflike, dress in tatters. The little hellion squirmed and kicked, cursing under her breath.

"Not so loud," I hissed. "You don't want to bring the cops." I twisted her arm around to catch the back of her to my body, then wrapped both my arms around her like steel bands. Up off her feet she went. Such a short thing.

"Who are ya?" she cried. "No lady."

I'd said *cops* instead of *police*. She was right. No lady would say that. This gal was a sharp little thing.

I gripped her tighter. "Nope. I may look like the goods, but sister, half my family died cleaning their guns."

She stopped moving at that. She knew that mafia expression and didn't like it one bit. What it actually meant was they'd died of lead poisoning … the kind you get from becoming target practice. The fact that I'd voiced it so openly put me at the top of the food chain in the mob world.

"Hell," whined the little thief. "I'm in trouble now."

"Sister, you don't *know* trouble." I swung around so her front was up against the wall, pinned there. So much easier to do without ladylike gloves on.

She whispered, "Where'd ya learn that move?"

"Let's just say I've been trained by the best," I said. The struggles subsided. I knew she was getting ready to kick backward, so I squeezed her chest hard, backed away, and let her drop to the ground. She wasn't expecting that! She landed in a heap with the wind knocked out of her.

It was rather pathetic. I watched as she huffed, desperate to get air back into her lungs, and something uncommon played upon my heart.

She was an odd little thing, painfully thin, with a pinched face that wasn't pretty. That would disqualify her from all but the lowest brothels, and even then, she wouldn't be in demand. Probably did time as a street beggar first and then graduated to pickpocket. There wouldn't be much of a good life ahead for her.

"How old are you?" I asked.

"Fifteen," she said breathlessly.

So older than she looked. And she may have shaved a few years off that. People tend to forgive young kids on the street, where they wouldn't an older thief.

I stared at her. She looked like a pile of rags had attacked her and died there. Here's where I got stupid, and discovered a better side to me I didn't know existed.

"So how about this," I said, surprising myself. "You look hungry, and I have time to kill before my ship departs. How about I buy you a meat pie if you know a place close by?"

She stared at me with dull eyes.

"I'm not going to harm you or get you in trouble. You can leave any time you want." I waved my hand. "See? Free to go. I won't stop you. But if you want a free meal, I can provide it."

"Why'd you do sumpin like that?" she said, the picture of suspicion.

I shrugged. "I know a bit about this life. And I'm leaving it all behind."

She grumbled and rose to her feet. It wasn't very far. She was shorter than my Italian grandmother. "I'd like ta leave it behind."

"Then why don't you?"

"You don't get it, miss." She rubbed her wrist. "They be watching me. I don't come back with the goods and I get knocked about."

I shrugged and looked around for my gloves. *Over there.* I reached down to pick them up. "That's a shame. I'm willing to spare you a meal, but only if you promise not to try anything. I get tired, see? Chances are, you couldn't outsmart me, but as I said, I get tired of having to be on guard. Besides, you really wouldn't want to get on the wrong side of me. I have connections with long shadows."

She wiped a grubby hand across her mouth. "Won't be fleecing ya. Can I have that pie?"

The blow came out of nowhere. I felt it hard between my shoulder blades, and I lurched forward. A big hand clamped on my arm, forcing me to my knees.

"What do we have here?" said a crusty male voice.

"No!" cried the girl. "Arnie, not 'er!"

"Shut your face," said my attacker. "She's prime, and I'll —"

Two things happened at once. I threw myself to the ground to throw my attacker off balance. At the same time, a knife flew across the alley. The big hand unlatched from my arm; the man teetered, mouth open, and fell hard against the brick wall, two big hands clawing at the knife in his throat.

The horrible choking sounds took a while to stop. There was a moment of unparalleled silence. My heart pounded; my mouth was dry. I recovered fast, rising to my feet while checking the alley for any other men. Then I dusted myself off and surveyed my suit for blood spatter. None, luckily.

I looked down at the thug to see if his open eyes were functioning. They weren't. The rest of him was huge, hairy, and motionless. My small friend knew how to throw a knife like a pro.

"Shite," she said, standing as if paralyzed. "Didn't mean to do it." Her whole small body shook like she was feverish. "Was supposed to hit his arm, not his throat."

"Not your fault. I threw him off balance," I said.

"Just meant to make him let go. I didn't mean to do it!" she cried. Her eyes were wild, and she was wringing her hands like you see in the silent films. "I didn't mean to!"

"Well, I'm damn glad you did," I said, controlling a shiver. "You probably saved my life." It wasn't an exaggeration. I can act cool under pressure, but I don't delude myself. This little mutt had taken a hell of a risk for me.

She sobbed out loud. "I'm done! They'll come after me."

"The cops?"

"Cops. Others. In the gang." She looked absolutely terrified.

I nodded. I knew about the law of the streets. She'd killed one of their own. No chance at all she could survive that, if the cops didn't get her first. Even then, prison wouldn't be safe for her. Nowhere in this city would be safe, and it was on my account. I felt it hard in my chest.

"I gotta get outta here." She seemed frozen to the spot, unable to choose which way to go. Which is why I made a sudden wild decision.

"Yes, you do," I said, checking my watch. *Just enough time.* "What's your name?"

In a little voice, she said, "Elf."

"Are you any good as an actress, Elf?" I said.

She hesitated, then nodded.

"Then act like you're my maid." I held out my hand to her. "You're coming with me to England."

CHAPTER NINETEEN

GRAY HAD STAYED silent through my whole story. I watched him shake his head then lean forward to refill my whisky glass. Gray had hardly touched a drop of his. He stared at me, wide-eyed. "I heard you had left because of a man. But that thug? They tried to marry you off to Marco Battalia?"

I should have known that would be the piece he'd latch on to.

"He did the Toronto-Dominion Bank job and took out two tellers. What a moron. No wonder you left." He sat back. "He's swimming with the fishes now. Did you know?"

I shook my head. "My letters from home are strictly personal. No business talk. I like it that way."

He nodded. "Brave of you, I'll say that. Ocean voyage, all by yourself. Not to mention the dash from Hamilton to Buffalo and on to New York. Don't know any other girls who would take the risk you did. And what, you were only eighteen?"

"Plus a day." I relaxed back with my whisky glass. "Yes, looking back, it shocks me that I actually managed to pull it off. Only thing in my favour was, I may have looked classy, but I knew how to handle myself like a street moll."

Gray rolled his eyes. "Still do, I reckon. So how'd you meet the mister?"

I smiled. "On that very voyage. Elf and Johnny came into my life on the same day."

"Your maid," said Gray, grinning and shaking his head. "So you got her on board that way."

"There was a slight matter of no documentation, but there are ways around that." I winked at him.

"And you know them all." I could see the admiration in his eyes. Of course, that could have been for my legs. I had swung them up on the other guest chair across from him.

"Of course, we picked up a few clothes for her at a charity shop near the dockland. I had her change out of her old duds right there, and we left them in a bin. Made her have a bath as soon as we left port." I wrinkled my nose in memory.

"And so you've been together ever since." He sat back in his chair at that, never taking his eyes off me, and took a large swallow of whisky.

I smiled at the memory. No one on this earth had been as grateful as Elf that day. I got such a kick out of watching her discover this new world I had brought her into.

"Yup," I said, feeling good about it all. "I admit it was risky taking her on, but no other thing I've done in my life has been so rewarding. People talk about loyalty without really knowing what it means. I know. Elf was always there for me, always had my back. When Johnny got TB, she knew what to do. Her own mother had succumbed to it. When Johnny died, Elf kept me alive when I wanted to end it all. My son adores her, and she, him."

"Plus we know she can throw a knife. How's she as a maid?" There was a saucy glint in his eye.

"Pretty crappy," I said, "but she's the best friend a gal could have."

"Not to mention a damn fine bodyguard." Gray lifted his glass to me. "I'm starting to like this Elf of yours."

GRAY WALKED ME back to my cabin. It was late. I wasn't really nervous, but Gray insisted. I had a feeling there was more to it. Like maybe he wanted to meet the woman I had just spent all this time talking about.

Elf met us at the door. Her mouth was set in a grim line. I introduced them. She gave him a long, cool look, nodded once, and stood back. The discrepancy in height was huge, and Gray always had a commanding presence, but on this occasion there was no question they stood across from each other as equals.

"You got it all put to rights?" he said, looking around the room.

"Not much to do," said Elf. "They didn't make a mess."

"Humph. Damn good thing you both weren't here when they broke in."

"For them," Elf muttered.

Gray caught that. I saw a slight tilt to the corner of his mouth. "No more tempting burglars, Luce, okay? Elf, make sure she behaves, will you?" Gray looked directly at her.

She returned his gaze. I watched as a silent message seemed to pass between the two. Wow. This was unusual. Elf didn't warm to strangers, as a rule.

"Needs watching, doesn't she." Elf gave a harrumph.

"Counting on you," said Gray. He made an odd salute and turned.

I stood with my mouth open. Elf closed the door behind him.

"What was that all about?" I asked.

She shrugged. "Man knows what he's about. Heard things. The stewards like him."

That was indeed a solid endorsement. Ship crews were not easily won over. You had to earn your respect.

"Not to mention he ain't bad to look at." A saucy grin split her face.

CHAPTER TWENTY

DAY FOUR AT SEA

EARLY NEXT MORNING, I was awakened by a noise. I lay still in bed, listening as hard as I could. It wasn't in this room, thank the lord. The sounds seemed to be coming from next door. Once again, someone was moving around in the room where Harry had met his end!

This time, I would get that darn steward.

I looked over at Elf, who hadn't moved. I'm a light sleeper, whereas she can be dead to the world for a full eight hours. She once told me that having spent the first fifteen years of her life afraid to close her eyes, she was making up for lack of sleep now.

I slid from the bed and reached for my dressing gown on the chair. It wouldn't hurt to peek out the door, I reasoned. I wouldn't take any chances, of course.

Still, I stopped to pick up something that could serve as a weapon if need be.

I tiptoed to the cabin door, opened it, and peeked out. No one in the corridor. I crept out, quietly shutting our door behind me.

The door to my right was closed. Would the intruder have stopped to lock it? Only one way to find out. I took a deep breath, grabbed the handle, and turned.

The door swung open, nearly knocking me over, and a male hand gripped my arm.

"You!" he exclaimed in a whispered voice. "You better come in." He pulled me into the room.

Mr. Mason! My heart was beating like a snare drum, and indeed I felt like I had been caught in a snare. More to the point, like a naughty child who deserved scolding.

"At least you didn't scream. Small mercies for that," he said, eyeing me up and down. He noticed my bare feet. The thin silk dressing gown was more for fashion than warmth, and I hadn't waited to put on footwear. "Good heavens, Lady Revelstoke. You must be cold. Sit down over there. Take my jacket first." He shrugged off his jacket and placed it over my shoulders.

Well, call me surprised. Mr. Mason could be gallant. Fatherly, in fact. I sat down on the bed, as he'd suggested.

"I heard something through the walls," I said to explain my presence.

"And you reasoned the murderer had returned?" He smiled at the alarm on my face. "Is that what the curling iron is for?"

I looked down at the tool in my hand ruefully. "I grabbed it, almost without thinking."

"He would indeed be shocked if you attempted to curl his hair." The big man shook his head. "But not a foolish move, to bring a weapon."

He seemed to stare right through me. "Tell me. What do you notice about this room that is unusual?"

I gazed around for sufficient time, while forming the words to say, "No luggage or personal effects. My maid told me she heard from the stewards that this cabin was unoccupied." I cleared my throat. "That's why I thought this might be the place ..." I drifted off.

He walked over to the rug and pulled it back.

"You reasoned well," he said. "This is where the murder took place."

I had no trouble looking shocked. The blood looked darker, dry now. But everything appeared to be the same as my previous visit to the room with Elf. I cleared my throat. "So the murderer used this cabin? But Mr. Mason, why didn't he just leave the body here? If the cabin is empty, the stewards wouldn't discover the body until we came to port."

Mr. Mason went down on his hands and knees to examine the crime scene more closely. "Yes ... curious, that. I've asked myself the same question. It seems he wanted the body discovered."

Now that was an explanation I hadn't thought of! Of course, Mr. Mason didn't know that Harry's body had actually been moved to my cabin. I was starting to feel bad about holding back information. So I offered up a tidbit that was darn close to the truth of what had happened.

"Could it be ... and I'm just thinking aloud here ... that he didn't know the lifeboats were below? He may have waited until night to do the deed, so as not to be seen. And it was foggy that night, as I recall. Maybe he couldn't see them, and he had hoped to drop the body directly into the ocean."

The detective vaulted up. For an older man, he was surprisingly agile.

"You have a good head on your shoulders, Lady Revelstoke, I'll give you that. It's something to consider." I watched as he looked in drawers, under the bed, and in the water closet.

"What are you looking for, Mr. Mason?" I was pretty sure I knew. Harry had gone overboard without his shoes. A seasoned detective would not have missed that.

I heard a grunt, then a pause. "Are there any hiding places in these cabins that you have come across?"

The question took me by surprise.

"You mean other than the safe?" I shook my head. "Not that I know of. Have you checked with Mr. West? But that reminds me of something I meant to follow up on earlier. This cabin is unoccupied, but someone may have left a parcel care of the line. Perhaps shipped trunks ahead?"

Mr. Mason stared at me. Then he smiled and nodded his head. "That is a prime piece of reasoning. You should write novels, Lady Revelstoke."

I smiled back at him in the most modest way I could. Men reacted to women in different ways, I well knew. Some liked a flirt. Others liked the helpless type. And I was beginning to appreciate that Mr. Mason was in some ways very modern. He appreciated quiet intelligence. It got me wondering about his wife. Had she helped him with his cases back home?

"The captain tells me you were a police detective in America. Are you hoping to make this a new career with the *Victoriana*? I'm rather hoping you are." I said the last bit to put him at ease. The question might have been seen as a challenge, otherwise.

"That remains to be seen. This is rather a new position for shipping lines. I may be a test case, and if so, this is certainly a trial by fire."

I smiled at that but made no comment.

He had been looking out the porthole at the sea. Now he turned and made his way over to the chair. He didn't sit down but held the back of it. "I wanted a new challenge after my wife died. I saw the shipping line advertise this post, and it seemed like a way to use my experience plus honour her memory. We had planned to visit England together, and I am merely fulfilling that dream of ours on my own. It's ... not the same."

"No, it surely isn't," I said, looking down at the curling iron in my lap. This, I could relate to. "I'm very sorry about your wife. The first year is by far the worst. Every anniversary — birthdays, wedding, Christmas — hits hard." It was still hard, but there was no point in depressing him further. He would find that out on his own, sadly.

"You are awfully young to be widowed." His voice had become fatherly again.

"At least we were married long enough to have a son. I don't know what I would do without him."

"I feel that way about our three daughters," said the detective. "They mother me something awful now. That is one of the reasons I felt the need to make a change."

"I'm glad you did," I said. And to my surprise, I actually meant it.

He smiled at that. "Let's get you back to your cabin. You must be cold."

As we made to leave, he said one more thing. "Let me give you my cabin number. If you hear any more movement in this room, please don't explore on your own. Don't take chances. This man is a killer, and he has already killed once. He won't hesitate to do it again. Instead, send for me. I will be more than pleased to come any time of the day or night."

He gave me a number for a cabin in second class, just one deck down. I promised him I would remember it and do as he said.

I truly meant to, but sometimes you just have to act.

CHAPTER TWENTY-ONE

I DIDN'T TELL Elf about the encounter next door. To be honest, I wasn't in the mood to face the scolding I would get for venturing next door on my own. I let her continue to sleep and dressed myself for breakfast. She was starting to stir, so I told her I was leaving, and she grunted once as the door clicked behind me.

I was going to breakfast. But first, I had another goal in mind. I didn't even have to ask for directions this time.

The purser was in his office, and alone this time, I was glad to see. I knocked quietly on the open door. He waved an arm at me and rose to his feet as I entered.

"You're up early." He smiled broadly. I could tell he was glad to see me. A tingling went through me. No man should look that good in the early morning.

I didn't take the time to sit down but braced myself on the back of the chair instead. "I won't keep you. I have a rather tickly question."

Gray remained standing. "Go on."

I cleared my throat. "And I don't mean to be disrespectful. But has anyone checked Mr. Mason's bona fides, to ensure he is who he says?"

Gray's serious look softened. "Yes. I did it myself when I hired him, through my own connections. There is indeed a Detective Mason recently retired from the New York police force, following the death of his wife. The physical description sounded accurate as well."

My whole body relaxed. I was truly relieved, as I had started to like the man. "Good," I said. "Although it would make a smashing plot for a novel."

"The detective on the case turns out to be the killer?" Gray lifted an eyebrow.

"Or ... the killer coshes the real detective on the head before he arrives at the scene, and then takes his place in the drawing room." I beamed with satisfaction.

Gray gave a throaty laugh. "You always did have a great imagination. Maybe you should become a writer."

"Actually, I do know one. I must remember to suggest this plot to my friend Agatha," I said on my way out.

I DIDN'T SEE Tony until lunch. Usually, he came to fetch me at my cabin, but this time I was ahead of him to the table. I smiled when he rushed over to pull out the chair beside me.

"You tricked me, arriving so early," he said.

I chuckled. "I merely wanted to get the choice of chairs so I could save one for you."

He seemed pleased at that. "What have you been doing with yourself this morning?"

I placed the monogrammed linen napkin on my lap. "Exploring," I said. "You know how I like a walk before meals." It was true too. Very early this morning, I had explored the cabin next door with Mr. Mason. And then I had explored the way to the purser's office, without getting lost.

Of course, I wasn't keen to explain why I had done both. Luckily, Tony wasn't much interested in walking as a pastime. I waited as he ordered a gin martini from the steward.

I smiled and toyed with the wineglass. "And you? What has occupied your attention this morning?"

"Sleep," he said. "I stayed up very late last night in the card room."

I nodded, but the smile left my face, and I felt my stomach drop.

Drew and Florrie joined us then. "Tony, my boy. Did you win any of it back?"

I watched Tony wince. I wasn't sure if it was due to being called by his first name, the affectionate "my boy," or the reference to a losing streak. Probably the latter.

Drew seated Florrie and then continued. "Big doings in the card room last night. That Sloan is a bit of a shark, I reckon. And watch out for MacPherson. I think he cheats."

I didn't know who MacPherson was, and that was just fine with me. It could stay that way.

Tony lit a cigarette, slowly and deliberately. I watched his hands and the hard set of his mouth. He didn't speak until after he had taken the first drag. "Better not cheat when I'm around," he said coolly.

A chill ran down my spine. I remembered the handgun I had seen in his room. Did he wear it under his suit jacket as a general rule? I couldn't see the customary bulge.

I like a man who can take care of himself, I admit. But there's a leap between that and men who simply invite danger. It made me uncomfortable, but I had to wonder if Tony was the sort of man he had talked about earlier — the type who had thrived on danger during the war and had trouble settling down to normal life after.

The table filled in around us, and lunch was served smartly. I nodded to the rest and then dug in. I savoured the savoury and devoured the main of lobster thermidor. Dessert was a bread pudding liberally laced with brandy, so I went without. Thank goodness for my dislike of rum and brandy — otherwise I would be having trouble fitting into these slim gowns of the season. Sometimes I think if one consumed a boiled egg, it would show through.

Florrie (why couldn't I remember her last name?) waited until Vera Horner and Amanda Martin were engaged in a spirited conversation with our hapless waiter concerning the uneven quality and temperature of the coffee. Then she turned to me and said quietly, "Lady Revelstoke, I've been wanting to ask you for tea. Will you join us in our cabin today at four? And you too of course, Mr. Anderson."

"Call me Tony," he said smoothly. I nearly laughed out loud.

We arranged to meet at their cabin at four. Tony excused himself with somewhere he had to be. I declined an invitation from Sloan to have a drink in the bar, pleading a headache. It was nearly true. Hearing Vera Horner ream out the waiter in her schoolmarm voice was giving me a whopper.

On the way back to my cabin, I got an idea. I took a detour and found myself across the main hall at the purser's office. As usual, Gray was there, signing papers. He was by himself again, which was convenient.

I knocked on the door, and when he looked up, he smiled.

"One more favour," I said, gliding into the room. "You know how you checked Mr. Mason's background? I'm wondering if you could do the same for a few others."

He frowned slightly. A lock of blond hair fell over one eye. "You think someone may not be who they seem. Mr. Sloan, perhaps? He strikes me as a strange fish."

I had to smile. After all, Vera Horner had called him a barracuda. "There's something off. I saw him flinch when Tony mentioned his Eton tie. Can you get me his full name? I might be able to do something there. Leave him to me."

Gray raised his eyebrow in question. I wasn't sure he knew about the schools in England and what a closed community they represented, so I let it pass.

"I'm also wondering about Drew and Florrie what's-their-name. They're from America. I don't know them from Adam, and neither do my companions. Vera Horner, I know quite well." *Unfortunately,* I thought to myself. "And Amanda Martin comes with a recommendation from Vera, so we can be clear about her."

"It shouldn't be too hard," said Gray. "I can look up their place of residence from the booking documents and put out the word to some contacts I have. Might take more than a day, though."

I didn't ask about the contacts. A purser had all sorts of business contacts, both respectable and those under the table. Gray had the additional benefit of a checkered background.

"Speaking of which," I said slowly, thinking back to this morning, "is there any way you can tell if the cabin beside me, the one booked to the name of De Beers, came with any luggage?"

Now I had his interest. "You're the second person to ask me that today."

I raised an eyebrow.

"Our security officer, Mr. Mason, asked me the same thing this morning," said Gray. "Now you. Explain please."

I mentioned my theory of how the cabin might have been booked for a discreet rendezvous and was never intended to be occupied. Then I took him through my version of what Mason and I had discovered in the cabin. He gave a resigned sigh.

"Dammit, Lucy. Do you have to poke your head in everywhere?"

I just shrugged. Yes, apparently I did have to.

Gray continued to grumble. "You've reminded me. I'll have to view the crime scene when I get through here and arrange for cleaners."

I'd forgotten about that. Sometimes it was hard for me to remember that the barefoot boy who'd shared my childhood hijinks was actually in charge of the operations on this ship. Small-town boy made good, for sure.

"I'm glad to see Mason is a good egg. I rather like him." He leaned back. "I suppose it's no good telling you to behave yourself and not go harrowing after murderers. In your night attire. Without even a weapon."

"I had a curling iron," I said primly.

It really wasn't polite of him to laugh so hard.

I'D BEEN UP at the crack of dawn this morning with Mr. Mason in the cabin next door and had been running around sleuthing most of the day so far. When I got back to the cabin, Elf insisted I nap until teatime. "Those looks won't last forever, ya know. Gotta rest yer face to smooth out those lines."

"What lines," I muttered grumpily. But I did as she said, and I slept like a baby until she woke me.

"Steward's at the door with a message for ya." She peered down at me. I wished she would stop doing that. It's a heck of a way to wake up, with that face in your face. I sat up and waited to hear it.

It was the short, well-muscled steward I had seen once before. He was no taller than my own five foot six, and may have been a prizefighter at one time, to look at his nose. He came forward with an envelope. "Mr. West asked me to wait for a response."

I thanked him and took the envelope. "Wait outside for a minute, if you don't mind. Elf, keep him company." I could see she was dying to.

I opened the envelope. On a sheet of paper, Gray had written three words, a name:

Maximillian Carver Sloan.

I smiled. Sloan might be a common surname — after all, we had Sloan Square in London — but the given names were unusual. That was to my advantage. Our suspect claimed to have been to Eton. There couldn't be more than one boy with those names who had gone to Eton in the correct time frame. Gray might not be able to do anything about checking that, but I could, as it just so happened my son, Charlie, was at Eton.

I decided to cable Charlie. Eton was proud of its heritage. There would be lists of graduates there by class, either in photos on the wall or in yearbooks. Charlie was a clever lad. He would find a way.

Of course, finding a way might mean breaking in to rooms he wasn't actually supposed to enter. I smiled at that. My lad was intrepid. Good thing I'd taught him a few things.

No need to mention murder and alarm anyone who might inadvertently see my message. But how could I word it so he would understand? Bingo! I had it. We were both fans of Sherlock Holmes, so I was able to come up with wording for the cable that would convey a message to him.

I went to the table, sat down, and picked up my pen. I used the other side of the paper and wrote, *Gray, can you send this cable?* I included the address.

Charlie, play Watson. The game's afoot. Maximillian Carver Sloan, Eton, age about 40. Anything you can find quickly. Love Mom.

I smiled to myself, pleased with the cunning cable. Charlie would be intrigued, for certain. I put the slip of paper back in the envelope and called the steward back into the room. He looked flushed, as did Elf. Message dispatched, I let Elf set about making me presentable for tea. We picked out a drop-waist lipstick-red dress with a pleated skirt. I look good in red, not so good in pastels. I paired it with long jet beads and a black headband.

"That's a strong-looking fellow," I said as Elf fussed with my hair.

She grunted. "Been around the block a few times."

"Nothing wrong with that," I said and left it at that.

Drew had given me a slip with the number of their cabin on it. I didn't look at it until I was dressed and out the door. Then I groaned. It was the Victoria suite, the very cabin I had tried to book and lost out on. Well, at least I knew where it was and wouldn't get lost.

Drew and Florrie welcomed me with open arms. "Come in, come in!" said Florrie. "How are you, my dear? Missing your son, I bet. I missed mine something awful when they were away at school."

I allowed myself to be folded into her arms, even though this was something "not done" by upper-class Brits, on pain of death. She smelled of fine powder and French perfume. It had been a long time since I'd been mothered, and it felt strangely good.

Drew gave my hand a good shake. "Sherry, or can I get you a cocktail?"

"Cocktail, please," I said, choosing a chair with swoopy arms. The Victoria suite was not exactly Victorian in design. The design principles of art deco had been beautifully applied to this cabin, including the colours of pink, silver, black, and chrome. I particularly loved the liberal use of mirrors, glass, black lacquer, and inlaid wood.

The Victoria suite boasted the huge advantage of a separate bedroom. The main area was designed for entertaining with several comfortable chairs, a curved mirrored bar on wheels, and a glass dining table similar in design. I knew it well, as I'd sailed in this cabin on my previous crossing.

Florrie was a fairly attractive woman a few inches shorter than me and a stone or two heavier. Her hair appeared to have been light brown at one time but was now running to grey. She wore it short in the modern way, and her clothes were definitely up-to-date, almost flashy compared to her English contemporaries at our table, but she wore them in a way that was comfortable, not competitive. I was embarrassed to admit that I'd not paid her much attention before. I did so now.

"You have sons as well, Florrie?" It occurred to me that I would have to use her given name, as I couldn't remember the other.

"Four, Lady Revelstoke! And oh, they kept me busy, didn't they, Drew? Four in eight years; the youngest is eighteen now. All of them missed the war, thank goodness. I don't know how mothers survived knowing their children were at the front." She shook her head sadly.

"Call me Lucy," I said, accepting the drink from Drew.

Florrie beamed. "See, Drew? I told you she wasn't like the others. Where are you from, dear? I know it has to be on our side of the pond. Your accent seems to be a blend."

"Hamilton, Ontario," I said. "Just over the border from Buffalo. Close to Niagara Falls." There didn't seem to be a reason to be mendacious. Always tell the truth when you can, as I've said before.

"Why, we've been to the Falls, haven't we, Drew!" Florrie clapped her hands. Her fingers were liberally covered in rings. "Fancy that. We're from Detroit. Drew even has business in Buffalo, don't you, sweetie?"

I had to smile at that. An English matron of her class would no more call her husband "sweetie" in public than kick off her shoes and dance on the dinner table.

"Got a dealership there, sweetums. Damned cold in winter." Drew stood leaning against the bar.

"What is your business, Drew?" I said casually.

"Motorcars," he said. "I own several Ford dealerships. That's where the future is, Lady Revelstoke."

"Lucy," corrected Florrie.

"Lucy," said Drew, toasting us with his drink. "Henry Ford

is right about that. Make the price right, keep people employed, and they will buy their own product. Soon those railways will be out of business. Everyone will have a car."

"And shipping lines? What about those?" I just had to ask.

He smiled indulgently. "Automobiles might go across water someday, but not the sea. The waves we get on the North Atlantic would present a problem. No, I think ships are a safe investment for a long time. Until, of course, the boys who fly figure out how to make air travel more lucrative, particularly for cargo. And they will, eventually." He toyed with his glass. "I have a finger in that pie too."

There was a shrewd look in his eyes. I suspected Drew had his fingers in a lot of pies. I wondered if all of them were legit. Although to be honest, I was relieved at this conversation. What Drew said about his business concerns sounded legitimate. I was beginning to like these people and wanted to think they were as presented. I hoped Gray's contacts would confirm that.

"Speaking of motorcars, I've been meaning to ask you ..." Drew paused to take a drink from his glass. "Your husband wouldn't have been John Revelstoke, the race driver?"

My heart quickened. "Yes. That was my Johnny."

Drew grew animated. "Wonderful driver! Knew his stuff, and was completely fearless. Good sportsman too, I heard. Truly a credit to the sport. I was sorry to hear he passed."

This was a total surprise. "Thank you, Drew. I appreciate the kind words. He was the love of my life. I miss him dreadfully."

He nodded. "Can imagine. Saw your husband written up a dozen times in the racing mags before the war. Never had a chance to see him race in person. Would have liked to. My dealerships sponsor racing back in Michigan. That's how I know the name.

Makes for good promotion, sponsoring cars that win. Especially for endurance. Everyone's all about endurance these days. No one wants a car that breaks down on you every thirty miles. That's where Ford is making great progress." He finished his drink.

I sat quietly — apparently, too quietly. Florrie was quick to intervene.

"Drew, don't bore her with business talk." She turned back to me. "He does go on, but he's a dear to me, so I forgive him. Now, I want to find out about where one should shop in London." Florrie droned on about a number of things that have escaped my memory. I tried to make the right responses at the right time, but I found my attention drifting.

Drew passed nuts every now and then. He kept looking at the door with a puzzled look on his face. I got the feeling he was itching to talk to Tony. It was pretty obvious girl talk didn't interest him a bit.

That did make me look at my watch. Why wasn't Tony there? He'd been invited. Perhaps he had settled down for a nap and was still out? Or was he at a card game somewhere and had lost track of time?

That was more likely. I felt my ire rise.

"Our tablemates are an interesting lot, aren't they?" said Florrie, bursting through my thoughts.

"Harrumph," Drew snorted. He obviously had a stronger opinion.

I smiled to myself and said, "Quite good company. The captain is charming."

Florrie leaned forward. "Dear, I wanted to mention about Mr. Sloan. He seems to admire you." She let the statement hang. In my experience, people will go on if you wait in silence long enough.

"It's just ... I'm not sure he's the best companion for you. Drew's heard things." Florrie looked to her husband.

Aha! This was just the sort of gossip I was hoping for.

Drew looked uncomfortable. "It's more like ... he doesn't play to type. I've heard things in the bar. He's a dark horse; sidesteps the most innocent questions. Plays hard with the cards and doesn't take losing well. Also won't stand a fellow to a drink. I don't trust a man like that, and you shouldn't either."

Now, this was interesting. First Vera Horner had stepped in with her two cents about Sloan. Now, the very people I'd asked Gray to investigate were warning me off the same man. And yet, I was inclined to agree with them. Something was off about Sloan, and it wasn't just the way he held his fork.

"You pay attention to Drew, Lucy. He knows men." Florrie reached forward to pat my hand.

"Can't make money in this world without knowing your fellow man," Drew added. He looked to the door again. "What's keeping the blasted man?"

"Drew! Language," scolded Florrie.

"Sorry," he mumbled.

No question Drew made the money in the family, but Florrie made the man.

"I appreciate your giving me this information," I said. "It's sometimes unnerving being a widow in new environments when you don't know all the people."

"Of course, dear! How it must be." She practically clucked at me. "You're far too young to be alone, of course. Now, that nice Lord Tony ..."

I put my glass down and rose abruptly. "I should see exactly what is keeping him. Perhaps he went to my cabin by mistake? I'll check."

"Oh, dear. Yes, do that. We'll meet at dinner, of course, if you can't hurry back."

I gave my thanks and left with more hugs.

CHAPTER TWENTY-TWO

ALTHOUGH I USUALLY tried to respect my friends' privacy, this was unusual and curious. True to form, that old unease was plaguing me. I worried there might be something wrong.

I'd not been quite truthful with Drew and Florrie. Tony wouldn't be at my cabin. The way we had left this at lunch had been perfectly clear. We were to meet at their cabin, not his or mine. This was very strange. Could he have forgotten? Or rather, *how* could he have forgotten? Unless the lure of a card game had obsessed him, and he'd lost track of time?

I didn't think it likely. Tony had never missed an appointment before, as far as I knew, and he was the consummate gentleman. Still, if he wasn't playing cards, where the heck was he?

I checked the card room first. Not there. He wasn't in any of the other salons, either. I checked the foredeck to see if he was taking the air with a hearty constitutional. He wasn't. In fact, no one I asked had seen him since lunch.

I hesitated to do it. A lady simply did not invite herself to a man's cabin. But something was wrong, I just knew it. It was one flight of stairs up to our deck. I skipped up the steps, smiling at the other first-class passengers I met coming down. I slunk along the corridor toward Tony's room, nodding to an elderly couple along the way. Then I dashed to the door and knocked quietly, so as not to draw further attention to myself.

No answer. I wondered what to do. Strange, about the female mind. We think of every possibility and seem to lock upon the worst ones. He could be ill, feverish. He could have fallen in the bath. Tony wasn't travelling with a valet, so who would know? The steward was nowhere around. He could be lying unconscious on the floor!

I looked around to make sure I was alone in the hallway. Then I searched my pocketbook for my little tool.

It's strange, while also serenely reassuring, how old skills come back to one. I had the cabin door open in no time. Almost too quickly.

"What the —"

"Oh, bugger," I said right out loud. Tony was sitting on end of the bed looking right at me. I stood staring back at him for several moments. How absolutely mortifying. I didn't know what was worse — my walking right into a man's room uninvited or having used a burglar's pick to unlock the door in the first place.

"Come in, for God's sake. Don't just stand there in the opening. And close the door behind you." Tony sounded irritable. He almost never swore in front of me. I nearly turned and ran, but there was something in his voice that had me responding to his command. The man had been a lieutenant in the war. I could see how he got his men to move on the battlefield.

I braced myself to enter a different battlefield and closed the door behind me.

He signalled with his arm for me to sit in the upholstered chair opposite. I did so.

"You didn't need to do that," he said. "The door was unlocked."

I must have gone bright red.

"But just to satisfy me, would you care to explain how?"

There was no point in being obtuse. I held out the pick, still in my hand. "My cousins taught me," I said.

His eyes went wide, and then he managed a laugh. It wasn't a nice laugh. More like the growl of an angry dog.

"I was worried," I said in a sad effort to find an excuse. "You didn't come to tea with Drew and Florrie. I thought you might have fallen and not been able to get up."

I waited primly with my knees together until the room was quiet, all the time looking around. The place was a mess. Papers everywhere. Drawers had been upended, their contents strewn upon the floor. My eyes went wide.

"Oh my God, Tony! You've been —"

"Burgled," he said, voice back to cool and formal. "It wasn't you, I take it?"

My mouth fell open. "No!" I said. He was staring at the pick still in my hand. "I couldn't! I would never do that!"

His mouth screwed into a grim smile. I'd just broken into his room. Suggesting I would never have burgled it was patently ridiculous. But he seemed to believe me.

"No. I don't suppose it was you. At first I thought it might be Elf. But I couldn't make sense of it. Of the why. I've been sitting here trying to figure it out."

That's what was odd. Tony, still sitting on the edge of the bed. He hadn't bothered to rise for me, either, which was odd for him. Usually, he was on his feet the second a woman entered the room. Or a man, for that matter. It wasn't just manners. You took the measure of a man eye to eye, I'd been told.

I swallowed a gulp of air. "Was anything taken?"

"Yes, as a matter of fact. Do you want to guess?" He seemed to stare right through me.

"A pair of shoes?" I said.

Again, that odd growl. "No, not shoes." He didn't elaborate. Still, he continued to stare blankly.

I looked around nervously. My brain worked to take in the scene. Cufflinks had been dumped among the clothes. Probably valuable ones. The thief hadn't taken them. None of this made sense. He didn't take the cufflinks, and he didn't take any shoes. Why would someone burgle Tony's cabin if not for the shoes? Or wait. Did they already have the shoes from my cabin? My mind was racing. If so, they'd found the heels empty. They knew of my friendly relationship with Tony and figured he might be the hiding the rocks in his cabin. So they ransacked the place.

"It may be I'm a few pages behind in this lurid tale we appear to be starring in. Why would they steal shoes particularly, darling?" he said. The words sounded a bit slurred. We'd had a few cocktails at lunch. Had he been drinking since?

I cleared my throat. "It was just an idea. When we threw Harry overboard, his shoes were missing."

I didn't bother to mention that Elf and I had caused them to be missing.

"Shoes. Hmmm. That's not what they took." Tony didn't bother to elaborate. His face went to a frown. I could see he was worried, and also that he wasn't keen to tell me why.

And that's when I had it. They had taken his gun.

I HAD A choice. I could own up and admit I'd seen it when I was here before or fake innocence.

I cleared my throat. "My grandfather taught me to stick as close to the truth as possible. It's easier for when you have to repeat a story."

Tony sniffed oddly. "Interesting man, your grandfather." He seemed to be balancing himself with both hands on the bed.

"He was," I said. "You can't imagine. Dead now. I'll tell you about him another time. You may know ... or maybe you don't. I'm a reader." I stood up and kicked through the clothes on the floor until I could see behind the lamp on the bedside table. "I have a thing about books. All kinds, fiction and non-fiction, although I must admit mysteries are my favourite. Agatha Christie and the lot. She's a friend of mine. I always bring loads to read on a voyage. The library is my favourite room at the castle. I'm telling you to explain myself." I paused and ran my hand along the table edge. "Last time I was here in your room, I saw the book beside your bed, and I was curious to know what you were reading."

His body remained still. His eyes appeared duller than usual. "And you saw the gun," he said.

"I saw the gun," I agreed, trying to meet his eyes. They were closed. "Is that what they took?"

He tried to nod, but it seemed to hurt him. One hand went to his head.

"That's bad," I said. My childhood training kicked in automatically.

"Yes," he replied slowly. "I don't like being without a weapon."

"No, that's not what I meant," I said.

His face had gone ashen.

"What's bad is they may use it," I said. "And it can be traced back to *you*."

Tony chose that moment to keel over.

"What the —" I caught his right arm before he hit the ground. "Tony! Were you here when the burglar came in?"

I got a groan as a response. He lay on the floor, not moving; I knelt beside him. The blood on the back of his head was obvious now. He'd been coshed!

"Oh, bloody hell! I'll get the doctor." I lurched to my feet and raced from the room.

CHAPTER TWENTY-THREE

"CONCUSSION," SAID THE doctor, coming around the corner.

Tony had been moved to the infirmary. I waited, seated in the staff alcove with the purser's assistant. My poor handkerchief had been twisted into a mess.

The doctor sat down opposite us. "Don't worry too much. I've cleaned him up. The skull wasn't fractured. I expect he will be fine, with rest and time. It's a good sign that he was upright and making conversation when you found him. But he'll need watching, both for medical and safety reasons, until we get to port."

Marcus Jones was an older man whose wife had died in childbirth. He had joined the shipping line some years ago and was popular among the staff and passengers. His quiet manner always inspired confidence. But that didn't help where violence was at issue.

I gulped. "Should we arrange for a guard?"

"Consider it done. I'll speak to Mr. West," said the young officer beside me.

I let out a stifled breath. Thank goodness ocean liners now had medical personnel. This ship employed Dr. Jones and one nurse. I hated to think what it must have been like to travel overseas in the Age of Sail. One heard there had been so many deaths en route. No chance for a decent funeral, either. With no refrigeration, bodies had to be disposed of immediately.

"Luckily, there are no contagious cases in the infirmary this voyage. We'll keep him safe, don't worry." The white-haired doctor reached out to pat my knee and then thought the better of it, I could see. He gave me a sympathetic glance and waved his arm. "Go. I'll let you know when there is change."

There was nothing I could do there. But there was something I could do elsewhere. When the purser's assistant rose to leave, I went with him and told him my plan. Once he had settled me in the empty purser's office, I sent him on two errands.

WITHIN MINUTES, MR. Mason arrived. He came in quietly and closed the door behind him.

"Thank you for sending for me. I'll speak to the doctor and examine Mr. Anderson's cabin after I've talked to you. But I first wanted to ensure that you're unharmed. You weren't there?" He turned the other chair to face me and then sat down on it. He leaned forward, face concerned.

I shook my head. "I went looking for Mr. Anderson after he didn't turn up for tea. We had made an arrangement, and it was unusual for him not to follow through." I stalled a moment. Luckily, I had thought about how to present the story during the time I had been waiting. "I knocked on his door and thought I heard something. A moan. So I tried the door, and it was open."

No need to tell anyone else that I had attempted to break in.

He nodded. "Mr. Anderson was conscious when you went in?"

I told him what had taken place, including the truth about the missing gun. Well, almost the truth. I didn't tell him that I had known Tony had a gun before today.

Mason looked thoughtful. "So the burglar was after the gun. That's interesting. It at least gives us a lead that should reduce the number of suspects. How would he know that Mr. Anderson possessed one?"

I gulped. "Tony told me he left it on the bedside table. He wasn't travelling with a valet, so I guess the steward would have seen it." That was true. I felt bad saying it, because now the steward would come under suspicion. But Mason would have figured all that out on his own, I knew.

"So I'll add talking to the steward to my list of things to do." Mason frowned. "Although it will be a useless interview, most likely. He'll deny that he told anyone about the gun, whether he did or not. They will close ranks." He was silent for a moment. "We will have to assume the entire cabin staff might have known."

"I see what you mean," I said slowly. I was feeling guilty. The culprit may have picked up the gun, but I didn't think that's what he'd come for. Most likely, he was after the gemstones that had been in the shoes. But I couldn't tell Mason that without checking with the other people involved. Tony, Elf, Gray ... we'd all been complicit in keeping silent about the shoes and, worse, Harry's trip through the porthole in my cabin.

"Is it possible Mr. Anderson told anyone else of the gun he possessed?" Mason asked. "One of your tablemates, perhaps? I seem to recall he is keen on gaming. Perhaps the topic of the gun came up when he was with other men in the card room. Was it a war souvenir?"

I considered it. "I expect so. He was definitely present at many card games. He's quite an ... enthusiast." That was a nice way to put it.

Mason's face lost its animation. His voice dulled to something resigned. "Drink helps loosen the tongue, and men will drink while playing cards. He very well could have brought it up in conversation, or someone may have prompted him. Men talk about the war when they are not with women."

I looked up to see a fleeting expression of sorrow pass across his face. I would have thought Mason too old to have served in the war. Which got me thinking. He'd talked of having grown-up daughters, but perhaps he had lost a son?

"I'll arrange for a guard to be stationed with Mr. Anderson. For now, we won't allow any visitors. I know you must be anxious, but to ensure his safety, I need to enforce this with no exceptions." Mason started to reach out a hand and then thought better of it. "Check with me tomorrow, and we'll see about a visit. And please, don't tell anyone. Word will get around, but we'll try to keep this quiet for tonight. In the meantime, let it be known that he has taken ill."

The door burst open. Gray stood there, taking in the scene. "I've just heard," he said. His eyes flicked to Mason and then settled back on me. "Tell me you're okay."

Before I could answer, Mason rose. "She is more than okay. She is wonderful. I will leave you now. Lady Revelstoke, thank you for sending for me. Please continue to do so." He smiled briefly, nodded at Gray, and made his exit.

Gray watched him go. "You've made a conquest there," he said. "However did you do it?"

"Never mind that," I said. "I've thought of something."

CHAPTER TWENTY-FOUR

"WHAT IF," I started, "this attack on Tony wasn't about the gemstones."

Gray swung around the desk and lowered himself into the chair. "First, tell me how bad he is. I only heard he was attacked."

It was good of him to ask. I knew he had no reason to be fond of Tony, but he had a heart, our Mr. West. I did as he asked, leaving out the fact that I had already known Tony had a gun. No need for Gray to know that I had visited that cabin before today. Men can be silly about things like that.

"Look." I pointed a finger in the air. "I assumed that Harry's killer was searching Tony's cabin for the gemstones. We know the killer stole the shoes from my cabin, and then they must have realized the stones were missing from the shoes."

"Okay, I get it." Gray leaned back in the chair. "So they didn't find the diamonds in your cabin. But they see you and Anderson are chummy, so they think you might have given them to him for safekeeping."

I nodded agreement. "That's exactly what I think. But they had bad luck again and couldn't find the rocks in Tony's cabin, so they took his gun as a kind of consolation prize."

"Once a thief always a thief," he muttered.

I found myself staring into his soft grey eyes. Golly, it was getting hot in here. I pulled off my wrap.

"Doesn't that prompt you to ask a question, Gray? It does me."

His eyebrows slanted down. I could see he was frowning, thinking hard. I helped him out.

"Okay, I'm just a woman, I know." I waved a hand through the air. "So I may not think like you men. Maybe you all carry around guns like little toy soldiers. Heaven knows, my family does. But this isn't the inner city or the Middle Ages. It's 1928. Why would you do that? On a cruise ship? When you're an aristocrat?"

Gray let out a breath. "Why the devil would he have a handgun on his bedside table?"

"Within easy reach. Not even hidden away in a drawer." I said what we both were thinking.

"He was afraid of something," Gray stated. "Something followed him here, and he was taking no chances."

I've heard people use the term *dead silence*, and I know now what they mean. The silence between us was heavy, like a dead thing. You wanted to avoid it.

I let it sit for a while. It was clear Gray was thinking deeply, pulling different scenarios through his mind. I knew to take him seriously. He had a sort of advantage in that he was a very much a man's man and knew what would motivate a male to do certain things, whereas I didn't claim to have any insight into the male mind.

"His past, Luce. I know nothing of his past. But something has caught up with him, for sure. What do you know of him?"

I sat back to think. Truth be told, I didn't know all that much. Only what Johnny had told me and a smattering of society gossip.

"His father's a viscount, quite respectable. Old family, very wealthy. The ancestor came over with William the Conqueror, I believe. But Tony's not in line for the title. Much younger third son or something, and the older two are married, with ample heirs."

"How do you know him?"

I shrugged. "Johnny knew him from the war. They were officers in the same company. He spoke well of him as a comrade in arms. But you get to know everyone in London high society eventually. Particularly bachelors. They are always in demand at fashionable dinner parties to even out the numbers, especially now, after the war, when so many of the younger men were killed in France."

We'd lost nearly a million men in the Empire alone. One could hardly believe the numbers — so much of a generation destroyed. It was horrible. I still felt my throat constrict, thinking of it. They weren't the only victims. It meant hundreds of thousands of women my age had no hope of marriage, of finding partners. Already, the newspapers were calling them "superfluous women."

Gray must have been thinking something similar, as he nodded and said, "Remarkable that he has remained a bachelor."

"I'm sure there was family pressure to marry, but he was the only one young enough to serve in the war. He was wounded and came back with shell shock. Spent some time in hospital."

I didn't mention what type of hospital. Gray could infer that.

"What was he doing in America?"

I frowned. "That's where it gets tricky. He left England over a year ago. I get the feeling he was a remittance man and didn't end up liking the colonies very much."

"What the devil is a remittance man?"

I smiled at that. Gray had been raised on the east side of an industrial city. He had cleaned himself up very well, but he wouldn't know all the practices of the British aristocracy, particularly those of inheritance.

"We have a saying in England. The first son is the heir. The second son is the spare. In previous times, the third son would go into the army or the clergy. Tony did go into the army because of the war. After he came out, there was nothing for him to do, I assume. He wasn't going to inherit the estate. So I expect they sent him overseas with an allowance." Even as I said it, it sounded heartless. Send the unwanted son with shell shock overseas where he can't embarrass you.

"Ah. That's what you mean by remittance man."

"They don't like to split up the estate, you see. It's a way of keeping the wealth and power in the family."

"Somewhat hard on the younger children, I'd say. Where I come from, we inherit equally. If there's anything left to inherit besides debt." He laughed at that.

"Johnny was a third son too. That's why there wasn't too much objection to his marrying a Canadian. He was never supposed to inherit the title." I paused in brief memory, then shook myself free of it. "Bad luck for the family that everyone else was lost at the Somme."

Gray nodded. "So the oldest gets the boodle. And everyone else has to stay in his good graces or pay the consequences."

"Pretty much. A daughter is actually quite valuable, once you have the heir and spare taken care of. A daughter, you can marry off to further your status or bring money into the family. But a pile of sons …"

Gray smiled. "So the ideal family for a British lord would be two sons followed by daughters."

"Something of the sort. Johnny's family was very pleased when we had a son. It's not just a whim, you know. It's the law. Most large properties are entailed, meaning they go to the firstborn legitimate son. A father can't change that, even if he wanted to."

"Seems damned unfair. What do the daughters get?"

"Usually a settlement for a dowry. And a place to live until they are married, as long as they behave to the satisfaction of the lord and master."

He shook his head. "Wouldn't want it. No amount of wealth is worth those chains."

I took a breath. I had been very lucky. Having a son instead of a daughter ensured that I would always have a home. I explained that to Gray.

"The worst thing for these old families is to have only daughters. Then the estate will pass to the next male in line, often a cousin. It's a disaster for the widow and her daughters, who often have to leave their home and live with other family, or hope for charity from the new lord. I've known that to happen, and if I hadn't had a son, it would have happened to me."

He shook his head. "And they call England a civilized country. It seems downright feudal to me."

"I agree," I said. "But back to my point. Tony would have a good allowance, and perhaps a little money of his own. Mothers can leave money to their children independent of the entailed property."

Gray looked at me, expectantly.

"My point is … he wouldn't have unlimited funds. He couldn't draw on the estate." I gulped air before speaking. It seemed a bit of a betrayal. "Have you seen how he spends his time here?"

Gray shook his head. "This position takes all my time."

I leaned forward. "Cards. He's a gambler, Gray."

A moment of silence, then he whistled low. "Now that will change things."

I rose from the chair, bounding with nervous energy. "It fits with the gun, doesn't it? Maybe he owes someone a packet of money, and they've come to collect. Maybe it's the very reason he's on this ship — to avoid debts he incurred in America."

I was pacing now, making a little half circle around the back of the chairs. "Heaven knows, it could be the reason he left England in the first place. Or maybe his father paid off the debts he left in London and insisted he clean up his act in a new country. But that didn't work out."

Gray watched me pace. "You don't know this for sure. You're just guessing, right?"

"Just guessing. But I know about gamblers, Gray. I saw my share of them back at my uncle's pool hall. They don't stop, even when it's dangerous to keep going." I stopped and held on to the back of the chair. "And if there's one thing I'm sure of, it's that Tony's not a coward. Johnny told me he was rather reckless on the battlefield. Drank his share of rum and never hesitated to join his men going over the top. I know him. He'd keep going until the money was gone."

Gray rubbed his chin. "That's the problem with war. It gives you a taste for excitement. Some of us come out of it wanting Mom and apple pie and a quiet life. But others never do adjust and keep searching for that blood rush. Gambling gives you that. Sounds like your Tony."

I stiffened. "He's not my Tony."

"Glad to hear it." Gray's voice was clipped. He shot right

ahead before I could respond. "So you're suggesting someone from his recent past may have come after him on board here to collect a debt. And that's why they ransacked his cabin. Looking for money, and they took the gun as a bonus."

I unwound myself and sat back down in the chair. "It's a possibility. We can't overlook it."

"They wouldn't be too particular about using violence, either." Gray shifted his weight in the chair. "Tell me again how you met up with him this time."

I hadn't told him how we'd met the first time. But that didn't matter.

"I spent two weeks at the Waldorf between sailings. Tony was staying there too." I slowed, using a few moments to figure out how to word things. "We'd been acquainted before in England, of course, and you know how things are with the British upper classes. If you've been introduced, you become instant friends in foreign places and ignore everyone else. He took me to dinner several times, and around to a few speakeasies."

"Of course he did," grumbled Gray.

I hid a smile. "He seemed to know his way around them. He didn't gamble when he was with me, but they definitely knew him in the places he took me." I sat back and reminisced. It had been exciting, going in cabs from club to club. He was fun, and I had liked him a lot. But always, there was a little something holding me back from getting too intimate. A prescient feeling haunted me, once again, that he wasn't entirely who he seemed and that danger went along with him as casually as his monogrammed cigarette case and flask.

Gray's voice interrupted my thoughts. "I'm going to ask you to remember something. Did he pay cash? Or did he run a tab?"

"A tab," I said. "Definitely. I remember thinking how easy it was for people with titles to pick up credit. The girls working in the places called him Lord Tony. The son of a Viscount doesn't get that kind of title, but Americans wouldn't know that. So I figured he was throwing the lord thing around to gain some status there, and consequently credit."

The silence around us was heavy again.

Gray spoke first. "To recap: Tony Anderson was attacked. It might be because Harry's killer — note how I've picked up your name for him — was looking for the gemstones in Anderson's cabin. Or it might be because he has enemies on board the ship looking to settle his gambling debts."

"Yes. That sounds about right." I was getting uneasy. Something there tickled my brain cells.

As it turned out, Gray was one step ahead. "I hate to bring this up, Lucy. But have you considered that a gambling man who is desperate for cash may have been tempted by your hidden diamonds?"

Curses! He knew my mind better than I did.

CHAPTER TWENTY-FIVE

WHAT A MESS. We didn't get to discuss it further because a steward came to the door. I took the opportunity to leap up and make my excuses.

"Walker, I'm late for my meeting with the captain. Can you accompany Lady Revelstoke to her floor, then meet me in the officers' lounge." It seemed Gray wasn't taking any chances with my safety. Or my sense of direction.

Walker appeared delighted. He was the same fellow from before, the one who looked like a prizefighter. He was smartly dressed in his steward uniform, with slicked-back sandy-blond hair. I was happy for his company, because I had something else in mind. I waited until we were out of earshot of the purser's cabin before revealing my plan.

"Mr. Walker, I wonder if you could show me where trunks are stored on this ship. My maid, Elf, was wondering."

"Of course," he said. "This way. We go a few floors below."

I was a little surprised he didn't ask why I wanted to see them. I had a whole story prepared. How I needed a gown that Elf had packed by mistake, and perhaps he could help me find this particular trunk. Surely they would be stored in order of room number.

But I didn't need to tell my story, as he seemed preoccupied. We walked side by side for several minutes without speaking. I could see he was fidgeting to tell me something.

"Well, out with it, Walker. I can tell you have something to say." I had a twinkle in my eye, as I was pretty sure what was coming.

"It's Elf, my Lady." He was so nervous, he blurted it out. "She's the tops."

"Yes, she is. I think the world of her." I waited for more.

"She's not like any of the others."

"No, she isn't," I said. *That* we could agree on. They had broken the mould when they created Elf. Or more likely, she had broken it herself.

"See, there's this do for the staff tomorrow night." He turned a corner and held open a big steel door.

"And you want to ask her to it." I smiled and walked ahead of him. "Go ahead. I can do without her for one evening."

"Thanks, miss! I mean, your Ladyship!" He beamed.

Wow. I had made him happy. If only it were that easy with all men.

Walker took me down several flights of stairs. The decoration of the stairwells became less and less magnificent as we descended. I had to hold the railing to keep my balance as the steps seemed to get deeper and more treacherous for one in heels.

As we got closer, I decided to tell him what I had in mind.

"Elf was a little overzealous with the packing. I'm hoping to find a gown in one of my trunks that was stored," I said.

Walker stopped on the stair below me and turned. "I beg your pardon, your Ladyship. We can't actually access the trunks. They're in the hold."

I stopped and faced him. "The hold?"

"Well, yes. With all the other cargo."

"Really?" Curses! Talk about disappointing. "I thought there would be a trunk room, where the luggage would be lined up by room number."

Walker smiled, and I could see he was holding back a chuckle. "This isn't a railway station or a hotel. All the trunks not delivered to rooms are stored in the hold with everything else. You have to balance the cargo in a ship, you'll understand. To make it stable."

"So no one can really go down there?" I was crestfallen.

He shrugged. "Not possible, I'm afraid. The packing is done while we're in port. We have a movable platform on this ship to lower cargo. It's the latest of its kind. That's what I thought you might want to see. All the cargo is packed pretty tightly. You can't have it shifting during the voyage."

Rats! Of course, that made perfect sense. Shifting cargo could put a ship off balance when strong waves hit. But there went my cunning plan.

"It is doubtful we could find your trunk even if we could go down there, my Lady. They are not in a specific order. The goal is to balance the load."

I held on to the stair railing, deeply disappointed. I had hoped that luggage would be lined up by room number so I could check if the cabin next door to mine had any trunks assigned to it. That way, I could see if the room in which Harry had met his end was ever intended to be occupied.

Walker waited patiently as I thought this through.

"Oh well," I said finally. "I'll have to do without that gown. We don't have to go any further, Mr. Walker. You can take me back to the main deck."

We retraced our steps up the stairwells, and I was breathing rather heavily when we got to the main deck. Walker, of course, was fit as a racehorse. I thanked him, and we parted, although he seemed reluctant to return to his duty. I thought he would have preferred to walk me right back to the cabin, in case a certain someone was there.

As I walked down the corridor, this thought came to me. Surely, they would have a list of trunks that went into the hold. Otherwise, passengers could complain of luggage being lost, and the shipping line could be sued. The name of the passenger would be on that list, and the number of pieces of luggage beside that, for sure. Probably even the room number allocated to the passenger.

I already knew the cabin next to me was booked in the name of De Beers. If only I could find a way to take a look at that list ... where was the most likely place it would be?

Wait a minute. I had an idea. Where did you go if you were a passenger on this ship and you wanted something? Room changes, staff issues. Who got all the passenger requests and complaints? There was one office on this ship that overflowed with paperwork. File cabinets wall to wall. Surely, somewhere in there ...

It was a gamble. Gray had said that he was meeting with the captain and Walker was to find him in the officers' lounge. That meant the purser's office would be empty right now!

Should I risk it?

I could just ask him instead.

But I'd asked him before — I was pretty sure I had — and hadn't gotten an answer. I couldn't remember why. Had we been distracted, or had he been stalling me? Why would he do that?

I felt that little niggle again.

I couldn't believe Gray was a killer. I refused to. Wartime was different. All sorts of men had been tested in ways we never wanted to see again.

Gray couldn't have killed Harry. I knew that in my heart. But he could have ransacked Tony's room looking for the gems, or one of his staff could have. No one was better placed to carry off a theft than the people who worked in the purser's office. And Gray had worked for my family in the old days ... was he still a little bit crooked?

I didn't believe it. I couldn't! Yet why take a chance? If I could get the information I wanted without asking for it, all the better.

I turned around and retraced my steps. When I got to the main hall, I made my way down the stairs to the office I had been in earlier. Luckily, it was a little way down a short corridor, away from the madding crowd.

The door was closed. I looked around to see if anyone was watching. Then I tried the handle. Locked! Rats. Well, I should have anticipated that. Luckily, I was not without options. I slipped my scarf from around my neck and let it drop to the floor. If questioned, I could always say I was bending over to pick it up.

I looked again to make sure I was not being observed, then took a small tool from my handbag.

When you are picking a lock, it always seems to take longer than it should. I had this down to a science after years of practice, but even then, I looked around nervously once or twice.

My training didn't let me down. In less than half a minute, I had the knob turning and was closing the door behind me.

I looked around. The usual mess on the desk. I had to smile and wonder if his own quarters were as scattered. This man needed a wife. Or at the very least, a maid.

I'd have to hurry. Yes, he had that meeting with the captain, but who knew how long that would take. Minutes? Or hours? Not to mention, Walker and I had wasted valuable time going down to the hold. Worse, it had accomplished nothing.

I geared myself up for the task. This search would be a race against time, so best to work methodically.

There was an in-basket on the corner of the desk with a few unopened envelopes in it, and two untidy piles of paper to the left of it. One appeared to be invoices to be paid and the other miscellaneous correspondence. I left them as is.

I started from left to right on the file cabinets. The first was a four-drawer locked cabinet. Damn! I hadn't thought about the cabinets being locked. It would take far longer if I had to break into them. To be honest, I'd never picked a cabinet lock before. Surely, this was a grave omission in my early education.

But maybe every cabinet wasn't locked? I tried the second one. Success! The top drawer pulled open. I quickly looked through the file tabs. This one contained supply orders, neatly arranged in alphabetical order by file. At least he was methodical in his filing.

Onto the second drawer. More supply orders and invoices.

Third drawer. More — this was getting frustrating. I pushed in that drawer and moved to the cabinet on the other side of the desk. Marvelous luck — it was also unlocked! Obviously, Gray had been using these cabinets earlier. I pulled open the top drawer and perused the files. Each was tabbed with a last name, A to Z. Could these be passenger names? I pulled one — employment records. Drat.

My ears went on alert. *Voices in the hall.* I stopped what I was doing and quietly pushed in the drawer of the file cabinet. The voices continued. One of the speakers was Gray! I stood stock-still, like a rabbit freezing to avoid a predator. *Stupid,* I told myself. I wasn't a bunny. The second the door opened, I would be caught.

The sound of a key turning in the lock ...

I looked around, frantic for a place to hide. The door handle started to move — I pushed the chair aside and dove for the hollow under the desk.

"I'll report back after the dinner hour, sir."

"Yes, do that. Mind the drinking in steerage tonight. I hear it got out of hand. Get Mr. Mason to keep an eye on it."

"Yes, sir."

"I don't mind the drinking, but we can't have fistfights. Get them dancing or something. We can't lose any more chairs."

The door closed with a solid click.

Silence. I could hear someone breathing.

"You can come out now, Lucy." Gray's voice was calm and low. "I'm alone."

CHAPTER TWENTY-SIX

CURSES! COULD THIS be any more embarrassing? I poked my head up above the edge of the desk. Gray was staring right at me. "How did you know I was here?"

He held up his hand. In it was the chiffon scarf I had dropped in the corridor. "I knew it was yours," he said.

"Bugger!" I said, coming out from under the desk. "How did I get so lousy at this? Honestly, I shouldn't be let out without a leash anymore."

He was chuckling now. "What the devil have you been up to?"

I straightened up and brushed down my dress. What the devil indeed. Now I was in trouble.

"You might as well own up to it. I know you must have picked the lock. I never leave the door unlocked when I leave the room. Caught is caught." That was an expression we had used as kids. Of course, we had played a different version of cops and robbers than most children. In our case, the robbers had been the good guys.

But the fact he'd used that expression meant he was more amused than angry.

"Caught is caught," I echoed. "I know." I turned to face him. "I'm just trying to figure out how to say it without looking like a complete fool."

He dropped the scarf and crossed his big arms across his chest. "I'm waiting. This is going to be good."

"Smarmy bugger," I said.

He laughed out loud then. "Spill."

So I spilled. I took a deep breath and told the truth. "I was looking for the luggage record. Trying to find out if the cabin next to me was booked for criminal rendezvous only."

His face held questions. "Go on."

I flung up my hands. "I mentioned it before, remember? If there were no trunks being stored for that cabin, see? Then we know the booking wasn't real. I mean, no one ever intended to occupy that cabin. They were just going to use it for meetings."

His face cleared. "So you were looking for the passenger assignment record. Or the trunk record. Why didn't you simply ask me?"

That's where it got tricky. I didn't want to tell him the real reason. So I stood like a simpleton with my mouth open.

He walked over to one of the file cabinets I hadn't touched yet and grabbed a dark green file off the top of it. I watched him shuffle papers, and then he dropped a stapled stack of paper on the desk in front of me.

"Here it is. You can check it yourself."

Now I was really embarrassed.

"Thank you," I mumbled. I plunked down into the desk chair, feeling awful. I kept my hands in my lap and looked down at the list as if it would burn my fingers.

"But why didn't you just ask for it?" He watched me closely. I couldn't keep the guilt off my face, and he saw it there clearly.

His eyes went wide, and his mouth reduced to a grim line. "Oh no, Lucy. Oh no. You don't trust me? Don't tell me you thought I might be a suspect."

I grabbed the scarf from the desk and twiddled it in my hands. "*Well* ... I didn't really think you were. Not really. Everything in me said you weren't. But I couldn't cross you off the list entirely. I mean, you say you aren't working for the family anymore. But you're still in touch, obviously, or you wouldn't have said what you said the day we first met here."

There was a pregnant pause. I could almost hear his memory click through past dialogue.

"'Bessie says hello,'" he recalled. Then he cursed. "That was stupid of me."

"Can you see why I might have doubts?" I said earnestly.

"Bloody hell." He was pacing now. "Yes, I can. And it makes sense that a purser could be the one with the right contacts to run a smuggling business. Contacts on both sides of the Atlantic. But I'm not. Here, I'll prove it to you." He stopped. "Sit still." He pointed at my hands. "And stop wrecking your scarf. Here, give it to me."

I put the wrinkled thing on the desk. He snatched it up, folded it haphazardly, and placed it on top of the cabinet beside him.

"First, I'm not working for the family. Haven't since the war. But yes, I am still in touch with them through your brother Paolo. And through Bessie, to a certain extent. Bessie takes care of my mother, makes sure she doesn't go without. I send money back home, and she manages it. You know how it is."

Paolo! Yes, that made sense. He and Paolo were the same age and had been fast friends. Even I was still in touch with Paolo. He was the best of the bunch, as far as I was concerned. Maddening, that my own brother hadn't told me about Gray. Would I ever tear his ear off when I got back to shore. Okay, only by letter, but still.

But then I thought, why would he tell me? Gray had been our childhood friend from the other side of the tracks. I was long gone and married. Why would Paolo think I would be interested in gossip about Gray? He couldn't have anticipated we would meet up on a ship in the middle of the Atlantic.

Worse, I hadn't even told Paolo I was making this journey. I felt guilty for that. But the trip from New York to Hamilton took almost a day, and I wasn't sure of my welcome in the family. Most important, I wasn't sure if once they had me, they would let me go.

So I hadn't told anyone I was coming. And wouldn't they kill me if they knew I had landed in New York and not made the effort to see them.

I would have to warn Gray not to tell them.

Gray! Good lord. He was standing over me, still staring. Whatever way you looked at it, I felt like a fool for breaking in to this room.

"I'm sorry," I said weakly.

"For God's sake, Lucy. Don't you remember when we were young and Paolo pushed you off the pier? I jumped in and brought you safely to shore."

His words washed over me like an awakening, and with no trouble at all, I remembered. Every minute came back to me in splendid detail. It had been a cool spring day, the sort that makes you glad to be alive after a ruthless winter. The robins were back, and small sprouts of green were poking through the brown grass. Paolo had been filled with energy, roughhousing with exuberance. The lake had been cold, breathtakingly icy, and we'd both come out of it shivering. Paolo had been full of remorse, begging that I not tell our parents. And I hadn't. We were enough of a pair for me to realize the punishment he would get. Paolo had given me his jacket and snuck me back into the house before anyone noticed I was dripping wet. Then he had mopped up the trail of water and made sure I had a warm bath.

I remembered all that. At the time, I had wondered if Gray had gotten into trouble with his mother, arriving home soaking wet. Memories from youth were now seen through the eyes of maturity, with more compassion. I hoped he hadn't ruined his shoes. They had had little money to spare, Gray and his widowed mother.

As the memories of that day came back, I also remembered that I hadn't needed saving. I swam like a fish. But Gray mightn't have known that, and I had been twelve, full of romantic notions. I'd imagined myself the heroine of lots of adventures. So when Gray jumped in to rescue me, I hadn't said a word.

"You trusted me then." He said it quietly, and his face had softened.

"Okay," I said in a little voice. "I believe you."

Maybe I said it too easily or too quickly, for his eyes hardened, and he came back with vigour.

"Not so fast," he said. "I don't expect you to take my word for it. We're going to settle this once and for all. Who do you trust back home?"

That was tricky. I had to think about it. "For what purpose?" I said.

He burst out laughing. "Yes, well, I suppose that's reasonable. I meant, to tell you the truth about whether I'm still working for the mob."

"I'd trust Paolo, of course," I said sincerely.

"Then you are going to send a cable to Paolo and ask him," said Gray. "Ask him whatever you like about me. Ask anyone, for that matter. I'm not proud of my past. But I'm damned proud of where I've got to now." His eyes caught mine and held them. I looked away first.

"Write down what you want to ask. I have pen and paper right here. I'll get Walker to take the cable to the operator. You can walk with him. He can send it, and you can watch him do it. I'm not involved at all." He held up both hands. "No interference. Fair enough?"

Wow. That put to rest any doubts. His openness and confidence won me over.

It was my turn to give. "More than fair. In fact, I don't need to do that anymore. I'm convinced." I rose from the desk chair. "I'm really sorry, Gray. Truly, I am."

"Yeah, well …" He paused. "I can understand it. Neither of us trusts easily. It goes with the territory." He picked up the list and handed it to me. "Give this back to me when you're done."

Even more faith! He was trusting me with his paperwork.

I looked down at the papers in my hand. "No need. Why don't we just check it here right now." I handed them back.

He took them and nodded. "What cabin number?"

I smiled at that.

"Lucy, do you have any idea how many cabins there are on this ship? Nearly a thousand in first and second class alone. I can't remember who is in each one."

"Right! Of course." I gave him the number and watched him run his finger down the list.

"No record of trunks stored. You were right."

I preened. It's always rewarding to be right. "So the brains behind this smuggling is someone with money."

Gray raised an eyebrow. "How so?"

"He booked an extra cabin just for a rendezvous, Gray! All because he didn't want to be identified by the courier or the authorities. That speaks to money and a big operation. At the very least, a person who knows what they're doing."

Gray whistled. "So not a novice, nor a crime of opportunity."

I leaned forward and rested one hand on the desk. "In a way, I have to admire Harry's murderer. This speaks of careful planning and a cool hand."

"Do you think he intended to kill Harry?" said Gray.

I shook my head. "No. That was unplanned, I think. An emergency measure. Still, I expect he considered the possibility when he booked the separate cabin. If any dirty work needed to be done, it wouldn't be in a cabin that could be linked to Harry's accomplice."

"Clever bastard," said Gray.

The clock on the wall bonged softly. I looked up, startled. "Hell's bells, I'm late! Must go. Elf will kill me."

Gray gave me a crooked smile. "Let me know if you survive."

All the way back to my cabin, my mind turned over the events of the last hour. I had accomplished something today. Gray was exonerated! I'd been so bothered by the possibility and yet couldn't bring myself to believe it in my heart. Nevertheless, it was a huge relief to know he wasn't involved with the criminals behind Harry's murder. I was sure of it now.

Things were looking up! By the time I got to my cabin, there was a decided spring in my step. I found Elf sitting on the bed cross-legged, darning her stockings again. That reminded me.

"What on earth have you done to that poor steward, Elf?" I said.

She went red. "What? What steward?"

"The well-built one called Walker. He's fairly itching to ask you to some staff do tomorrow night. Even asked my permission."

"Silly git," she mumbled.

"I said sure, but watch out for her left hook."

"You *didn't!*" she screamed.

I chuckled. "No. I didn't." I ducked the pillow she heaved at me.

I braced myself for the scolding. Yes, I was far too late getting back to the cabin. No, no maid should be expected to put up with it. Yes, dinner would have already started and —

"*Basta!*" I said, plopping down on the bed. Funny how the Italian comes out of me when I'm dealing with Elf. "I don't have the heart to change into a dinner gown or mingle with the others after all that has happened to Tony."

That got her attention. Before long, I had brought her up to date on Tony's assault and my discovery about the room next door. Even Elf had to admit I'd been pretty brazen, but of course she had a different take on it all.

"See what happens when you don't 'ave me along? Things go topsy, and that's a fact."

I accepted the second scolding with grace.

Elf ordered us both dinner trays, claiming I had a headache. Explanations to my tablemates could wait until tomorrow.

To my surprise, Elf voiced the same suspicion that Gray had about Tony.

"Can't trust gamblers," she said, munching through a sandwich. "They always need dough. Coulda been him what stole the shoes."

I pointed a carrot at her. "That's ridiculous, Elf. Tony wouldn't ransack his own room and cosh himself on the head."

She shrugged. "Not saying he's the killer. Just sayin' he could be *our* thief. And maybe egg that killed Harry knew that and trashed his room to look for the rocks."

I didn't believe it. "Far more likely that they saw we were chummy and thought maybe I'd given the diamonds to him for safekeeping."

She muttered something while stuffing the rest of the sandwich in her mouth. Probably best I didn't hear it.

Elf asked permission to meet with some of her friends in the crew. At least, that's one version. I don't think she actually knew the definition of the word *permission*. In any case, I waved her off with a hand and got myself ready for an early bed. Before long, I was dreaming of a costume ball where every man there was dressed as Raffles, the gentleman thief.

CHAPTER TWENTY-SEVEN

DAY FIVE AT SEA

I ROSE AT dawn the next morning. As always, the first thing I did was go to the porthole and look out at the sea. My cabin was close to the stern. The sun shone down, creating mesmerizing sparkles. Our wake rippled out, repeating itself in symmetrical waves that would probably travel many miles before disappearing from the surface. The angry dark-blue surface we had seen earlier was now a shimmering grey-blue.

I never got tired of looking at the water in all its manifestations. A wild sea was exhilarating, with an energy that seemed to transfer itself to my heart and soul. The calm of the morning was contemplative. Just what I needed to sort out where we were in this mess of burglary, assault, and murder.

I needed to think it out logically and make a list in my mind of the most important points.

- Harry is killed in the cabin next door and dumped in my room.
- Harry goes overboard that night, with help from Elf and Tony.

- Harry's body is found in the lifeboat the next morning. Now everyone knows about the murder.
- Elf and I discover the diamonds in Harry's shoes. Elf hides the shoes in one place and the diamonds in another.
- My room is ransacked, and Harry's shoes are taken.
- Sloan acts suspicious about his profession and background at the dinner table.
- Elf and I discover the crime scene in the room next door.
- Elf learns that the cabin next door is booked in the name of De Beers, but it is strangely unoccupied. We now know there is no luggage in storage for it.
- Mr. Mason discovers the crime scene, with me in tow.
- Sloan is a key suspect after he persists in his pursuit of me.
- It becomes clear that Tony is a gambler, and he needs money.
- Tony is assaulted and his room ransacked.

I wanted to figure out suspects for all of the above, based on motives and opportunities. I needed to write it all down because it was getting too complex. Too many combinations and permutations for one simple brain like mine. For instance, the person who'd killed Harry had most likely ransacked my room to get the diamonds. That seemed obvious. But Tony's room was also ransacked; was it by the same person looking for the diamonds? Or was that break-in related to his gambling debts? Whoever the culprit might be, he wasn't shy about using force.

That made me gulp. One thing I knew for sure: Harry's killer still hadn't found what he was after, and he didn't appear to be giving up. What would he try next? I felt a chill and backed away from the porthole.

No question, I needed to talk this over with someone who would be open but also discreet. Tony wasn't going to be of use to me as a fellow sleuth in his condition, sadly. But I would see Tony today. Yes, I would, even if I had to hoodwink the guard at the door of the infirmary by creating a distraction. Elf could do that for me. I smiled to myself. She was great at creating distractions. True, there had been that unfortunate time with the vicar and the hedgehog, but no hedgehogs around here that I could see, happily.

I could hear Elf stir behind me. I thought about discussing all this with her but changed my mind. Elf had a tendency to take things into her own hands without giving enough attention to potential consequences. I didn't want her setting cockamamie traps that could put us both in more danger.

There was no getting away from it. The only other person I could completely open up to was Gray.

And as I was thinking about him, a strange thing happened. In my mind, the name Gray mysteriously translated into the colour, and I reached into the wardrobe for a grey dress with a pleated skirt and pink-banded drop waist to wear.

We had breakfast trays sent up, and right after dressing, I excused myself.

"Going to the purser's office," I mumbled. "Won't be long."

"No rush. I got something planned," Elf said mysteriously.

I should probably have been more worried about that. But I was already on my way.

THE DOOR TO the purser's office was closed. My heart fell because that most likely meant Gray wasn't there. *Silly woman,* I told myself. *You're getting too attached.* I stood still for a moment, listening to determine if anyone was inside. I could hear some movements and rustling of papers, so I made a fist and knocked three times.

"Who is it?" said Gray in a clipped voice.

Unusual. Normally he would just say to come in.

"Lucy Revelstoke," I said quietly.

"Wait there," he ordered. Again, unusual.

I waited until he opened the door. He stood to the side and opened it only a foot or so, then signalled with his arm. I squeezed through the opening and heard him shut the door firmly behind me, then click the lock.

I was about to question all this peculiar behaviour but was stopped by shock.

The office looked like someone had picked it up and shook it. Or worse, like a small tornado had blasted through it. The file cabinets were open, papers strewn everywhere. Pictures had been taken off the walls, the backs removed. Even the garbage pail had been overturned.

"I'm not the neatest person," said Gray behind me. "But even I wouldn't leave a room like this."

"Jesus Murphy," I said, falling back to my Canadian roots. "When did this happen?"

Gray came around into view. His naval uniform was less than immaculate, and his visage was dark. He swept a few papers off one of the guest chairs and pointed for me to sit. "I worked late last night. So sometime after midnight. When I get my hands on him ..." I'd never seen Gray look so fierce.

"But why? For payroll? Or do you think ..." I gasped. "Harry's murderer!"

"Yes, Harry's murderer," said Gray, throwing himself into the desk chair. "Ransacked your place first and then the cabin of that faithful dog of yours later. Didn't come up with anything, but he must have seen you come in here."

"And figured I may have given something to you for safekeeping." I gulped. "Oh, Gray, I'm so sorry. What a mess." I looked around, shaking my head.

"I have a hell of a lot of work ahead of me," he agreed. Gray picked up a pencil and played with it between his fingers. "What worries me is he must have followed you here yesterday."

I shifted uncomfortably on the chair. "That doesn't make me feel good."

Someone had been following me? Who could it be? I hadn't detected anything, which left me uneasy and bewildered.

Gray threw down the pencil and drummed his fingers on the table. "So who besides you and that loco maid of yours would know how to pick a lock?"

I could feel the blush climb up my face. Before I could answer, more knocks hit the door. We both jumped.

Gray looked at me then left his chair to answer the door, repeating the procedure he had followed with me. I turned to see our Mr. Mason squeezing through the opening.

"My lord," he said as the door clicked behind him. He glanced around, saw me, and smiled weakly. Then he continued his observations, walking carefully to avoid standing on papers.

"Did they take anything?' he said finally to Gray.

"Not that I can tell." He removed the pile of documents from the other chair and offered it to Mason.

"Well, I have news," said Mason. He included both of us in his gaze. "Mr. Anderson's cabin was ransacked again in the night. This time a little more thoroughly."

Gray cursed. "What the hell is going on? Didn't we have a guard on that?"

Mason shrugged his shoulders. "Not on the cabin. His Lordship was moved to the infirmary yesterday, so that's where we placed the guard."

"Bloody lot of good that did," grumbled Gray.

"I judged his safety to be most important," countered Mason. "If we could spare more men ..."

I heard Gray grunt.

"So Harry's killer is still looking for something," I said.

"Harry?" Mason raised an eyebrow.

Oops!

Gray gave a dry laugh. "She and that crazy maid of hers are calling the murdered fellow Harry."

"It's not really his name," I quickly filled in. "Or at least, I don't know if it is. But it just seemed heartless to keep calling him 'the body,' so Elf and I felt we should give him a name. To be respectful. I picked Harry from Tom, Dick, or Harry."

"Oh," said Mason. "Of course." He seemed to find it amusing.

So did Gray, apparently. "Just like a woman. She'd probably name a spider on the wall."

"And you'd probably kill it," I shot back.

Oh dear. This was beginning to sound like a quarrel between spouses, and there was Mason witnessing it. I snuck a glance at him and found he was observing me with interest. Then his face shifted to a frown of unease.

"Lady Revelstoke, I have some concern now about your safety. This person has taken big risks to search your cabin, your friend's cabin — twice — and now the purser's. There is every reason to expect he might try to do a more thorough search of yours again, and probably tonight." He turned to Gray. "Can we find some other accommodation for Lady Revelstoke and her maid for this evening? An empty cabin somewhere, perhaps?"

Gray came to attention. "Excellent idea. I believe first class is fully occupied, but I should have something in second class."

Mason leaned forward. "That is even better. Let's put you on a different deck entirely. Can we get it fixed up before dinner so that we can have a steward move her essential belongings while others are occupied eating? The key is to keep this move completely confidential. No one should know about it beyond ourselves and the steward you choose."

"Okay," I said slowly. "I see the sense in this. Just one thing. You don't want my cabin to appear empty, do you? You want it to look like we are still staying there."

Mason's eyes twinkled. "Correct, my lady. Take essentials with you, but toss some clothing over chairs and leave your trunks to be searched."

"And," I said, catching on to his plan, "you will ensconce yourself within the cabin tonight to catch the thief red-handed."

"Right again, my lady. You are indeed a quick study."

"Brains as well as beauty," muttered Gray. "Plus a goddamn castle."

CHAPTER TWENTY-EIGHT

"LET ME WALK you back, Lady Revelstoke. I have something to discuss with you."

"And I'll get busy on that cabin for you," said Gray, rising from his chair. I liked that his manners were impeccable. Pretty good for a boy from the east side of Steeltown.

We said our goodbyes and left the office. When the door closed behind us, Mason put his hand on my arm. "I have arranged for you to see Mr. Anderson when you wish. Just tell the guard at the door who you are."

"Oh, thank you!" I was truly grateful. "How is he?"

"I've just come from there. He was conscious, and the doctor feels he is out of immediate danger. I knew you'd want to know as soon as possible."

I clapped my hands. "Oh, that is the best news! Thank you."

He took my elbow. "We are keeping the assault confidential for now. Best to spread the word that he has taken ill. If you could do so at dinner? I won't be there, of course."

I nodded. We walked in companionable silence for a bit. I let myself be guided to the staircase and took hold of the railing while he walked beside me.

Mason spoke softly. "You understand that he will need to be kept quiet and watched, for his safety and for any other signs of symptoms resulting from the concussion. We'll keep him in the infirmary until we get to port."

"He won't be happy about that," I said, shaking my head.

"He has no choice," said Mason firmly. "The doctor has plans to sedate him to ensure his staying quiet. No bright lights. No getting excitable. His brain needs rest to recover. You will likely find he is asleep when you visit him."

"I just want to see that he is okay." My voice sounded a bit shaky to me.

"I understand." Mason held open the door at the top of the staircase for me to walk through. "This is your floor. I'll leave you here. Can you arrange to have your maid pack an overnight bag for you? I'll have one of the stewards move it during dinner."

I turned and smiled at him. "Yes, certainly. Thank you for this, Mr. Mason. You've been such a comfort through all of this."

His face turned an odd shade of pink. "My pleasure," he said with a slight head bow.

We parted on easy terms, and I spent no time loitering in the corridor, for good reason. Coffee at breakfast.

I rushed into the cabin, waving a hand at Elf, and disappeared into the water closet. Sometimes a gal just has to vanish with a reason. Men seemed to have the vernacular for this. I'd heard my uncles talk about "seeing a man about a dog." One day, we women need to come up with something similar. Perhaps something along the lines of reapplying makeup?

I washed my hands, dried them, and re-entered the bedroom. Elf was at the door talking softly to someone. Female voice, definitely east end. Another maid? I waited.

Sometimes the eyes notice what the mind fails to register. I had rushed by everything on the way in. But now, as if pulled, my gaze drifted to the floor against the wall. It was lined with men's shoes. Mostly black dress shoes, in various states. Lace-ups, brogues, short boots. Some traditionally British. Others more daringly American or Italian. I stared, completely baffled.

The curious exchange at the door was ending. When Elf turned around, the other girl had gone. In her hands was another pair of men's shoes. Black leather lace-ups, well-shined. I watched as she added the new pair to the lineup.

"Are we starting a haberdashery, Elf?" I said.

"Nah. This is me, being smart." She stood up to her full height of not very much and waved a hand at the shoes. "Someone broke in and stole Harry's shoes, right? So I'm trying to find the bastard who took 'em."

"Ah," I said, catching on. "So you arranged with your lady steward friends to sneak shoes that match the description out of various cabins. That's rather clever."

She beamed. "We'll return them later. Course, if guy has a valet, it's a no go. Valet knows what shoes his master owns and shines them himself. So this isn't all o' them."

She meant shoes, not valets. "But it's a start," I said. "Have you checked? Do any of them look familiar?" I moved closer to the wall.

"Not yet. But we have the name of that maker. You wrote it down, right?" She poked a shoe with her foot.

"Yes, I'll get it in a minute. We should be able to tell by the height of the heel, though, and whether it's been tampered with." Something else had occurred to me. "But Elf, your point is, if we find Harry's shoes in this pile, then we will know in which cabin the killer resides. Correct?"

She nodded.

"So my question is: how do you know which shoes belong to which cabin?"

She froze. I wanted to giggle. Elf couldn't read. Therefore she couldn't write things down. I'd tried to teach her, but we were a long way from agreement on the importance of the skill.

Which meant we had a dilemma. At least ten pairs of shoes lined the floor, and we had no idea where they'd come from. So even if Harry's shoes were there ...

"Bloody hell," she grumbled. "Thought it was a good plan."

I couldn't stand to see her so crestfallen. "It *was* a good plan. Very ingenious. So here's what we do. Once we find it, we mark the pair that is Harry's. Say, put it closest to the door. You bring the stewardesses back here one by one. And when Harry's pair is picked up, you can pump that stewardess for the cabin number."

"Cor — brilliant!" said Elf.

Our plan encountered a slight snag. This became evident when the first Elf-friend, Maggy, came by to retrieve her shoes.

Maggy was a sturdy blond girl in her twenties. She looked as if she had come from farm country and milked all the cows by herself. She had a crooked smile, crooked teeth, and a way of talking that matched our Elf for colour.

Elf met her at the door.

"You finished? Can I have them back now? My gent's getting sloshed in the bar, but he'll be back afore dinner."

I cleared my throat. Maggy stole a glance in my direction. Her eyes went wide.

I put up both hands. "Don't mind me," I said. "I've seen a few men sloshed. I've even been the cause of it."

She grinned in relief, then turned back to Elf. "So hand them over."

Elf shrugged. "Over there. You can get them yourself."

Maggy came further into the room. She stared at the wall of shoes. Then she turned her head to Elf. "Which ones are mine?"

I covered a snort.

"Whaddya mean, which ones are yours?" said Elf, bracing both hands on her hips. "The ones you brought in here!"

They stared at each other. I started to laugh. This was turning into a farce.

"But I gave them to you," argued Maggy. "Black shoes, shiny. You took them, put them somewhere. I don't know which of these are his." She waved a meaty hand at the pile. "Not my usual gent, like you and this ladyship here. I just serves him for this crossing."

Elf's jaw had dropped. "Bloody hell," she muttered. "Don't ya even know what kind of shoes they were?"

I interceded. "What she means is, did they have laces? Can you remember that? And if not, were they slip-ons? We can start there. It's simply a process of elimination."

Maggy's face screwed up as she thought. "Had laces," she said.

"Elf, bring all the lace-up shoes to this table," I ordered. Elf did as she was told. We were down to six pairs of shoes, almost identical.

The three of us stared down at them.

"How do we choose 'em from that?" Elf wailed.

"Easy," I said. "Maggy, go back to your man's cabin. Bring another pair of his shoes to us here. Actually, just bring one shoe. Can you do that now?"

"Yes, your ladyship," she said, dropping into a short curtsy. She didn't even question me. Elf, meanwhile, looked puzzled.

"Go now, and hurry back."

She sprang to it. I waited until she was out of the room and had closed the door behind her. Then I explained our room change to Elf and that we'd be sleeping somewhere else for tonight.

"Both those places ransacked?" she exclaimed. "Blimey! Sure as shootin' he'll try here again next."

"That's why Mr. Mason is going to lie in wait."

"Just like in the Westerns!" Elf was really enjoying this, I could see.

"So pack up an overnight bag for us, and include my jewellery." I didn't want to lose that if things went wrong!

"Should I bring Harry's rocks?" Elf said.

I smiled. "Yes. Bring those. Let's not take a chance, even though I can't imagine anyone would think to look there."

At this point, I should probably admit that I hadn't decided what to do with the diamonds. Ownership was — to put it bluntly — nebulous. No innocent party seemed to be involved who would suffer by losing them. And I've never trusted the police. Things disappeared in police custody, never to be seen again.

Of course, uncut diamonds were not the easiest things to get rid of. You had to know the right fences, and to be frank, I didn't. Nor did I want to contact those people from my family who would know. For one thing, I didn't need to. Money was not something I required. Johnny had left me well off, and Charlie would inherit a fortune along with the title.

For another, I wanted no part of reawakening that part of my life.

All the same, these rocks could be a welcome gift of security to someone who had nothing much of her own. I was playing with the idea that no one deserved them more than Elf. They might serve as her retirement fund if something were to happen to me. Yes, that made me happy to think of. Besides, I was willing to bet she could find a fence easier than I could.

Meanwhile, Elf got busy on the floor. "Harry's shoes didn't have laces, right?"

"Correct. And the heel was big, remember. A little higher than normal, to accommodate the rocks. With four screws on the bottom."

"Can't see any here that match our Harry's," said Elf.

"Well, it was a long shot." I sighed. This wasn't going to be as easy as all that. "Remember, these are only the shoes from first-class passengers. And frankly, I would have gone about it another way."

Elf rose to her feet. "How so?"

I sat down on the edge of the bed. "I would have had Maggy check for any shoes that weren't the exact size of the others in her man's cabin. Ones that were out of place."

"Cor," said Elf. "Good one."

Something else niggled at me. Oh, but there were too many thoughts roaming around in my mind. I kicked off my shoes and lay down on the bed, hoping for a little shut-eye.

Elf saw what I intended and left the cabin. I don't know how long passed before she returned. I had lapsed into that semiconscious state where you're having dreams that almost seem real. They could be real, and almost too graphic. It shocked me that I could go for Gray in that way …

My dream was interrupted by the door opening. "You awake, Luce?" A small face peered down at me.

"Don't call me Luce," I muttered. I waved her off and sat up slowly, swinging my legs over the edge of the bed.

Maggy stood obediently in front of me. I took the shoe she'd brought from her hand.

"Size ten," I said. "Look for any that are size ten."

Elf made herself busy.

"British or American?" asked Maggy. She was a sharp little thing after all. Well, not so little.

"Doesn't really matter," I said. "You'll see."

"Two pair," said Elf. She separated them from the others.

"So how do we choose between them?" Maggy sounded defeated. "They look almost the same."

I checked the inside of the single shoe and then both of the pairs. "Ta-da!" I said. "Check this out. Same make as the one you just brought me." I handed all three shoes to Maggy. "Stands to reason he would get his shoes at the same store and favour a particular make."

"Cor, that's clever," said Elf. "She's a bright one, she is."

I grimaced. How many times had I told Elf she shouldn't comment on her mistress to other people? Particularly with her mistress in the room!

"Get rid of the rest of these before dinner," I ordered her, reaching for my own T-straps. I caught her eye so she'd understand. All this had to be cleared out in time for Mason. "I may be out for a while. First, I want to check on Tony."

CHAPTER TWENTY-NINE

IT WAS A little while later when I made it to the infirmary. Very well for Mason to say I need only give my name to the guard at the door. One has to first *find* that guard and that door.

So of course, I took a wrong turn somewhere, and that's when Amanda Martin found me staring at the line of corridors converging onto the main hall.

"Lost?" she said from behind me.

I turned to see her and smiled. "Sadly. I have a terrible sense of direction."

Today she was dressed in a more contemporary two-piece slate ensemble that suited her recently widowed status. She clucked in a maternal way. "Where are you headed?"

"The infirmary. Tony's been taken there, ill."

"Oh dear," she said. One gloved hand swept to her mouth. "Should you be seeing him? It's not anything contagious, I hope?"

Now, didn't it just figure she would worry about that. But then, I thought, I should be more understanding. We'd all been through the Spanish flu years. The fear never leaves you.

"I don't believe so," I said. "He was gassed in the war and has recurring problems due to that."

"Ah! Well, Mr. Sloan will be glad of that."

Glad that Tony was gassed?

"Oh dear," she clucked. "That came out wrong. I meant about him not being contagious. They sat beside each other for hours yesterday after lunch, playing cards."

"Really? All afternoon?" I said, sounding much too interested.

Her brow wrinkled as she thought. "Until about four. I was reading my book and could see them. Then I convinced Mr. Sloan to join me for tea in the library salon." She gave me a very satisfied smile.

I had to stop myself from chuckling. No doubt, Amanda had been lying in wait for Sloan, using the book as a cover to watch his movements from a distance. When he got up, she nailed him.

But wait. This was important. I had to make an effort to veil my excitement. If Sloan was having tea with Amanda Martin, he couldn't have been the one to cosh Tony on the head!

This was big news. Sloan had an alibi. I'd have to rejig my thoughts.

She clucked again, then gave me directions to the infirmary. I marvelled that she knew where it was; she must have deduced that from the expression on my face, because she explained. "It's a silly thing, but I like to walk for exercise. I make it a habit to check the location of all the services when I first board a ship. You never know when you might need to know these things."

I nodded and thanked her. She smiled in a way I hadn't seen her do before. There was intelligence there, and satisfaction; less of the fussy-muss, as Elf would say. I watched her walk away, wondering if she could indeed be the person I saw the other day sneaking into that cabin on the lower deck. Was it possible she could be having an affair? She'd had tea with Mr. Sloan and had seemed eager to let me know. Was she trying to send a "hands off" message to me? Maybe she was, but wanting a man wasn't the same as having him.

At last I shook my head. How likely was it that Sloan would dally with her? A woman of late middle age who was neither a beauty nor rich. No assets to exploit. Besides, Vera Horner would be sure to know if such a thing were taking place. And Vera would never have held back a choice piece of gossip like that.

I found my way to the infirmary and walked up to the guard in charge, who rose stiffly. He was an older gent in a steward's uniform who looked as if he might have fought in the Napoleonic wars and not come through them well. He opened the door for me when I gave my name and then went back to sitting and daydreaming.

The infirmary looked the same as it had when I took my initial tour of the ship last year. It was scrupulously white and clean, with two portholes and locked glass cabinets to the right. I knew those held medical supplies, including drugs. A slate table stood off to the left. It would be used for surgery if need be and could be shrouded by curtains that wrapped around but were now pushed out of the way.

In front of me were two well-appointed medical beds, with only one occupied.

Tony was alone in the room when I entered. He was partially upright, bolstered by pillows. I could see a thick bandage covering the top and back of his head. As the door clicked behind me, his eyes opened. The smile on his face was thin, but I was happy to see it.

"Sight for sore eyes," he said. "I'm bored beyond expression." Then, "Help me sit up here."

I rushed forward. "Should you be doing that? Where's the nurse?"

He pushed himself to sitting and instructed me to pile the pillows behind him.

"Don't know and don't care. She reminds me of my great-aunt Ermintrude. Did you ever meet her? Big woman, right out of a Wagner opera, with a face like an overripe cabbage. Eyes in the back of her head. Scared the devil out of me when I was a kid. Even more so now."

I settled into the chair beside him. "That wouldn't be a bad thing, from what I've heard."

Tony frowned. "And just what have you heard?"

I shook my head. "First, how are you? How's the head? You gave me an awful scare there, Tony."

He grimaced, putting a hand to the bandage. "Head hurts like the devil. Bad hangover without the fun time before. Feel a bit dizzy if I try to get up."

"You shouldn't try to get up!" I scolded.

His face took on that reckless look. "You have no idea how hard it is to keep still. Hand me that cigarette case over there." He flicked his free hand to the table out of reach.

I got up, made my way to the table, and clamped my hand over it. Then I stopped dead. "Wait a minute. Should you be smoking? No, of course you shouldn't. Jeepers, Tony." I let it go.

He gave a sheepish grin. "Been worse on the battlefield. That never stopped me from smoking."

"Just …" I sat down again and took his hand. He liked that. "Can't you behave until they give you the all clear? It won't be long." I didn't mention what they had said about keeping him in the infirmary until port.

"So. What's been going on? What have you been doing with yourself?" he said.

"Touring the boat with that nice steward Walker. The short one who looks like a prizefighter. Did you know we have a state-of-the-art cargo lift on this ship?"

"Whatever got you interested in that?" he said, waving a hand dismissively.

"Nothing whatever," I said. It wouldn't do to tell Tony what I had been planning for the hold — or what was going down tonight in my cabin, for that matter. No need to worry him more than he already must be.

I turned to whisper, "The poor steward has a crush on Elf. He actually asked my permission to take her to some party with the other crew members."

Tony snorted. "God help him! The fellow has more courage than brains." He leaned back into the pillows. "Speaking of which, any idea who gave me this cosh on the head?"

"We still don't know. Mr. Mason is working to find that out. But please tell me what happened to you before I got there. Everything you can remember."

He frowned. "Not much. I remember coming back from lunch. Had planned to visit the card room, but nothing was happening there. I hadn't slept well, so was thinking about taking a nap before we met for tea. I remember walking down the corridor. Opened the door to the room —"

"Was it locked?" I interrupted.

His eyes squinted. "No. That should have warned me. Damn, but I'm a fool."

"No matter," I said, patting his hand. "What then?"

His face took on a look of deep concentration. "Door didn't open all the way. Seemed to hit a wall. I walked in a few feet, not far, and the cabin looked strange. I wondered if I was in the right room. Everything appeared out of place. To tell the truth, it was bewildering; I felt as if I had fallen through the looking glass. The floor was littered with things that had been knocked off shelves, the closet was emptied, and it seemed like the Mad Hatter had been jumping on the bed. You know, from that Alice book."

"I know it," I said.

"Then — nothing. Before I could register what had happened, I went down." He put his hand to his bandage. "Bastard must have been behind the door."

I nodded. "Do you know how long you were out?"

He shook his head. "No. I was on the floor when I woke. Crawled over to the bed eventually. I couldn't think properly or see well. Something was in my left eye. Guess it was blood."

I shivered, imagining it all.

"Finally put two and two together, in a simplistic way. Head was hurting something awful. I tried to neaten up a bit, but that made me woozy. I sat down on the bed for a long while, just trying to remain upright. May have drifted off for a bit. Must have, because then you came in, and — well — you know how much sense I was making."

I told him about the discussion I'd had with Mr. Mason.

"So they were after the gun, you think." He seemed to relax.

"Maybe. Or they could have been after money. Just how much do you owe those people, Tony?"

My words came at him like a bullet out of nowhere. I heard

the air intake, then the quick exhalation. His face took on a dark look, and he took his hand back.

"How much do you know?" His voice was gravel.

I looked off into the distance. "I don't *know* anything. But I know gamblers; you might say they run in the family, so I've seen it up close. And you're one of them. I figure you've lost a pile in America, and you're going back home to avoid the debt collectors. Not a bad plan. But maybe one of them caught up with you here."

He grunted. Pretty clear he'd thought of that himself. "So I owe a few boys some money. No big deal. It's just they're so unreasonable about paying it back. I need more time," he insisted.

"How much money do you need?" I asked.

He shot me a look. "Oh no. You're not bailing me out. I'll get out of this on my own terms, even if I have to hit up the *pater* again."

It was the "again" that did the trick. It confirmed everything I had surmised to date. Tony *was* a remittance man, sent away by his family because his chronic gambling was an embarrassment to them. No doubt his father had bailed him out at least once before in England. Probably more than once. I knew what those families were like. If Tony was expecting a warm welcome home, he would most likely be sorely disappointed. In fact, there was a good chance they would turn him around and send him off again to South Africa or Australia or another of the colonies.

His handsome face looked at me earnestly. "Look here, Lucy. I know I'm not the best fellow to take a chance on, but I'll beat this, you'll see I will. I'm not an addict. Just find it a fun way to while away the hours. Things have been boring since the war."

"Sure," I said, knowing perfectly well that words were cheap. Right then, I knew any possibility of a romance with Tony was over. I'd never seen anyone recover from gambling until they hit rock bottom. And even after that, put a little money in their hands and you could wave that goodbye too. But it would do no good for me to say so. Especially not while he was recovering from a pretty nasty head wound.

For the same reason, there was no point in mentioning that others thought Tony might be after the diamonds himself in order to pay off his debts. No point because if it *wasn't* true, he'd be furious that we'd spent even a minute thinking it could be possible. And if it *was* true, he'd only deny it.

To be honest, I didn't believe he was capable of doing that. Tony was a gambler, and possibly reckless with his own life, but I'd never thought him dishonourable. Johnny had known men through and through, and he wouldn't have been friends with someone he thought a cad.

To pass the time, I told him about the ransacking of the purser's office, and he gave a low whistle. But before he could say anything, the nurse returned. I thought her a rather pleasant-looking woman, in late middle age and a trifle overweight. Not harsh but firm, as we witnessed immediately.

"Now, Mr. Anderson. What are we doing, sitting up like that?" Her Scottish accent was thick, and she marched right over.

"*We* aren't doing anything," Tony muttered. "*I* am sitting up, while *you* are being a fussbudget."

"Lie right back down, as the doctor ordered." Whereupon she proceeded to be a first-class fussbudget. I smiled, watching as she held his back up with one strong arm and fluffed pillows with another, scolding him all the while.

In some ways, I think he enjoyed it.

I DECIDED TO stay with him for the next meal, which turned out to be a cream tea. We had left it too long for lunch. That suited me fine. The nurse arranged to have two trays brought in, and although she stayed a discreet distance away, I didn't feel comfortable talking about the case.

But Tony was grateful for the company, so I brought him up to date on gossip about our set back home. He'd been in America for over a year, virtually out of touch for all that time, and a lot had happened. Marriages, babies, affairs ... a few financial collapses that were shocking in this time of prosperity. Divorces rarely happened in our set; too much money involved. But a man taking a mistress, or a woman taking a lover ... that was the stuff that kept our grapevine green and flourishing.

As I talked, I had the chance to observe him up close. His face looked strained, more lined than usual, and I would have sworn he looked thinner. But how that could be possible in just a day or two, I didn't know. Perhaps he was thinner than my memory of him from past years. The jackets men wore these days had padded shoulders and could disguise such things.

"Say, would you do me a favour?" said Tony. "I could use some clean duds. Before Florence Nightingale here forces me into some godawful cotton gown and nightcap." He pretended to shiver.

"Sure. Nightclothes and some underthings?" I queried.

"And a clean shirt for tomorrow." Tony was always fastidious in his appearance. "And my shaving kit."

Before I could answer, the steward arrived with our meals.

Portable trays are never as exciting as plated dinners in the dining room, but I happen to love sandwiches on really fresh bread. Plus the scones with Devon cream and strawberry jam were divine. I munched happily, devouring every crumb, and it was some time before I became aware that Tony was looking at me.

"I've never seen anyone enjoy her food as much as you do," he said, shaking his head with a smile.

"Nuts," I replied, pointing my last bite of scone at him. "I'm only an amateur. You should see Elf."

He snorted.

I looked down at my near-empty tray. There was a small teapot with hot water and a bag ready to put in it. I made a face. "No coffee," I said sadly.

"You heathen. And you call yourself English. Aren't you going to drink your tea?"

I shook my head. "I only like tea one way."

"And how is that?" he enquired.

"Left in the pot," I said.

He burst out with a laugh, but it quickly changed to that hacking cough. The nurse was up and over in an instant. She fluttered around him and then chased me out. "His lordship needs to sleep," she said in that thick brogue.

"Feel like I'm back in the nursery," Tony mumbled as I waved goodbye.

CHAPTER THIRTY

I WENT DIRECTLY to Tony's cabin from the infirmary. Or at least, I intended to. There seemed to be a fiendish gremlin on board this ship who kept moving the corridors. The second-class reception areas were really quite nice, it turned out.

A pretty young kid and her new husband were quite happy to direct me to my own deck. In fact, they walked up with me as an excuse to see the first-class grand foyer. I enjoyed watching them ooh and ah and then made my way alone to Tony's cabin from there.

The corridor was pretty busy at this time of the afternoon. I found a steward I knew and asked that he open Tony's cabin for me, explaining my mission. Better to play by the rules since there were people about, even though I could have opened the locked door on my own.

He was pleased to oblige, although he was on his way to another task. "Do you mind if I leave you alone? I'll lock up on my way back," he said.

I didn't mind at all. In fact, that fit in with my plan.

The room had been left as it was, in complete shambles. Tony hadn't brought a valet, I remembered. I shook my head and set about putting it back in order. At least that was something positive

I could do to help him. I picked up the clothes on the floor and folded them neatly. I found socks that were separated and put them back in pairs. Then I tried to imagine which drawers he would put them in. Underthings and socks in the top drawer. Nightclothes in the second, along with sundries like collars. Shirts, he would hang in the closet, I knew.

I took a set of nightclothes, underthings, and socks and put them on the bed to take with me.

Tony's shaving kit was in the water closet. It had been emptied into the sink. What on earth had the burglar been looking for that could possibly have been in with his shaving things? Well, I guessed it was possible the gems could have been hidden in with the shaving cream. Actually, that would be rather clever. I decided I simply must remember that. I put the kit back together, zipped the case shut, and brought it to join the other things for Tony on the bed.

I turned my attention to the closet. Shoes had been kicked out of it, and all the contents had been removed from hangers. I sighed and picked up the shirts first, putting a not-too-wrinkled one on the bed to take with me. The others, I hung up, along with the jackets and pants that had been in a pile.

Most of his clothes had English tailor tags. That made me wonder. Hadn't he bought any suits during the year he was in New York? One year was not enough time for men's clothes to go out of style, and perhaps he liked playing the part of a lord abroad, clinging to his Jolly Old English styles. However, some of the shirts looked pretty worn.

I looked at his shoes on the floor, gathered them up, and put them in order. They were well-shined but also not new. All makers from London.

But what did I know of men? As a woman, I would have spent my year in New York picking up all the latest fashions. I'd done a pretty good job of that in just two weeks. Maybe men weren't interested. Or maybe — I finally had to admit this — he'd just spent most of his time and money at the gaming tables.

I stopped what I was doing and stared into space. Tony had certainly shown me some fine establishments back in New York. Prohibition hadn't stopped the night life, nor the drinking. He had run a tab in most places and paid cash in some. I had no idea if he'd paid off those tabs before he left New York.

I looked around for something to carry the clothes down to Tony. A large trunk stood in the corner of the room. It was open and empty. On the floor across the room on the other side of the bed was a small brown leather overnight bag. I went to that and checked the contents. Empty. I filled it with the items I'd put aside. At the last minute, I picked up the book that had been swept to the floor in the break-in. He might want some reading material. That was a quiet activity.

I'm always curious about books. This one was a recent edition of *The Sun Also Rises* by Ernest Hemingway. I hadn't read it yet, but I knew it had references to the war and its aftermath. That would interest Tony. I must remember to ask to borrow it after he was through.

I sat down on the bed and read the back cover. Then I turned to the beginning pages, with an eye to maybe reading a few pages. As I have said, books are my guilty pleasure.

It was all right there on the title page. Yes, the title of the book in the middle of the page, but also a list of last names running down the left side with numbers beside them. At certain points, he had added up the numbers and put the sums to the right.

My heart threatened to choke me. I recognized some of those names. Not my family, but ones we had cause to know, names from New York in a similar business. The sums started small, but when you added them up … I gulped. A working-class person could labour their whole life to earn that much. Yet it was clear to me this was no record of income.

I'd discovered the list of Tony's gambling debts.

CHAPTER THIRTY-ONE

I DIDN'T LINGER. With overnight bag in hand, I made my way back to the infirmary. This time, I got there with no detours. Our Scottish Florence Nightingale came to the door with her finger to her mouth. His lordship was asleep, apparently. She took the bag from my hand and waved me away.

There was still a little time before I had to dress for dinner. I decided to go to my favourite spot, the bow of the boat, to do some thinking. It seemed a little chillier today, so I decided to make a short detour back to my cabin to pick up a wool wrap.

I never got there. Elf came at me in the grand foyer, where she had been lying in wait.

"Figured you'd pass through here eventually," she said. She grabbed me by the arm and pulled me over to the starboard corner. There were passengers milling around, so I was pleased to see she was wearing a newly pressed maid uniform, complete with the starched cap. It wasn't always so. Even still, it was unusual to see a maid drag her mistress by the arm in a public hallway. Or anywhere, darn it. I would have to deliver another lecture.

"Walker brought me a message from his boss. He got a cable this morning. Your American couple checks out." She had a throaty whisper that belied her childlike stature. I gently removed her hand from my arm.

"So Drew and Florrie are who they say they are." I was secretly relieved. I'd come to like both of them. It was also good for my soul to hear that. Not only did it show me that my instincts were still worthy, but it simply wasn't good for a woman to have to suspect every single person she knew.

"Puts us in the muck." Elf wiggled nervously.

I knew what she meant. More suspects eliminated, and that meant we were running out of people.

"You still think Tony-boy is in the clear?"

"Don't call him that," I hissed. I stood still, watching the passengers come out of the first-class public rooms to make their way to the staircase. If you stood perfectly still, sometimes people didn't see you. I had been taught that by my older brothers. It's something to do with our being predators, designed to look for movement. Right now, I didn't want any acquaintances inter-rupting us or even seeing me conferring furtively with my maid in a corner.

"I'm not sure," I said finally. I hadn't told Elf about Tony admitting to having gambling debts. And I wasn't sure it was fair to tell her about the list I'd found in his cabin. There were some powerful names on that list, names that would frighten Elf … well, the fewer people who knew about Tony's connections, the better. "I'll do a little more checking," I said.

"Break into his cabin?" Elf was a sharp little thing.

I froze. She couldn't know I'd already been in there this after-noon. Or could she? I decided to play innocent. "That could be risky. They could be watching it. Promise me you won't do that, Elf. It's not necessary."

She fiddled with the belt on her uniform. "Doesn't have to be him. There's still that Sloan guy. Plus, it wouldn't have to be someone at your table. Could be someone sitting near it. They could overhear stuff."

I groaned. "Or not even that. It could be someone not even close to us in the dining room, if they were willing to take a lot of chances and got lucky. We have to face this, Elf. It could even be one of the staff. They go back and forth between New York and England and would know people on either end. And they might be in a position to need money." I knew what they got paid, and while it was decent money for this type of job, it wouldn't make one rich.

"Possible. Could be a steward. He'd have keys. Some bloke under pressure to come up with dough."

"We can't overlook an officer," I said, feeling my heart sink. I didn't want to go back to considering him a suspect. And logic told me that since his office had been ransacked, he wasn't the villain of this piece. Yes, he could have staged the break-in, but why would he? Also, I would swear that anger I'd seen seething beneath the surface was real.

Still, Gray wasn't the only officer on this ship. He had an assistant, and we had to consider the possibility that an officer could make the same connections as a steward. Oh, but I hoped not. I adored the captain of this ship and hated to think of his staff betraying him.

Wait a minute — I suddenly remembered the buns. Quickly, I told Elf about the steward who had dropped the tray in the dining room and had seemed a little too interested in my cabin break-in.

"Same guy as the one who snuck out of the cabin next door the other night?" she asked.

"I think so. It was hard to tell in the dim light." I described the fellow as I remembered him from the dining room: average height, average looks, wavy brown hair, very young.

"Seen him about. Might be a gun or diver. Doesn't have to be Harry's killer. More likely, light-fingered hisself and got a shock to hear 'bout another second-storey man workin' the ship," she said.

I agreed that that was a possibility.

"Let me explore the steward angle. See if any have a rep for dark deals. I got connections in the right places." She gave me a wink that I hoped no one else saw.

She left me there, but not before making me promise to stick around where she could find me. There were times I really wondered who was working for whom.

CHAPTER THIRTY-TWO

I CONTINUED ON my way back to the cabin. There wasn't really much more I could do in the way of sleuthing until Elf came back. I thought about Agatha Christie's detective novels, particularly the Tommy and Tuppence book. Why couldn't I be like her? Tuppence always seemed to have a clue drop into her lap at just the right moment. Real life wasn't nearly as convenient, I was discovering.

As I turned into the vestibule, Mr. Mason stepped out of the empty cabin next to mine. The cabin where Harry had met his end. The security officer looked startled to see me, and I admit I jumped a bit.

"Is everything all right?" I asked.

He made a strange face, as if making a difficult decision. "Come in here for a moment. And keep silent, whatever you do."

He signalled with his hand, and I followed him into the room he had just exited. The first thing I saw was Gray, looking ashen by the porthole. I was about to say something when the floor drew my attention.

Mr. Sloan lay there on his back, facing up. The hole in his chest had bled profusely, adding fresh red colour to the rug underneath him.

"Oh lord," I whispered. Mason caught my upper arm and steered me to the single chair in the room. I wasn't feeling faint, but I was shocked.

Poor Mr. Sloan. This wasn't supposed to happen! I wasn't fond of him, and I had suspected him of being more than just a lady killer. But no man is an island. He didn't deserve to lie there cold on the floor, his life ended long before his time.

What the deuce was going on? I'd had Sloan pegged as Harry's murderer! And yet here he was, another victim on the floor.

Two victims? How many people were involved in this diamond smuggling?

"I sent a steward to assess the cleaning process needed here." Gray's voice was grim. "He came straight back to me. This is what he found."

My eyes went from him back to the body. "Shot this time." I looked up at Mason. "Why was he shot? Harry was knifed. Surely a knife would be safer. Not as loud."

"You didn't hear anything?" Mason asked.

I shook my head. "I was with Tony from the time I left you until just now." I heard Gray grunt but ignored him.

I looked down again at the body. "Looks like a large calibre."

Mr. Mason watched my face. "Always, you surprise me. Yes, a .38 most likely."

I gulped. "The same calibre as Tony's gun."

"Yes," said Mason. "We will assume for now it was the same gun."

I thanked my lucky stars that Tony was in the infirmary. At least he couldn't be accused of this killing, not with a guard on the door all the time. Imagine. The guard had been posted there to keep Tony safe. Who would have guessed the same man would serve as his alibi for this murder?

"Do you think that's why the killer ransacked Tony's cabin? To get the gun?" I looked up again.

Gray spoke this time. "Probably not. Remember, my office was ransacked too. Expect it was just a lucky bonus to find the gun there."

I cleared my throat. "So there's even more urgency for you to keep watch tonight, Mr. Mason."

He rose to his feet. "Yes, Lady Revelstoke. We'll get this man, never fear."

But I did fear. I was totally lost now. Sloan had been my favoured suspect. This threw all my theories in the trash. Worse, it made me face something I hadn't wanted to. There had to be *three* people involved in this business, not just Harry and one more. Unless Sloan had just gotten in the way.

"He was killed here, correct?" I felt both sets of eyes on me. "I mean, there's a great deal of fresh blood …" My voice trailed off.

Mr. Mason spoke first. "Yes, he was killed here."

"But —" I couldn't keep my thoughts to myself. "What was he *doing* here?"

Gray laughed. He waved an arm in the air. "Look around."

I felt a fool. The body on the floor had taken all my attention. I'd never even noticed that the cabin had been in the process of being searched. The bed had been stripped clean, and bedclothes were thrown in a corner. One of the drawers was upside down on the bed. I guessed Sloan had been looking for something taped underneath? The diamonds? They could be made to fit in a narrow package or envelope.

I watched Mason explore all parts of the room. He lifted the sheets and bedspread from the floor, opened all the remaining drawers of the dresser, and even got down on his hands and knees.

Gray stood at ease watching in the military position, feet apart with his hands behind his back. I caught his eye, and he said earnestly, "The important thing is to keep you safe tonight. Keep out of it for once, Lucy. Leave it to us. I beg you."

Mason's head shot up at the name "Lucy." That had been a slip of grave proportions. He smiled slightly and went back to his work. I don't even think Gray noticed. Meanwhile, I didn't miss that Gray had used the word *us*.

"You'll be around to assist Mr. Mason tonight?" I said aloud.

He nodded firmly.

It was hard not to shiver. I knew he would be armed. Chances are, this wouldn't go down without some violence. No criminal gives up easily, and this one had already killed twice.

I told myself that Gray had grown up on the east side and survived a world war, so he knew how to take care of himself. Yes, I told myself that. It should have helped, but it didn't.

I rose from the chair. "I'll stay in my cabin for now, in case you need me. It's almost time to get ready for dinner, in any case."

"That's right," said Mason. He peered up. "Please do your best to appear normal to your tablemates. No mention of these latest events, nor the plan for tonight, to anyone except your maid. You don't know anything more than they do. Can you promise me that?"

I nodded. Normally I don't respond well to being given orders, but it was easy to appreciate this thoughtful, solemn man who actually seemed to care about others.

I left them both and returned to my room. Elf was in the water closet, so I moved to the porthole to get some air. My head was spinning. I simply had to get my mind off murder, at least for the evening. Mr. Mason would be keeping vigil in our cabin tonight, and he would be armed. Gray had said he would be on hand to come to Mason's aid if needed. I didn't know exactly what he'd meant by that. They hadn't been forthcoming. For all I knew, they would both be in my cabin, or maybe Gray would stake out the one next door, ready to move at the sound of a struggle. I shivered. The body of Sloan would be moved by then, surely. Or would they leave it in situ until after midnight to avoid passengers seeing anything being transferred? Maybe they could use a trunk to move it. Or did they have a stretcher in the infirmary ... *Stop! Stop thinking about it.*

It was crazy to keep going over it. There was nothing more I could do tonight. For once, I needed to leave the investigation in the hands of others. Elf and I would move into the cabin Gray had reserved for us. My, but I hated to be left out. Things would happen in the night that I would probably not hear about until morning. That is, if anything happened at all. Nothing was for sure. But we had hit a wall in this investigation with Sloan's death. Surely, Mason was right, and my cabin was next on the hit list. This killer had murdered two men and assaulted a third; he wouldn't stop until he found what he was after. Mason had a golden opportunity to catch him in the act.

I shook myself as I stood looking out the porthole. *Clear your thoughts and get ready for dinner.* I couldn't miss another meal without raising suspicions. Most important, I had to play a part tonight. No one was to know that Sloan had been killed or that Tony had been assaulted. Keeping those horrible events to myself was going to take every bit of concentration.

I could be an actress. Listen, if Elf could pretend to be a maid ...

She was pretending now.

"Sit," she ordered. For the next twenty minutes, I watched her fuss around me, getting me presentable for yet another meal. Not that I didn't adore meals. Especially dinner. Dinner came with dessert. I always felt sorry for those women on the *Titanic* who had passed on dessert.

But it was a fact of life. If you were a lady, you had to make as many as six dress changes a day. And with fashions as they were, you couldn't manage that by yourself. Yes, the dreaded corset. One day, I was going to chuck mine into the sea.

A lady travelling with a husband could do without a maid, I suppose. But a woman travelling alone simply had to have her maid along. That's why it was so important to like your maid. If she was going to change you at all hours of the day, then she had to be on hand. And that meant sleeping in the same suite as you.

Elf was no trouble at all, that way. She didn't snore, and she was so small she hardly took up any room. In fact, it was kind of like having a sister. An extremely eccentric and amusing sister.

My thoughts were taking me way far away. I'd never had a sister. Just my brothers, who had gone into the family trade. Mom had died giving birth to the last one, who'd also died. Two more had died of the Spanish flu. I was the youngest, with Paolo two years older. We kept in touch by mail, but it was a poor substitute for company.

I looked up to find Elf staring at me. Her face was grim.

"So. Whatsit gonna be," she said. "The faithful doggy lord or the dangerous one from back home?"

"What?" I said, snapping out of the past. "Doggy lord? Do you mean Tony?"

"Follows you around like a mutt," she said.

Wait a minute ... hadn't Gray called him the same thing?

"I got a right to know, Luce," said Elf. She sat cross-legged on the bed. "It's my home too."

My mouth was wide open. It didn't appear to work. But then, my brain had no words to feed it.

"Doggy Lord would provide a nice home," Elf continued. "Good food and duds. But you already got that. Main thing is, would we be bored?"

"We?" I said weakly.

"Probably wants a wifey at home. Trot her out to entertain now and then. None o' this travel that we've been doing. Nah, can't see it. You'd go bonkers."

She twisted her legs to swing them over the side. "Now, Danger Man might be a lot of fun. Probably, we'd get to go places a lot. Not sure he would want me hanging around all the time, though."

"Danger Man?" I echoed in a voice too high.

"Sure. Got that look in his eye. Scrappy past. Not to mention, that bod of his was made for the ring, know what I mean. Knows how to handle himself and don't often lose a fight, I bet my last shilling. Whereas Doggy Lord is rather —"

"Stop!" I threw up my hands. "Just stop. Why are you doing this? Aren't things okay the way they are?"

I actually managed to surprise her.

"Sure they are! I gets worried when you get starry-eyed, that's all. Runnin' to the purser's office. Then off to the infirmary. You thinkin' them both the duck's quack."

"The duck's ... what?" I was absolutely baffled.

"The shark's bite, the bee's knees ... you know," Elf snivelled.

"I'm not ..." I shot up from the chair. "Sure, it's nice to have the attention of two handsome men. But believe me, Elf, I'm not about to jeopardize my freedom. Women are finally getting the vote this year, thank God, but we don't have a lot of property rights yet. If I were to marry again, think of what I'd lose."

I had climbed on a soapbox. Except if there had been an actual soapbox, I would have fallen off it while pacing. "Think, Elf! If I got married again, I'd practically cease to exist. All my assets would become his. My husband would own all my property and money. He'd even have control over my children. I have Charlie to think about. And you." I pointed a finger. It was true. A husband could fire a maid whether the wife liked it or not. And Elf was not the ideal picture of a maid. My Johnny had been an exceptional husband, kind and supportive. He'd accepted my friendship with Elf easily, as he'd also accepted my past. In fact, it had amused him immensely. But I knew of many other husbands who were not so fair-minded.

"It's in the Magna Carta." I slowed to a halt.

"The who?" said Elf.

"The ancient law of England, drawn up after the Norman invasion. Widows can't be forced to remarry. They get to keep their freedom and their worldly goods." I stopped pacing and met her eyes. "Plus they can live with whomever they want. Come on, Elf," I said gently. "We've got a pretty good life. I might take a lover. But a husband? Why would I risk all that?"

For the first time ever, I saw tears in her eyes. There was a long silence. "Phew," she said finally, with an audible sigh. "They aren't Johnny, that's all. Don't know if they'd want me along." She wiped her nose on her sleeve. "So it's the merry widow for you, is it?"

"Count on it," I said firmly. "And for a long time to come."

She snuffled. "Don't like to think about the future."

"I know." I put my hand on her shoulder. "But whatever comes, we'll do it together."

For a brief second, almost too short to measure, she put her head down on my hand.

CHAPTER THIRTY-THREE

ELF'S STEWARD — the fellow named Walker — came to the door
with news of our cabin number. I was to go down to dinner now,
and Elf would accompany Walker to the cabin later, when all the
first-class passengers were at dinner. Then Mason would move in
to this cabin for the evening.

Elf had dressed me in my favourite gown — a sapphire-blue
silk with a handkerchief hem that did something extra special for
my face and figure. Even Walker stood bug-eyed when I rose from
picking up my beaded shawl and evening bag from the bed. I was
dressed for war, even if it was to be an undercover part I played.

I waved at the two lovebirds (wouldn't Elf take a swipe at me
for that if she heard!) and left the cabin. Elf would have some
time with her new *amore*, which made me smile.

It was strange to walk the corridors to dinner without Tony
at my side. He almost always met me for meals. I wished him
a speedy recovery, but I knew in my heart that he wouldn't be
escorting me to any more meals.

While passing through the dining room, I nodded to several
first-class passengers I knew by sight, including the table of men
who played cards with Tony. They made no secret of their

admiration for my gown. Yes, a woman knows how to dress for war, and it can be just as effective as a weapon.

I reached our table and made my greetings to Drew and Florrie, Vera and Amanda. For the first time this voyage, I pulled out my own chair.

THE TROUBLE WITH travelling on an ocean liner is there are only so many things you can do. Reading. Card playing. Walking the deck for exercise. Taking tea with other passengers. Dancing to the band after dinner. I'd learned recently that one of the French lines had installed moving picture projectors in small theatres aboard their latest ships. That seemed like a wonderful addition, one worth looking into. Space is always at a premium on a ship, but that entertainment might be worth it.

Since there is so little to do, gossip is a favourite activity. News travels fast on a ship. Faster than the ship itself. Faster, if it is possible, than the speed of sound.

So I shouldn't have been surprised to learn the main topic at dinner. It wasn't Sloan's murder or Tony's assault, both of which were carefully guarded secrets. No, it was something far more entertaining.

There were just five of us tonight. The captain had sent word that his spot would be vacant. Mr. Mason was conspicuously absent. Word had spread about Tony being ill in the infirmary, and Mr. Sloan … well, he had no more need of food, alas. I noticed no one mentioned him, nor did they seem to wonder at his absence.

I explained my own absence at the earlier meals as due to a long-lasting migraine, and I had barely sat down when the absurdity started.

"Did you hear about the shoe thief?" said Vera Horner, leaning across the table. Her hazel eyes danced with excitement.

"What?" I said ungracefully.

"It's true," said Drew, pointing with a knife. "Someone stole a pair of my good brogues. I confronted the purser about it, and he admitted I wasn't the first."

"It's an epidemic," said Vera triumphantly. It was common knowledge she prided herself on being the first to share the latest gossip. "Several men have reported it to the purser. I heard it from that young steward."

"But why?" said Florrie, looking flustered. "Why would anyone do that? It's not like it's romantic, stealing shoes."

Drew laughed. "Florrie has visions of a regular Raffles, wearing a black mask and climbing the side of buildings in search of florid gemstones."

I choked on my wine at the mention of Raffles.

"Well, at least I can see the point of that," she defended. "If you are going to take a risk, it should be for something fabulous. Not shoes."

"And so many. The damned fellow must have taken a dozen, according to our steward. Beats me. You can only wear one pair at a time," said Drew with an amused smile.

"What will be next?" said Amanda Martin in a shaky voice. "First that poor man was murdered and thrown in the lifeboat. Now this." She shivered.

"It's a disgrace." Vera shook her head. "This has always been a respectable company. But now thieves! Whoever heard of such a thing? It must be one of the stewards. Who else would have access? I can only say, this is what comes of hiring people who are not from the Empire."

I had to smile. What would she think if she discovered my parents were Italian?

"How are we to be safe in our beds?" Amanda almost whispered it.

"Well, I hardly think you need worry about someone killing you for *your* shoes, Amanda." Vera Horner sniffed. "Besides. It's only men's shoes they're stealing, so I heard."

"Apparently all the officers are baffled." Drew shook his head. "It must be a prank."

All this time I had listened with my mouth open wide enough to catch flies. Darn that Elf! When I said to get rid of them, had she taken me literally? What had she done with all the shoes? Thrown them overboard? Jeepers, would we find all twelve pairs in a lifeboat tomorrow morning?

"Where's Mr. Sloan tonight?" Amanda asked finally. I had expected her to be the one to miss him. I hadn't forgotten how she'd triumphantly told me they had shared tea yesterday, and all those other times she'd vied for his attention.

"Don't know. Haven't seen him since cards last night," said Drew.

None of the others seemed to know. Amanda didn't look upset, and she changed the conversation to something else. That surprised me. No doubt I'd got it wrong. I guessed Amanda hadn't been having an affair with Sloan. It was strange, though. I watched her face for signs of despondency, but she was talking with animation. She didn't seem at all concerned that Sloan was missing. Why this sudden change in attitude? She had made a habit of trailing after him in a pathetic way that we had all noticed. Her disinterest now didn't make any sense.

And that gave me the most astonishing idea ...

CHAPTER THIRTY-FOUR

I NEEDED TIME. I needed to be alone. The puzzle pieces were starting to come together in my mind, and it left me almost breathless.

On a previous night, I had told the table that dancing was a trigger for my grief. So when the band started playing "My Blue Heaven" after dinner, I made my excuses.

"Of course, dear," said Florrie. "But don't forget we make port tomorrow. We'll need to exchange addresses so we can keep in touch. Perhaps share a farewell lunch or dinner?"

I smiled at her. Such a nice lady, so keen to include me. I promised her I'd be pleased to join them tomorrow and left the table.

While walking, it occurred to me that I was going to be on my own for the next little while, and my cabin was not an option. Gray would be staking out the cabin with Mason. Tony was still out of commission. I knew Elf and Walker would have moved our things by now, and then … Best not to ask what they would be doing now. If you did, you'd get the whole story, and it could be rather indelicate, to say the least.

I looked for a quiet place to think, but the bar was crowded with loud men smoking cigars. I swept past them, nodding to one or two on my way. It would have to be the foredeck then.

A perfect place to be alone when everyone else was occupied with drinks and dancing.

I walked the empty corridors, feeling excitement that the solution could be close at hand. I wanted to piece things together with the knowledge I had gathered. We would be reaching shore tomorrow. In one more day, I would be settling into my country home, and the opportunity to solve this mystery would be swept from my hands into those more official. Chances were, they'd never get to the bottom of it once we were off the ship. I hated to think of Harry not getting his proper due.

The foredeck was deserted, as I had expected. I walked to the bow, enjoying the wind through my hair. It was always windy on the foredeck as the ship rushed through the water, and I found it invigorating. You wouldn't think a thing could go wrong on an evening like this. The sky seemed to be bigger and blacker on the open water. The stars twinkled above, and the bright quarter moon seemed to welcome me. It was a beautiful night, cool but not cold, with light seas. A calm before the storm? I grimaced. We'd had stormy seas aplenty, this trip.

Back to the task at hand. I told myself to go through it logically, drawing out each discrepancy to see if the hypothesis fit. Two men had been murdered, the first with a knife. That was a man's crime. I'd seen enough stabbings back home, and this had been no delicate effort. You needed brute strength to overcome a healthy male opponent and drive a knife through his ribs. I knew that well because I had been taught by my cousins how to hold a knife when I was twelve. And even I, with all my training, couldn't have managed the blow that killed Harry.

Sloan was a different story. Anyone can shoot a gun, and his horrifying murder had blown up all my former theories. I had thought there were two people involved in the gem smuggling: Harry and the man who'd killed him. But surely, that would have been Sloan. I had assumed (which one should never do) that there had been a falling-out between comrades: the courier and the receiver. I'd heard of that happening before in my own family. One of the two gets greedy without the big cheese around, and that seals his death warrant. Sloan must have killed Harry — it just made sense. You couldn't have two unrelated murders in one cabin of an ocean liner, could you? Of course not. It defied logic.

So the question was, who had killed Sloan? It was "elermentry," as Elf would say. There had to be a third person involved in the gem scheme. Harry, Sloan, and one more. A person who was so cool, they would risk a second murder in highly dangerous circumstances, when everyone was on alert after the first death. True, there was a lot of money at stake. Those gems were worth a boodle. But it would take a really ruthless hand to gun down an American gangster in the close quarters of a crowded cruise ship. But why a gun this time? Guns make noise, which is always risky. Why not a knife, like for Harry?

It had been a stunning feat of sheer bravado. No escape on the high seas. Nowhere to run to. The ship was a floating prison. Who would risk that? And why?

A tingly feeling came over me. Oh lord, I had it. I knew why a gun had been used for the second murder. That made complete sense when you considered my new information: it wasn't an affair. The missing puzzle piece was now in my hand, and I marvelled at it.

Sherlock Holmes was right: *When you have eliminated the impossible, whatever remains, however improbable, must be the truth.*

Everything fit when you manoeuvred that final puzzle piece into place. Holmes himself would be intrigued. Because it was improbable. More than that, it was fantastic!

Names can be changed, as I knew from my own experience. And in this case, all it would have taken was omitting one letter.

Which brought me back to the puzzle piece. *Sloan's alibi.* I'd thought he couldn't have coshed Tony on the head because he had been given an alibi for the time it took place. But every alibi has a weakness in that it's only as good as the person who gives it.

Sloan was dead. I knew now he most likely was the one to have burgled Tony's room. Yet he had an alibi for the time of the burglary that must have been false.

Why would she have given him an alibi if she wasn't having an affair with him? Furthermore, why had she been keeping track of him so diligently if she wasn't in love with him? There was only one reason I could think of. Holy hell! *She was the brains.*

I gasped out loud. Here it was 1928, and I called myself a champion of women's rights. Yet not even I had considered the fact that a woman could be behind all this.

I stood at the railing watching the waves crawl away from our bow below, appalled at my own deduction, yet also grotesquely fascinated. I had to admire her — oh yes, I did. It would take a brilliant mind to pull this off and to play the part without giving it away. For she certainly had played a part. It would explain my unease that one time at dinner, when her eyes had registered fury over the slight Sloan had given her. The one slip in her performance. Oh, why hadn't I clued in to that before?

I would need to be equally brilliant to catch her out. How to do it? How to set a trap that she would walk into and give herself away? I felt my heart pump with excitement.

It was incredible. *Two* mob women, taking on each other. I wanted to laugh out loud at the sheer outrageousness of it. Talk about the emancipation of women!

I pushed myself forward. I could do it. I had a mind just as devious. I would set a trap. I just needed to think of a way to get her alone by tempting her with the gems …

So it was an abominable jest of fate, what happened next.

"So easy to push you over," said a voice behind me.

I froze, clutching the rail like a lifeline.

"Too easy," said the voice again. "I like a little more drama than that."

I spun around then and cursed my own carelessness.

Amanda Martin faced me. But a different Amanda Martin than I had seen before. Not the meek fussy-muss, as Elf had called her. This version was all confidence and swagger. In her gloved hand was a gun. I didn't have to ask if it was loaded. Her face said it all.

"You're going to tell me where the gems are," she said. Even her voice was different, deeper and confident. "I know they were in the shoes. That's the only reason you would have removed the shoes before throwing the body overboard, and we all heard about the missing shoes from the gossip mill. Just bad luck I didn't think of that hiding place first, before we left him in your cabin. Believe me, I've kicked myself black and blue. So don't bother to pretend the gems don't exist."

"I won't." I nodded to the gun. "But if you shoot me, you'll never find out."

"I might," she said. "You're pretty chummy with that pint-size maid of yours. I could make her tell me."

My heart thumped wildly. Not Elf! She'd found my weak spot, damn her. I sucked in air and tried to think straight. Amanda

Martin! If only I had pieced it together before tonight. It was so incredibly cunning. The dull, fluffy matron of our table, wearing her outdated dresses. Falling into the shadow of her richer friend Vera. Now she stood before me like a demented Valkyrie in worn gold velvet that had probably done time in the teens. The gun made a stunning accessory. She didn't look a bit fluffy now.

I recovered myself by shrugging. "You think I would share a boodle like that with my maid?"

"You willing to take a chance?" said Amanda. She gestured with the gun. "I'm a pretty good shot, as I expect you are. Quite a family you come from, back in Canada. Amazing, how you've kept that quiet. Wouldn't the others love to know."

I felt a deep chill creep down my spine.

"You've got some fine connections there." She chuckled. It wasn't a nice sound. "Prohibition has made your family quite wealthy, if not respectable. Yes, I know your background. But I bet you can't guess mine."

I wanted to scream. We had researched the backgrounds of Sloan, the American couple — even the detective. But Amanda? Because she was English and a friend of Vera Horner's, it had never occurred to me to check on hers. But I had it now. Oh lord, I had it now.

"I'm a quick learner," I said, leaning back against the rail. *Stall for time. Maybe someone will come.* "You married an American with big money, from Chicago. I've heard about the mob in Chicago. You obviously know of my family, which few people do. And you're holding a gun on me now. That speaks volumes to me."

She nodded. "Go on."

The name! Now I was sure I was right.

"Last name Martin. Maybe originally Martini?" I'd surprised her. You could see it on her face.

I continued, thinking swiftly as I went. "Strangely, it was a love match. Young Italian-American fellow comes over to England, making connections with dubious industries on behalf of the syndicate, and chances upon the love of his life. Who also just happens to be short of money and looking for someone to bail out her family. New husband does the minimum for her kin, then brings her back to Chicago, where they live happily ever after, dodging bullets. I can relate to that. Both sides of it, actually."

"Yes," she said darkly. "It was a love match. So many people didn't understand that." She giggled then. "Gaetano caught me stealing a silver snuffbox from the country house where we were both guests. I thought I was done for, but he laughed it off. Said it only went to convince him I was the girl for him."

I nodded, oddly enthralled. It was a common enough story — rich American marries an English title — but with an absurd mafia twist. I cleared my throat. "The devoted husband died recently, probably from lead poisoning. A slug from a gat will do that. So now you're the one working for the mob."

The gun had dropped slightly. She brought it up smartly.

I put up my hand like a stop sign to stall her. "I figure you were the brains of the business and the drop for the rocks. But something went wrong. Courier didn't want to part with them? That's the usual scenario."

She snorted. "You ought to write scripts for those moving pictures."

"But you had an accomplice. You didn't do the dirty work the first time on Harry. I simply don't believe it."

She glared at me. "Why not me?"

"You're too classy to do knife work. A gun is much more your style. Clean and neat. I assume our dinner companion was your assistant?"

She stared at me. Then nodded. "He got too greedy. Wanted more than his share and thought he could strong-arm me out of it. Why is it that men are so stupid? Always, they underestimate me. Everyone does! Always did, even at school. That fool Vera Horner, for one. If only she knew." Amanda laughed bitterly. "She thinks I'm a poor cousin, some impoverished colonial widow with no means and no brains. Someone to be pitied. She likes to pity others, the stuck-up cow. That's the sad part about all this. She'll never know who I really am."

I could hear the whining regret in her voice.

"It doesn't have to end this way." My heart was racing now. "You can have the rocks. I don't need them. I have a castle."

"Don't be ridiculous," she said. I saw her finger move and heard the gun cock. "You know too much. And your connections have long arms. I don't like loose ends."

"Shame, though," I said, desperately taking a new tack. "You're going to shoot the one person in the world who knows how clever you are. It must be frustrating to be taken by everyone for such a nin—"

"Amanda, dear! There you are. I've been looking all over —"

Amanda swung around, and the second she did, I smashed into her with all my strength. I heard her grunt. The air went out of me. The gun went off. We both came crashing down. I rolled, frantic to grab the gun from her hand, but it wasn't there, and she didn't move.

CHAPTER THIRTY-FIVE

STILL STRAINING FOR breath, I looked up to find Vera Horner looking down at us with her formidable cane at the ready.

"Are you all right, Lucy?" The concern on her face looked genuine.

I nodded from my very ungraceful position on the floor, still fighting for air.

"Your beautiful dress is torn," she said, tutting. "I don't think your interesting maid will be able to salvage it."

I followed her eyes. Yes, the gorgeous sapphire silk was shredded down one side. My headdress lay on the floor about six feet away. My evening bag lay near it. And I was pretty sure at least one heel of a shoe had broken off.

Vera turned her gaze on Amanda.

"Dear me, I believe she shot herself," said Vera, following the trail of blood with her eyes. "Too bad my cane couldn't reach her gun arm in time. You had a close call, my dear. But then, so did I. She would have shot us both if you hadn't tackled her."

I gulped air. "Let's call it even." I had to smile.

And here she was, gazing down at me calmly. Vera Horner, ever the high-born lady, stoic and in control of her emotions, even when confronted with a grisly scene and her own near death. I nearly pointed it out but for the panting. No doubt she would have answered me, "My dear. Whatever do you mean?"

Wow, had I ever gotten Vera wrong. No one, simply no one could have been more shocked than me to find this gal had guts galore in an emergency. Plus the tenacity and courage to put her own self at risk for *me*.

I was full of awe and respect.

The handgun lay less than a yard from me. I took a good look at it. A blunt revolver. Sure looked to be Tony's. Oh, what a web Amanda had spun! I would be shot with Tony's gun, and he would take the blame for it. Just like he would take the blame for the death of Amanda's accomplice. She wore evening gloves, of course, and his prints would be on the gun.

If it hadn't been for Vera Horner …

I shivered and rolled myself to a sitting position. "I didn't hear you sneak up," I said.

"I can be very quiet on my feet," said Vera, clucking with satisfaction. "All those deportment classes had to be good for something."

"How long had you been listening?"

She peered down at the body. "A while. 'Stuck-up cow,' indeed. Nasty woman. Even as a girl, she was horrid. Stole my gold locket before we left school, I was sure of it." She poked the body with her cane. "I had a feeling she was up to something. The way she looked at you during dinner! My blood ran cold. So when she followed you after dinner, I decided to follow her."

Finally my heartbeat was returning to normal. I raised myself from the floor. "I thought you were good friends."

"Amanda?" she said with her eyes still on the body. "Hardly. I hadn't seen her in years, and even back then we weren't close." She moved her gaze to me. "She pounced on me as soon as she saw me. You know how it is on a ship. Only so many people we've been introduced to, so one makes do with the acquaintances one has. Beggars can't be choosers," she said firmly.

I brushed myself off. "Well, this beggar is extremely grateful you came along when you did. Like the Furies, you were. Boadicea on the battlefield, brandishing that cane."

"Absolutely my pleasure," said Vera, eyeing me with a smile. "I raised five boys. It's been a while since I employed this as a weapon." She gestured with the cane. "And I'm sure you will fill me in as to the reason Amanda Martin was holding you at gunpoint."

"My dear Vera, you will dine out on this story for months," I said.

WE CERTAINLY CAUSED a sensation. Gray was on the scene first. He burst through the steel door and made straight for me.

"You okay?" he said, clutching my upper arms with both hands. I nodded and signalled with my head to the body on the floor. His eyes stared into mine for a moment, and then he released me to survey the scene.

He was quickly followed by the captain, more officers, and Mr. Mason. The gunshot had been heard as far as the bridge. Looking at the amount of brass around us right now, I wondered briefly who was actually commanding the helm.

After checking on me, Mr. Mason took charge. Vera Horner stomped right up to him and relayed the events with startling clarity. She deployed her cane to demonstrate the necessary punctuation, causing a few of the men to back away. I filled in bits where need be, but honestly, I was content to make this Vera's show. It occurred to me then how very fortunate it was that she had been there to witness the struggle and not just to provide me with the necessary distraction to take down my opponent. Vera's word as to my good character seemed to carry all the weight needed.

The captain said as much to me as we watched Vera replay our movements for the benefit of the detective. "Lady Revelstoke, you seem to be born under a lucky star. I will forever be grateful to Mrs. Horner for proving to be such a formidable witness."

I felt myself shiver. "Yes. The notoriety will be fierce enough. If she hadn't arrived when she did, I might not be here to even face the spectre of self-defence."

"We'll keep this quiet," he said. "You'd be surprised how we can do that."

I smiled at his naiveté. With Vera Horner arriving like a Wagnerian heroine just in time? It would be all over London society before midnight the day we landed. No chance of keeping her quiet. And frankly, I didn't mind. She deserved this little bit of celebrity.

It also wouldn't hurt my stance in society that she appeared to have taken me under her wing. Vera had seemed quite fond of me in her retelling of the events. In fact, as we were about to be herded off to separate cabins to give our statements, she gave me a generous bear hug and insisted we meet for breakfast the next morning.

CHAPTER THIRTY-SIX

AN HOUR OR SO later, Gray was comforting me in my cabin. It was an enthusiastic sort of comfort that might eventually have led to strenuous exercise. Unfortunately, we were interrupted.

"Cor!" said Elf, barrelling into the room. "What's this I hear about old fussy-muss?"

A partially-clad Gray rolled off me. I sat up and patted down my hair. "You missed all the fun, Elf. So did Gray, nearly, but he arrived in time for the wrap-up."

Elf frowned at Gray, who was struggling into his jacket. "Saved her, did ya?"

Gray laughed. "Hardly. She single-handedly took down the Martin woman with a full-on football tackle. Your mistress doesn't need a man to save her."

"Yes, but it's nice to have a man there afterwards." I smiled at Gray, and he grinned back.

Elf looked from one of us to the other. "Humph. Wrecked another dress, I'll wager. And what's this about not waiting for me?"

"Couldn't be helped," I said, reaching down for my shoes. "I didn't expect Amanda Martin to come following me after dinner. Besides, I expect you had your hands full where you were." I turned to Gray. "Elf has been seeing that well-built blond steward of yours. I'm pretty sure she saw even more of him this evening." I winked at her.

Elf had the surprising decency to blush.

"Bloody hell!" she said suddenly. "Forgot to tell you. This came for you." She handed me a cable. I ripped it open. It was from Charlie, and it said:

Name completely unknown here. Write me!! C

On no! Too late. The last twenty-four hours had rendered this news moot. Ah well. Charlie would have enjoyed the sleuthing, even if it hadn't produced results. I sighed. Poor Sloan. He hadn't gone to Eton, as I had expected. And he wouldn't be requiring that misappropriated Eton tie anymore. It made me sad to think we might never know exactly who he was, or even if that was his real name. *And don't forget Harry*, I reminded myself. It was such a shame that the two people who could name him were also dead. I hoped someone somewhere would mourn him. No one should leave this world completely unloved.

"Should I leave you both?" said Gray. He had done up his jacket.

I put the cable down and looked over at Elf.

"No matter to me," she said. "You can fill in the bits ladybird here finds too raw."

We spent the next while bringing Elf up to date.

"One thing I'd like to know," Gray said when we'd finished. "I know you've got the rocks. That's fine, as far as I'm concerned. Better you than the mob. But just where the hell did you hide them? Will you tell me?"

Elf looked at me, and we exchanged a measured look.

"What do you think?" I didn't see a problem with telling him, but I'd leave it up to her.

Elf looked him over from tip to toe with a frown and tilted her head. "He's one of us, after all," she said, finally.

I nodded, then turned to Gray with a twinkle in my eye. "We left them with her mother for safekeeping."

That confused him. Elf giggled at the face he made, went to her old trunk, and dug to the bottom. She pulled out a slightly battered pewter funeral urn.

IT WAS SOME time later. Elf had run off to tell her favourite steward "the goods," as she put it. I was recuperating from a formidable amount of exercise and was feeling cheerfully serene. In contrast, Gray appeared to be grumpy.

"So," he said, getting up from the bed. "What happens now? What do we do about all this? Sure, it's been fun, but I'm damned if this is a satisfactory conclusion, at least for me. I've just got you back in my life, and I don't want to lose you." He stood over me, looking down. "Yes, that's me, baring my heart. To me, you'll always be Lucy from back home. To hell with your money and title and the goddamn castle, you hear me?"

I smiled nicely. "I hear you."

It was unusual, this violent declaration. The war had made our generation afraid to care too much, or at least to appear to. Love was a game to be played, not to be taken seriously. I gazed at him, and through our eyes, the truth shone bright, without any need for clarification.

It wasn't a game anymore.

"We dock tomorrow, and I'll be on duty for the sail back." He frowned. "When will I see you again?"

"Say in two weeks? I need to return home to see my son. But perhaps," I said, reaching for my dressing gown, "the owner of this shipping line might find it prudent to make a return trip on the *Victoriana* across the pond. To check on the quality of service."

He looked baffled. "What owner?"

"That would be me, darling," I said. I twinkled at him.

ACKNOWLEDGEMENTS

THOSE WHO KNOW me well will recognize that this book, number seventeen, is a rebirth for me. And as with any birth, there are many people who have helped to give this story life.

Much credit goes to Brenna English-Loeb from Transatlantic Agency, who offered great advice and supported me through revisions of this manuscript, then went on to place my baby in very good hands.

From Cormorant Books, I can't say enough about Marc Côté and Sarah Jensen, whose warmth and professionalism have made this journey such a pleasant one. May we take more trips together!

Don Graves, Chris Nielsen, Joan O'Callaghan, Cheryl Freedman, Lynn McPherson, Des Ryan, Thom Bennett, Ang Tisiot — your encouragement on this particular book has meant the world to me.

And Mike. You have held my hand, heard my angst, and taught me that when one door slams shut, another truly can open, with enough time and love. This book is for you.

We acknowledge the sacred land on which Cormorant Books operates. It has been a site of human activity for 15,000 years. This land is the territory of the Huron-Wendat and Petun First Nations, the Seneca, and most recently, the Mississaugas of the Credit River. The territory was the subject of the Dish With One Spoon Wampum Belt Covenant, an agreement between the Iroquois Confederacy and Confederacy of the Ojibway and allied nations to peaceably share and steward the resources around the Great Lakes. Today, the meeting place of Toronto is still home to many Indigenous people from across Turtle Island. We are grateful to have the opportunity to work in the community, on this territory.

We are also mindful of broken covenants and the need to strive to make right with all our relations.